PORTAL TO EVIL

The Adam Barrie
Paranormal Investigations Book 2

First Published in the UK 2025 by Mirador Publishing

First edition: 2025

Any reference to real names and places are purely fictional and are constructs of the author. Any offence the references produce is unintentional and in no way reflects the reality of any locations or people involved.

ISBN: 978-1-917411-25-7

Portal To Evil

By

Elizabeth Revill

To my dear friend, Sue Taylor who has always supported and encouraged me. Your friendship is very precious. Long may it go on.

~ 1 ~

ADAM BARRIE AWOKE IN A sweat. He was literally dripping wet and yet it was not a hot night. The remnants of a dream too elusive to capture fully, had left him unsettled and if he admitted it, scared. The music of drums being played repetitively thundered through his mind together with alien howls. He had seen young girls, dressed in white robes giving fawning obeisance to a man in an extraordinary costume with a wolf's head. He was flanked by two very large Alsatian wolf-type dogs. He raised his arms, and the girls appeared to faint and fall on the ground before him in some kind of stupor.

The wolfman raised his arms and ordered, "Lilith! Come forth."

A stunningly beautiful woman dressed in a tight fitting gold lamé catsuit, in which she moved fluidly, made her clothes seem like a second skin. She wore a partial mask with seven eyes and had come forward propelling the sixth form student, Michelle, who had attended Caroline Mitchell's art exhibition with Leonard Shaitan and was dressed all in black. They had all been part of his second paranormal investigation of the schoolgirl murder case after Adam had moved to Black Head Ridge House. The discovery of Caroline Mitchell's body and her killer had been his first. Adam struggled to remember more of the dream but as footsteps in the sand vanish with an incoming tide, his mind refused to recollect any more of the dream. The more he tried to remember the more it slipped away.

He sat up and rubbed his eyes. The drumming was still playing in his head although fainter now. He knew it was to do with Gilbert Bray Boarding School for Girls, near Penmyron, and the deaths of the young student and the previous groundsman, Kenneth Parkes. In his gut, he knew the reason the groundsman was dead was because Kenneth had talked to him and Vanda, his investigative journalist girlfriend.

Vance the DCI of Brinkworth's police force had requested his help in identifying a headless victim and uncovering the truth behind the murders and whatever was happening at the boarding school. Adam glanced at the time on his bedside clock and saw it was five past five in the morning. Shaking off his need for sleep he scrambled out of bed, walked to his bedroom window, and stared out at the sea as the sun was rising. The lighthouse was still shining its bright, friendly beam across the water serving as a navigational aid to help passing ships to a safe harbour and to warn them of impending doom, and the treacherous jagged rocks that lay hidden under the surf. He had a flash of memory of the lighthouse keeper who had fallen to his death after Adam tackled him about the killing of talented artist Caroline Mitchell. He was waiting to see who would take over the duties for this one, one of the few manned lighthouses in the country but had not seen anyone new, yet.

Adam stood there for a further few minutes admiring the crimson dye that washed the sky as the sun rose until the temperature suddenly began to plummet. He shivered and dived into his ensuite to shower. As the hot water warmed his body, he soaped himself vigorously but at the back of his mind, voices were niggling and nagging him. He could just about hear the name, 'Lilith', being praised as if adored. He shook his head as if to clear it and as he lifted his eyes to the misted shower screen he recoiled. There in the mist was the clear outline drawing of a wolf's head with its teeth bared and with it came a snarling growl that filled the enclosed space and drowned out the other voices. He hurriedly wiped out the misty picture on the glass and the snarling stopped. He breathed a sigh of relief and quickly exited the shower feeling unsettled and very unnerved.

Adam hurriedly dried himself and dressed. He ran out from his bedroom and down the stairs to the kitchen, where Vanda's Dictaphone rested on the worktop. He made himself a pot of coffee before sitting at the counter and playing the tape he had recorded at the school. The white noise he had noticed in the car on the way back from Gilbert Bray Boarding School was more apparent. In amongst the conversation the whispered murmurings registered with him and the names Lilith and Sabrina were clear. There were faint howls and another rasping voice that claimed to be Beelzebub. Adam shivered, each time he tried to grasp what else was being said, the sounds were drowned out by unintelligible whisperings, which crowded his mind and seemed to be calling to him.

It was then he heard the key in his lock and Vanda Sullivan swept in. Adam looked up curiously, "You're early."

"I know. I awoke really early and couldn't get back to sleep. I just had a feeling that you'd be up, too. So I thought I'd chance it and pop across."

"And what if I had been tucked up fast asleep?"

"Then I would have come and woken you."

"Mmm, that would have been a nice surprise."

"You're only saying that because it's true," she replied with a giggle.

Adam stood up and wrapped his arms around her. "So, what disturbed your sleep?"

"I had a very strange dream," she whispered, as she snuggled into him.

"What a coincidence. So did I."

"Really?" she asked and pushed away from him. "What was yours about?"

"I can't remember much, but it wasn't very pleasant. It was enough to disturb my sleep and force me to get up. What do you recall?" pressed Adam.

"A vicious looking wolf come hybrid Alsatian. It made an horrendous noise."

"Anything else?"

"Some kind of chanting and a pentacle on the floor of a forest."

"Could you make out what was said?"

Vanda screwed her face up, "Not sure, something about lilies I think, and it was said with a lisp."

"A lisp?"

"Yes, you know… a 'th' sound instead of an 's'."

Adam gasped. "It sounds similar to mine except I don't remember a pentacle."

"What do you think it means?"

"It means, either we've got someone rattled, or…"

"Or?"

"You've connected to me."

Vanda studied Adam's face. "You mean your sixth sense is catching?"

"Not quite. I just believe that you are in tune with me, close to me, so you pick up on certain things."

"Hmm!" Vanda flounced away and went to pour herself a cup of coffee and asked casually, "So, what's next?"

"More research and another visit to Moss Woods. But, I'll have to see Vance first."

DCI Vance sat staring at a handful of scene of crime photographs spread out on his desk. He scratched his head. The man, Kenneth Parkes, had died with a look of terror frozen on his face. There were scratches on his back and bite marks on his neck and bruising but nothing that would have caused his death. His cursory look at the postmortem report had revealed no definitive reason why a healthy forty-eight-year-old man should suddenly drop down dead in the night. They were waiting for the toxicology report to come back to see if there was evidence of any suspicious substances. Frustratingly, there was some kind of hold-up in the labs.

Vance picked up the few statements that had been taken and began to re-read Lola Parkes', Kenneth's wife's, testimony. It didn't make sense that a grown man had begun to suffer with extreme nightmares, which he was unable to fully recall. He had taken to sleeping in the spare room for the last few nights before his death, so he wouldn't disturb her or the children. Lola had woken to the sound of his horrific screams and heard her husband begging for his life and to leave him be. She had rushed to his room but there was no one else there. Kenneth was gibbering incomprehensively, and she tried frantically to calm him. He died in her arms. She watched as the light left his eyes. It was then she attempted resuscitation and worked on him for fifteen minutes until the ambulance and paramedics arrived that her daughter, Jody, had called. She, too, had been woken by the screams.

The bedroom window was wide open, and Lola mentioned that it was as if a vampire had entered his room and sucked him dry, but of course, she added, there are no such things as vampires. The paramedics could not explain the bruising, scratches or bite marks, nor could the pathologist. The cause of death was unknown and deemed inconclusive, but Vance knew in his gut that it was murder, but how? That was the question.

There was a knock at the door and Paul Jacobs popped his head around. "Sir, Adam Barrie is here to see you."

"Send him in."

Adam hurried past Jacobs who admitted him before shutting the door.

"What can I do for you?" asked Vance.

"I'm keen to know how the investigation is going and if I can do anymore to help," said Adam. "I have some major concerns."

"Any help gratefully appreciated. What have you got so far? We can pool ideas."

"I've warned you about this before but... I have been experiencing strange dreams, so has Vanda, and what's more we are both getting images of you and two aggressive dogs."

Vance looked up. "Both of you?"

"Both of us. It's all tied up with the school and Kenneth Parkes' death."

"There's something going on there, for sure."

"Haven't you been yet?"

"Sergeant Jacobs went out and called in a team of SOCOs. I was still working on the schoolgirl murder case, Melanie Parker. You were right about that. Once we had a name it was easy to track down her family. Our schoolgirl was definitely Melanie. I went to see the parents at their business premises whilst my sergeant went to Kenneth's house. He did the initial interviews and brought the information back to me. I'm just going through it now."

"May I?" indicated Adam with a jerk of his head towards the evidence.

"Be my guest," said Vance and shivered as the temperature in the room began to drop.

Adam picked up the pictures and studied them before reading Lola Parkes' statement. As he read, his head was filled with whispering voices. He heard again the name, Lilith. Adam swayed and grasped the back of the chair at the desk facing Vance to steady himself.

"What is it?" asked Vance.

"I'm not sure, but I know that when you return to the school, I must come with you."

Vance raised one eyebrow, a habit he had when he was uncertain about what someone was saying. "Okay…" he said slowly. "What have you got to tell me?"

Adam launched into what he and Vanda had discovered during their research and again reiterated his warning about aggressive dogs. He concluded, "As I said, it's not just me who has received these images, but Vanda, too. That confirms it for me. There is something very wrong at that school."

"So, Vanda had exactly the same visions as you?" queried Vance, trying to get his head around it.

"Yes, I don't know how but we both had similar dreams that featured you and two snarling dogs."

If Vance was shaken he didn't show it. "Weird."

"We thought so, but how are we to explain me accompanying you to the school?"

"If I have to explain, I will just say you are a police consultant. Otherwise, I'll say nothing."

Adam stiffened as he heard his mother's voice in his head, as if speaking through a mist. He asked Vance, "Tell me, do you have the coroner's report?"

"I do."

"Was Kenneth's bed wet?"

"Wet?"

"As if he'd ejaculated?"

"I haven't read through it all properly yet, I only quickly scanned it. I was just studying the photos and then you came in."

"Can you take a look, now?"

Vance picked up the sheaf of papers in the file and sorted through them. He found it and searched through the findings quickly. He looked up into Adam's questioning gaze. "Yes… Yes he did. Is it important?"

"It could be. I don't know yet. But it should be looked into."

Vance assented with a nod and continued, "I will be heading out there this afternoon after I've had time to digest all of this." He gestured to his various reports.

Adam nodded. "I'll pop back about two. Is that okay?"

"Yes, you can travel with me. And before you say anything, I'll be careful driving, I remember what you said."

Adam nodded and added, "What about Melanie?"

"We wouldn't have known anything about that but for you. We'd still be bumbling about in the dark. I went to her house, not a very good experience. Very humbling. Her parents were in complete shock, and I promised them I'd find answers. We need to know how she died and why."

"The answers to these questions are all at the school."

Vance nodded. "See you at two."

Vanda was poring over information she'd found online and was so absorbed that she didn't notice Adam's return. She jumped nervously when Adam stepped up behind her and rested his hands on her shoulders. "You frightened me half to death," she complained.

"Sorry. What have you learned?"

Vanda scrolled back up the page. "Here, read this." She had opened up a number of pages about Lilith. "That was the name we both heard except I thought it was Lilies, remember? Apparently, she was the first wife of Adam and primordial queen of demons."

"I thought Eve was Adam's first wife."

"So did I."

Adam leaned over her shoulder and began to read, "Authorities say that the Bible was edited and references to Lilith were removed from Genesis. She was made from the dust of the earth like him; problems occurred when Adam tried to exert dominance over her. She claimed equal status with him and wouldn't lie under him during sex because of it. Lilith fled the garden of Eden and refused to come back, when three angels tried to persuade her to do so. The three angels found Lilith in a cave bearing children, but Lilith refused to come back to the garden. The angels told her they would kill a number of her children every day for her disobedience. After the angels' departure, Lilith tried to return to the garden but upon her arrival she discovered that Adam already had another mate, Eve. Out of revenge, Lilith had sex with Adam while he was sleeping and 'stole his seed'. With his seed she bears 'lilium', earth-bound demons to replace her children killed by the angels. Lilith is also said to be responsible for men's erotic dreams and night emissions. She was then cursed to be the mother of demons and would seek to kill Adam's sons. Adam, now having no wife, was given the more submissive Eve who would listen to and obey him. Huh! That didn't work when you think of the story of temptation with the serpent and the apple…"

Vanda urged him, "There's more… It seems Lilith is a very beautiful woman evoking desire in men, but she is a succubus. I didn't know what the hell that was. But I found actual cases of men being enslaved by a demon female lover who comes to them in their dreams to have sex with them. The men would suffer a deterioration in their health and state of mind, and it would lead to death. Some died after the sex, others took a little longer. There are references to succubae in every culture and country although called different names."

"Then it makes sense," said Adam amazed.

"What? How?"

"Think about it. Kenneth Parkes was suffering from nightmares, so began sleeping in another room. His wife thought him delusional. He died after he had ejaculated. I heard my mother's voice in the station she said the word succubus… Somehow this cult or whatever it is in the school, is something to do with it."

"What do we do now? This is way out of my experience."

"Mine, too. But I am going back to the school with Vance this afternoon."

"This seems so farfetched. We'll have trouble making anyone believe us. Heck, even I don't really believe it. Do you think I should come?"

"No, you stay here and do some more research."

"Won't it be dangerous for you to return?"

"We'll get over it. And we need to take a trip back to Moss Woods. See what else we can learn."

"All right. But I don't like it. I don't like it at all."

~ 2 ~

THE WEATHER HAD TURNED CLOUDY, thick bubbling clouds that hung in a layered ceiling of decaying grey. There was no sign of the sun. Trees shadowed the ground, making strange and grotesque shapes resembling alien beings from another world. Adam hoped it wasn't some kind of portent as he travelled the coast road to Brinkworth. The atmosphere was heavy, almost as if a thunderstorm was due. He sighed wearily and concentrated on the road, dismissing the many thoughts that crowded his brain. As he approached the small market town, a few people he knew, spotted him and gave him a friendly wave, which he acknowledged with a smile and a nod of his head.

Adam made his way through the streets to the police station and parked carefully. He met Vance coming down the stairs, who indicated he should follow and ride with him and Jacobs. Adam fell into step behind them to Vance's car, an unmarked BMW, and climbed in the back. Vance switched on the engine, but the car refused to start. Puzzled, Vance alighted and lifted up the bonnet. He couldn't see anything obviously wrong and got back in the driver's seat and tried again. Still nothing. Adam got out, as did Jacobs, and they both stared into the engine, not that it revealed anything.

Jacobs murmured, "I'll call Ernie at the garage and get him to come and take a look. We'll have to take an official car."

"And that's what I didn't want to do. It's like an early warning system announcing that the police are here!"

"Don't think we have much choice," said Jacobs.

Vance sighed heavily. "We could take your car, Adam."

"I don't really want to advertise the fact that I'm back. I'm hoping they won't remember me."

Vance snorted. "Okay. Jacobs go and fetch a car, whilst I ring Ernie."

Jacobs returned driving an Audi A3. They swapped places and Vance took the wheel, and Adam, once more, got into the back and using the Sat Nav, they travelled on towards the boarding school. Conversation was lively as they turned off from the small market town and into the countryside. Jacobs was testing out his questions for the next quiz night at the local pub. Inexplicably, as they travelled a more remote lane, they became quieter and eventually fell into silence.

They were passing along a deserted single track country road, with fields on either side, when the sun finally burned through the clouds that were now slowly dissipating. There was a thundering cracking noise as a stout oak tree close to the hedgerow came crashing down, coming right through the hedge at an acute angle, which completely blocked the road. Vance yelled and slammed on the brakes. The car skidded wildly and ploughed straight through the hedge, down the bank and into the field, and stalled. Vance thumped the dash in exasperation. He turned to the others, "Is everyone all right?"

"I'm a bit shaken up, but no damage," answered Jacobs, looking dazed.

Adam rubbed his shoulder, where his seat belt had pulled tightly. "Glad I was wearing my belt."

"Well, you were right about me driving," said Vance remembering a previous warning from Adam.

"Yes. I just didn't think I'd be with you," said Adam. "Let's get out and inspect the damage."

They exited the vehicle and walked around it. Adam got down and looked under the car. "It looks okay."

"What do we do now?" asked Jacobs.

Vance finished giving the vehicle the once over. "Fortunately, the car doesn't appear to be too bad, a few scuffs and scratches. They will T cut out. We need to get it out of the field. At least it's dry. If the grass was wet it may be a different story, and we'd be stuck here," said Vance.

"You get in and drive. The sarge and I will push if and when we need to," advised Adam.

Vance got back in the driver's seat and started the engine. He slipped it into first gear and gently manoeuvred the Audi around and took a run at the bank, but it rolled back. Adam and Jacobs hurried after it and heaved against the car, now in neutral. It took a monumental effort but the wheels finally gripped the ground and reached the top of the bank. It plummeted down, back through the hedge and Vance just managed to stop the car from hitting the huge tree trunk about a foot away.

Jacobs and Adam scrambled after the car and got back in as Vance cursed and swung the car around. He manoeuvred the vehicle in four attempts to return the way they had come in order to take a different route.

"We must call it in," said Vance. "Someone will need to get out here and clear that away. Sat Nav is useless now. It will keep telling us to do a U-turn." As if to concur with what Vance had said, the efficient female voice said, "Make a U-turn as soon as possible." Vance cancelled the guidance.

Jacobs swore, "Dammit! Adam, can you check the map? See if there's a decent route for us to take. The map's in the pocket in the back of the seat."

Adam pulled out the map and studied it, and as he did so, a strange tickling sensation ran down his spine and he heard the voice of Bob Dylan singing, 'Lay Lady Lay' cutting into his thoughts. He shook his head and his mother's soft tones whispered, "Ley lines, Adam... Ley lines... Take a straight line from Copse Corner and the small church there, passing through the ancient burial mounds..."

Her voice dissolved into a soft hissing noise as Jacobs spoke again. "Can you see a way through?"

Adam suddenly came to and concentrated on the map. He could see Copse Corner marked next to a tiny, abandoned church where the road veered off and passed close by some Iron Age burial mounds. His finger traced a straight line passing through an old abbey and through Gilbert Bray School and beyond to a medieval church. "Yes, back the way we came and veer off right at Copse Corner..."

"That's not the most direct route," said Vance.

"But the road will lead to Gilbert Bray. You'll see."

"Bit like going through Jerusalem to get to Jericho," quipped Vance. "If you're sure?"

"I'm sure."

"Okay," said Vance with a sigh and he turned off at the left fork from Copse Corner and pursued a much rougher single track road. They drove on and as they neared the small, ruined church, with its tiny graveyard there was a bang. The car shuddered to a halt. Vance got out to check the car and found the rear passenger side tyre had blown on a particularly sharp stone that had cut into the rubber threads.

"Oh, no," groaned Vance.

"What is it?" asked Jacobs.

"We've got a flat."

Jacobs and Adam alighted to inspect the damage and as they did a number of crows circled around them. One landed on the roof of the car and eyed them beadily. A cloud passed over the newly shining face of the sun and the temperature dropped.

"There's nothing for it, we'll have to change it." Vance took off his jacket, rolled up his sleeves and walked to the boot and opened it. He lifted up the floor panel and removed a jack and the spare wheel. "Jacobs, I haven't notified the authorities about the blocked road, yet. Can you call in about the tree?"

Jacobs nodded and took out his mobile phone. He lifted it up to try and get a signal and as he raised it above his head the crow on the car flew at him and knocked the phone from his hand, which landed with a clatter on the stones, smashing the screen. Jacobs went to retrieve it as more crows flew down to attack him. His face was scratched and one bird landed on his head and tried to peck at his eye. Jacobs raced back to the car flapping his arms in a wild attempt to stave off the attack and he dived in the front passenger side door and locked it as the body of one crow thudded against the glass. Adam glanced up and called to Vance, "Get back in the car, now." Adam quickly clambered in and shut the door as other crows batted against the glass. Vance scrambled up from the floor and dashed to the driver's door. Two crows landed on him, and one pecked at Vance's hand as he struggled to open the door. He managed to fling it off but not before its needle sharp talons had dug into his hand, which was now bleeding profusely. He hit out at the other on his shoulder that was pecking his cheek, and it fluttered to the floor allowing him time to get back inside the car and lock it.

The murder of crows landed on the fence by the road and some on the car bonnet. They fixed their baleful eyes on the occupants in the car and waited. "What the hell was that?" exclaimed Vance.

Jacobs exclaimed, "I've never seen anything like it. What do we do?"

"Wait… do you hear that?" said Adam.

"What?"

"That!"

All three men listened closely and on the wind came the sound of drumming. A repetitive rhythm that echoed around them. The birds lifted their heads and began to caw. One by one they flew up and away into the sky and the drumming stopped.

"Is it all right to get out now?" asked Jacobs.

Vance looked at Adam. "What do you think?"

Adam nodded. "I believe we're safe now. Let's get that wheel changed."

Vance was the first to get out of the car. He stepped out warily and kept looking about him. Adam was next and Jacobs last. They all stared about them in trepidation before Vance wrapped his hand in his handkerchief and knelt down. He then set to, trying to jack up the car to change the wheel.

Fifteen minutes later, with help from Adam, the spare wheel was in place and the three got in the car again. Vance glanced at his watch. "What now? Look at the time. Those two mishaps have taken so much time out of the afternoon, I think we should leave it until tomorrow. What do you say?"

Jacobs nodded. "I agree. Try again tomorrow."

Adam added, "I think something, or someone is trying to stop us going to the school. If we go on today, it will only invite something else to prevent us travelling and I think that might be worse."

A hush descended on them as they digested Adam's words.

"What? That's terrible!" exclaimed Vanda as Adam finished telling her everything that happened. "Those crows sound frightening."

"They were. You should have seen Vance's hand and Jacobs' cheek. It was like that film of Hitchcock… The birds."

"Don't think I've seen it."

"It's really old, made around 1963, I think. I remember my mum and dad watching it on a classic streaming service. I was only a tot. I woke up and crept downstairs and watched part of it through the door. It scared the pants off me. I had nightmares for a week. My parents didn't realise I'd been watching from the doorway and couldn't understand why I was so upset. I daren't tell them in case I got into trouble. I've never forgotten it."

"So what now?"

"The answer is in Moss Woods. Someone doesn't want us poking about in Gilbert Bray School and surrounds. We need to discover what is going on. Well, we are going to… It's a full moon tonight. We are going to take a look."

"Don't you think you should tell Vance?"

Adam shook his head. "Shaitan and that art teacher Russell Draper won't be expecting us after today. They will think they're safe. It's the best time to go. Strike while the iron is hot, as they say."

"Well, I don't like it. I think you're asking for trouble," said Vanda with a toss of her head.

"You don't have to come."

"What and leave you with goodness knows what to come after you? No, I'll be there. Remember, I'm the voice of reason."

Adam sighed, he knew it would be hard to dissuade Vanda. "All right. But first some more research."

"What kind of research?"

"Ley lines. What they mean and how it fits in with the school."

"Ley lines?"

"Something my mother said. I heard her voice in my head when we were travelling. Well, I heard Bob Dylan first."

"Bob Dylan?"

"Singing, Lay Lady, Lay."

"I see," said Vanda hesitantly although it was clear that she didn't. "Okay. How do you spell it with an a or an e?"

"An e."

She picked up her laptop and typed in Ley lines and waited to see what the search produced. "It says here that Ley lines are straight alignments drawn between various historic structures, prehistoric sites and landmarks."

"Yes, I know. I studied the map and Gilbert Bray School is on such a line."

"How does that help us?"

"It doesn't. It means we need to be aware of the power likely to be present."

"What sort of power?"

"I don't know very much, that's why we need to research it. But I believe the energy created by these lines supports and accelerates spirit activity. People used to say it was to help alien spacecraft."

"Now you've lost me."

"Let's just read it together," said Adam and he drew up a chair alongside Vanda and they scrolled down the screen together, whilst Elsa, Vanda's cat watched unblinkingly from the sofa.

The moon had risen and its full, glowing, silver face shone down on Gilbert Bray School and Moss Woods. A group of girls of mixed ages was gathered in the clearing all dressed in white robes, with flowers plaited in their hair. An aged, huge, gnarled oak tree stood tall at the head of the clearing. Ravens and crows adorned its branches. Nailed to its bark was an upside down cross and in front of that was a tall athletically built man wearing a wolf's head, and black and gold robes.

A bonfire with a cauldron type cooking pot held aloft by two stakes with an adjoining bar bubbled over the fire. In front of the man was a large pentacle that had been scorched into the grass and earth and further delineated by white chalk pebbles that shone eerily in the moon's light.

The man, Leonard Shaitan, whose eyes had turned blood red, held an ornate chalice aloft, filled with milky liquid taken from the pot. Either side of the man sat two very large dogs, which seemed subdued but whose eyes glinted malevolently in the flickering light of the fire. Shaitan ordered them away, "Go, guard the entrance to the woods until our ritual chants reach their peak and then return." The animals loped off.

Shaitan led some sort of chant and one by one the young women stepped forward to drink deeply from the goblet. When emptied, a flaxen haired man, Russell Draper, dressed in forest green, took the vessel and refilled it from the bubbling cauldron, whilst two women clearly intoxicated with some kind of drug beat a regular rhythm on Haitian Tanbou drums.

Once all the girls had drunk from the elaborate chalice they sat inside the pentacle and swayed to the unearthly drumming music. Shaitan called out, "Lilith, I command you to come forth!" A stunningly beautiful young woman with long dark hair that flowed down her back and dressed in gold appeared in the shadows. She was with the student Michelle, who wore a tight-fitting black catsuit that clung to her shape. It fitted her as if her clothes had been turned into liquid oil that had set on her body. Lilith pushed her forward to kneel before Shaitan.

He lifted his arms and with his flowing robes he resembled a giant crow with shredded feathered wings. He stepped forward and placed his hand on Michelle's head. "Daughter of darkness, disciple of Lilith, you who will know men and bend them to your will are to be renamed Sabrina, and with that name I invoke all the powers of Lilith to be duplicated in you. I shower you with all the arts and gifts you will need to go forth to tempt and destroy our enemies to bring our lord's kingdom here on earth." He brought his other arm down and shrouding her as would a hawk with its prey she disappeared from view.

Shaitan let out a groan of ecstasy as he shivered in melting delight and his eyelids fluttered. His knees buckled and he called out, "Sabrina has become. Sabrina is."

The girls echoed his words and swayed in unison, "Sabrina has become. Sabrina is."

Shaitan continued, "Sabrina will stop our enemies. Sabrina is."

The girls chanted again, "Sabrina is. Sabrina is."

A howl went up in the forest and the two wolf-like dogs emerged back into the clearing and flanked Shaitan as he unwrapped Michelle now Sabrina and she rose before him. She stood and walked seductively to Lilith who welcomed her into her arms before leading her to stand by one of the animals and Lilith glided to the side of the other. Then the drums began to beat and the girls in the pentacle swayed and rocked as if possessed by some kind of internal music.

Betty Buswell, the receptionist moved from the shadows and knelt before Shaitan. He offered her the chalice from which she drank freely before untying two silken cords at her waist. She attached one to each of the dogs' collars and moved off into the woods leading both animals.

Another mournful howl was heard and the girls in the pentacle swayed and chanted in time to the beat of the drums. Shaitan, with Lilith and Sabrina lifted up their arms and called out in a strange language. The metronome rhythm of his words stilled the drums and silenced the girls in the pentacle before he clapped his hands and called them to attention. One by one they became quiet. He gestured for them to rise and disperse. The girls stepped out of the pentacle and ran back from the clearing, through the wood, and back towards the school.

Vanda and Adam had arrived at the outskirts of the school. The full moon shone its ethereal silver light appearing to highlight Moss Woods, whilst the school was submerged in cloud. They parked securely and stealthily crept into the woods trying not to make a sound. They were both wearing dark tracksuits and trainers. They heard the drumming stop and the unworldly howls that echoed mournfully in the trees. There was a sudden rush of voices murmuring something unintelligible and they tried to take cover as a stream of young girls ran past them towards the school. Their eyes looked wide and distracted and although passing within only a few feet of the couple they appeared not to see them. Adam and Vanda held their breath, which Vanda let out in a huge whoosh when she deemed it safe to do so.

Adam whispered, "We've missed whatever it was they were doing. Come on."

"If we've missed it, why not just go?"

"No. There is something else here. I can feel it."

They waited a few minutes and attempted to continue to thread their way through the woods, when Adam raised his hand to stop Vanda moving. They heard a dog growl, the sound carried on the night air like an imam's voice on a minaret. Adam signalled to Vanda that he was going to climb a tree. She nodded and watched as he shinned up a large sycamore tree with low slung branches. A dog barked and the sound seemed much closer now. Vanda began to panic and she, too, searched for a suitable tree to climb. Driven by adrenaline she struggled up another tree and crouched with difficulty in the branches.

A fierce snarling could be heard and the school receptionist dressed in golden robes came through the leaf littered path with the two dogs. They approached the trees where the couple were hiding and the animals began to bark furiously at an opaque white substance, which seemed to emanate and grow from nowhere and transform into a woman that appeared before the creatures who salivated and went wild. The receptionist struggled to hold onto them as they pulled her after the strange apparition, which darted on through the woods leading them away from the trees in question.

A few minutes later, Betty Buswell, the receptionist came back the way she had come without the creatures and passed by Adam and Vanda without seeing them and returned to the school. Once she was out of earshot, Adam jumped down and went to help Vanda from her precarious perch. She had torn her track bottoms and grazed her knees in the climb.

"What the hell was...?" whispered Vanda, but Adam put his finger to his lips to quieten her. She gingerly followed Adam, who moved on through the woods until he came to the clearing. The bonfire had died down now to a small flickering ember mass. The cross had vanished from the tree although the nails could still be seen in the trunk where it had been fixed. There was no sign of the chalice but there was a spillage of the milky liquid that had come from the cauldron, which had also gone. Adam gathered up what he could of the seepage on the leaf detritus and placed it in a freezer bag. He had come prepared.

The pentacle could still be seen, and Adam removed his mobile phone from his pocket and took a few pictures. He gestured to Vanda, and he followed the path that had been taken by the receptionist through the woods. They continued past the trees they had climbed, along the route taken by the dogs and moved deeper into the trees where the tracks from the dogs led them. They appeared to stop at a huge hollow oak, with a large girth, resembling something from a child's fairy story. Adam peered inside. It was quite cavernous and there was an empty wire metal crate sitting on the leaf litter. Adam pulled his head back and stepped back out.

"There's no more for us to see today, let's get back to the car, we can talk there."

Vanda nodded. They carefully picked their way back and got into the car. Vanda burst out, "What the heck was that in the clearing?"

"What?"

"It sent the dogs mad."

"The apparition?"

"Apparition? I didn't see any apparition."

"No. But those creatures did. They chased after it. It certainly helped us."

"Do you mean there was another ghost?"

Adam nodded. "Yes. I believe it was the spirit of my grandmother."

"This is just too weird."

"Guess, you'll have to get used to it! Come on. We have to see Vance."

"Now?"

"Now," Adam affirmed.

~ 3 ~

VANDA AND ADAM REACHED THE police station in Brinkworth late that night but there was no sign of Vance. "You can hardly expect him to be on duty 24/7," said Vanda.

"I know. I just thought if he was here we could tell him what had happened."

The duty sergeant said kindly, "I know he left work early today, some kind of family emergency but he did leave a message for you. Mr Barrie, isn't it?"

Adam nodded, "Yes, that's me." The duty sergeant rummaged under his desk and pulled out an envelope. "He asked me to give you this, if perchance you came into the station."

Adam took the proffered note. "Thanks. Come on, Vanda, we'd best get back."

"Aren't you going to open it?"

Adam tore at the envelope looked at the letter and passed it to Vanda who read it avidly, "He doesn't want you to go with them tomorrow. Thinks it will be safer."

"Well, it won't. He needs me. Dammit, he needs to see what we saw."

Leonard Shaitan stretched out on his bed, Michelle lying next to him. She lay her hand on his chest and played with his nipples, making them taut and erect. He leaned across to her and stroked her hair. "So, Michelle, Sabrina renamed, how are you feeling now?"

Michelle said dreamily, "Empowered, strong…"

"But are you compliant?" Shaitan asked.

"I will be whatever you want me to be, Master."

"It is good," murmured Shaitan as he began to caress her. "Soon we will begin the next stage of initiation, where you will join Lilith, and you will be my chosen one. That time is coming. Are you ready?"

"I am ready," said Michelle in a monotone, her eyes wide and blankly staring.

"Are you able to leave your parents, remove yourself from their care?"

"I am ready."

"Will you do my will and bow to me?"

"Whatever you wish, Master."

Leonard Shaitan's eyes turned red as he clambered upon her and joined with her in a frenzied bout of sexual passion.

The next morning, Adam left Vanda continuing her research into Gilbert Bray School and relevant local news stories. She was also looking for evidence of Leonard Shaitan and Russell Draper on social media. She could find no trace of Shaitan himself but did uncover references to him. Vanda discovered much more about Russell Draper who had begun life as an artist and lived in a commune in France for many years belonging to a cult, 'Children of the Light'. It sounded fairly innocuous in its pledges, advocating love, tolerance and freedom of expression. The members worked in the community and gave up their possessions to the cult. But she also found a disturbing number of stories of interventions by parents and family who endeavoured to rescue their children and bring them back to settled 'normal' family life. Some were successful but other rescues had been tragic, resulting in suicide and a few youngsters being sectioned in mental health facilities where doctors attempted to de-programme them. Following the actions of an Anglican vicar, Melvyn Thomas, who infiltrated the group and did an exposé on the workings and management of the cult, it was finally disbanded. The members and leaders in the hierarchy went their own separate ways, some were never heard from again. She then learned that Draper had trained for the priesthood, but against all God's rules he involved himself in a torrid affair with a young married woman, who believed he was the Messiah, which saw him defrocked and he forcibly left the profession. Vanda had to agree that he did bear a physical resemblance to her own idea of Jesus and thought that might be part of his attraction to the young. However, Draper didn't crop up in any more stories and his social media page showed him as a hardworking art teacher who nurtured his students' talent.

Vanda then decided to do a search for Melvyn Thomas, covering all the platforms that she used. She found him on Facebook, but nowhere else. She did find a couple of news stories about him and the fact that he was the vicar in a local parish just twenty-five miles away. She was able to access his address and phone number and determined to ring him as soon as she had finished her searches.

Adam had arrived at the police station and argued his case with Vance. "So you see, you must let me come with you. I know what to show you in the woods."

"What if the receptionist recognises you?"

"Let's hope she doesn't."

"We can't trust hope. Put a hat or cap on and keep your head down and averted from any CCTV. Don't engage with anyone and listen to my instructions. Understood?"

"Yes, yes, of course," said Adam happy to comply.

"Okay. We leave in an hour. We will use an unmarked car and Jacobs will drive. I don't want to chance anything else."

Adam nodded, he knew Vance was referring to the accident when he was driving, just as Adam had predicted. "Just make sure you take a catchpole," said Adam.

"I will. I know better than to ignore your warnings."

"Good. I'll grab a coffee and get a cap in town. I'll be back in..." he checked his watch, "exactly one hour."

Vanda had printed off all the relevant results from her searches and set them aside for Adam. She picked up the phone and dialled the number for Melvyn Thomas. It rang a number of times and then a breathless Welsh voice answered, "Hello?"

"Melvyn Thomas?"

"Yes... Sorry, you'll have to excuse me and let me catch my breath. I was outside when I heard the phone ringing and had to run back to answer. Okay... who is this and how can I help?" His voice was gentle, and his tone was kind.

"I wonder if I can come and see you?"

"Why? What's this about?"

"I'll explain when I see you but it's to do with The Children of Light."

"Oh, no. They haven't started up again, have they?"

"Not to my knowledge."

"That's a relief."

"But I do need to talk to you." It sounded to Vanda as if he was turning pages of a book, maybe a desk diary.

"Um... well, all right. Can you get here for 2:00pm? After lunch? I have a prayer meeting before that."

"That will be perfect," purred Vanda.

"And may I ask your name?"

"It's Vanda, Vanda Sullivan and it is urgent."

Melvyn didn't ask any more questions. "I'll see you at two. Do you know where to come?" Vanda reeled off an address. "Yes, that's correct. I'll see you at two. I must admit you have made me very curious."

"Thank you, Mr Thomas. I will explain everything then."

Adam had enjoyed a latte at a local coffee shop in the High Street and had ventured into a Scope charity shop and purchased a black baseball cap, and a tweed jacket with leather covered buttons. He kept the items on, and the assistant parcelled up Adam's linen coat. He thanked the woman politely and made his way back to the police station, where Vance and Jacobs waited on the steps. Vance was standing with a catchpole in his hand. "Ah, there you are. I feel a bit stupid with this in my hand but never mind. Jacobs, get the car." Jacobs went off to the car pool and Vance gave Adam the once over. "Hmm, I suppose that will help. What did you wear last time?"

"Nothing like this."

"I'm glad to hear it," said Vance as Jacobs arrived with the car. Vance placed the catchpole in the boot and got in the front passenger side as Adam clambered in the back and they set off.

This time the journey was uneventful, no falling trees, flat tyres or marauding crows. They drove the recognised route to the school and Vance warned Adam, "Keep your head down and no asking questions."

Adam nodded. "Understood. Did you find out what the substance was that I found in the woods?"

Vance shook his head. "Nothing yet. But it was confirmed from your previous visit that the blood on the bark of the tree was a mixture of chicken and human blood."

"Was it, indeed?"

"Yes. I can't tell you anymore except one was a rare blood type."

Adam digested this information, and the rest of the journey continued in silence.

On the approach to the school Vance reminded him, "Remember, no questions or interference and keep your head down."

Adam nodded with a rueful smile. He knew the fact that he was impulsive could get him into trouble. "Yes, okay but after you've done your bit at the school, drive around to the woods and I'll lead you in by foot and you'll see it all for yourself."

The majority of children were still on their summer holiday, so there was a skeleton staff to look after a number of students that had boarded on the premises through the break.

Adam hung back as Vance approached the receptionist and hoped she wouldn't recognise him. The woman, Betty Buswell, was this time, dressed in her normal attire. She glanced at Jacobs and him but there was no flicker of recognition and Adam inwardly breathed a sigh of relief but still kept his head down.

Betty Buswell was quite gushing with her answers to Vance. "Such a shame about little Melanie Parker. What a horrible way to die. Who on earth would do such a thing? And Kenneth Parkes, too. He was a pleasant man. I was sorry to see him leave. He'd worked here for years. Such a shame. But I don't think I can tell you anything about Mr Parkes. You'd be better off visiting his place of employment at the other school. I don't really think I can tell you anything else...Will that be all?"

Vance thanked her and turned away signalling to Jacobs and Adam to go to the car. "Jacobs, you can drive." And then, he stopped and turned. "Ms Buswell, you have been most helpful."

"I have?"

"Yes, all the background you have given me on Melanie Parker is very useful... Could I trouble you for a couple of more things?"

Betty Buswell beamed brightly. "Of course. What is it?"

"I'd like a list of all the staff members, teaching and ancillary. Also, Melanie Parker's peer group, can you furnish me with her class list?"

Ms Buswell hesitated and then smiled again. "But of course, hold on, I won't be a moment." Vance urged Adam and Jacobs to return with his eyes and they left the foyer, whilst Vance waited for the lists. Miss Buswell examined the files in the cabinet and exclaimed, "Ah, here we are." She passed Vance a list of all the staff.

Vance prompted, "And the class list?"

"Oh, my... Of course, how silly of me." She returned to the filing cabinet and selected another drawer, removed some papers and looked through them. She selected three and crossed to Vance. "These are Melanie's year group. Three tutor groups in all. Will there be anything else?"

"No, no. That's fine. If I need anything else..."

"Please don't hesitate to ask." She smiled again and fixed him with her eyes, watching him carefully as he walked away. There was a tap, tap, tap, on the office window and a large black crow was pecking at its reflection in the glass.

Betty Buswell stared into the devilish eyes of the crow and waved her hand, "Shoo! Go on. Be off with you." The crow cawed raucously and flew off into the sky. She gave a small shudder before returning to her workstation and continuing with her copy typing.

Once outside, Vance approached the others in the car, where the crow now sat on the bonnet. Jacobs and Adam were staring at it, willing it to go away. Vance waved his arms and the creature flew up, its powerful wings taking it across the school to the woods. He climbed into the passenger seat. "Okay, Adam, which way?"

Adam directed Jacobs back down the sweeping drive and they circled the school arriving at the back of the woods where they parked securely out of sight of the road. Adam had a niggling feeling and heard a whispered word, "Keys". He reached forward and took the car keys after Vance and Jacobs alighted. Once Adam was out of the car the three of them ventured into the woods. As they penetrated further into the trees a strange serpentine mist began to writhe along the ground wrapping itself around the base of trees and rising up into the canopy. Adam stopped. "This isn't normal." As he said this he could just hear the sound of drums on the air. He raised his hand to stop them. "Listen!"

"What?... I can't hear anything," said Vance.

"Nor me," asserted Jacobs.

"It's very faint." They all stood rigidly hardly breathing and listened. Jacobs and Vance shook their heads and reiterated that they could hear nothing. Adam closed his eyes as he focused. "No, it's gone now. Come on." They moved further into the woods and a crow, with a white tip on the end of one of its tail feathers landed on a branch of a tree close to where they had been standing but none of them saw.

The mist grew thicker and swirled around them as they approached the clearing where Adam had seen the pentacle and remnants of a bonfire. The white pebbles defining the mystical symbol had gone. There were marks on the grass that showed the grass had been scorched and more evidence of a fire. Adam pointed at the tree, which bore scars of nails that had been driven into the bark and the blood residue. "It was here, the pentacle and other things I reported to you."

"Well, there's not a lot here now," murmured Vance. "Is this where you found the milky substance?"

Adam nodded, and a low mournful howl filtered through the cloying mist. "Did you hear that?" he whispered.

Jacobs spoke in his normal voice making them jump. "Aye and I for one don't want to stick around to find out what made it."

Adam shook his head. "No, but you must see what else I found. Come this way." Adam began to walk cautiously along the path that had been left by the dogs although it was getting harder to see in the encircling fog.

Jacobs and Vance trooped after him. "We mustn't get separated," asserted Vance.

"No, these woods are dangerous enough at night," said Adam. "Keep together."

They slowly meandered their way carefully through the woods until they reached the hollow tree, where the temperature dropped rapidly. Again there was an eerie howl that appeared to emanate from the hollow. Adam looked about him nervously. "Perhaps this isn't such a good idea."

The fog seemed to swirl and thicken so much that they could no longer see each other or the tree. There was a low growl that developed into a snarl, which was joined by another different rumbling warning. There were other sounds of twigs snapping and leaves crunching underfoot. Jacobs whispered, "What do we do?"

"Stand still and wait," said Vance.

They waited for what seemed like an eternity as other strange sounds drifted towards them in the sinister fog. The mist began to dissipate revealing two large aggressive looking Alsatian-type dogs with their lips curled revealing mouths full of viciously sharp teeth, standing in front of the hollow tree opening. They were looking straight at Vance.

~ 4 ~

VANCE TOOK A STEP BACK and the snarling dogs drew closer. Their jaws dripped with saliva. Jacobs was rooted to the spot as he looked on in horror. Adam was nowhere to be seen. It seemed he had vanished.

Vance attempted to calm the animals talking soothingly, "Steady, boys. Good dogs, Steady."

But with hackles raised and the lips continuing to curl back on those wolfish teeth, the creatures would not be pacified. They continued to creep forward until they were within springing distance. Sounds of someone crashing through the undergrowth alerted the dogs that turned their heads to see Adam enter the clearing carrying a catchpole. He moved gingerly towards them. The animals were uncertain where to look and Adam attempted to reassure them, "Easy does it. Easy, now. I'm not going to hurt you, come on. Good dogs... Sit. SIT!" he said more forcefully. One creature whined softly and put its head on one side, and sat, the other continued, snarling and salivating as Adam drew nearer with the catchpole. He attempted to ensnare the creature in the head ring when there was a fierce hammering of a drum, and the animal crept back and charged into the undergrowth. The other dog yelped as if stung or hit with something and streaked off squealing.

Vance took in a huge gulp of air, not realising he'd been holding his breath. Jacobs heaved a sigh of relief and they both looked at Adam questioningly. "What?" he asked when he saw their expressions. "I made a dash back to the car when I could to retrieve the catchpole. I just hoped I would be in time."

"How did you get the keys?" asked Jacobs.

"I took them before I left the car."

"Why?"

Adam shrugged. "I just had a feeling…"

"Good job you did. Come on, let's get out of here. I've had enough for one day," ordered Vance.

"But we haven't investigated that hollow tree," protested Adam.

"And I don't think we should. Let's go. We'll come more prepared next time," said Vance.

As he spoke the crow with the white tipped feather landed on the branch of the tree and eyed them. Another one landed next to the first and it was enough to make them move, and they scrambled back the way they had come.

One of the crows cawed and shook its feathers before flapping its enormous wings and taking to the sky. It cruised overhead observing their path back to their vehicle and landed in the canopy of a spreading horse chestnut tree and watched as the three men hurried into their car and accelerated along the road. The crow took off and circled above the trees before a series of drumbeats echoed through the forest, and it flew off following the car.

Vanda had arrived at the vicarage of The Sacred Heart Church in Entwhistle twenty-five miles away from Brinkworth. She parked on the gravel drive next to a small pond and fountain, locked her car and crunched towards the stone steps that led to the front door of an appealing looking stone cottage with wisteria growing in abundance and climbing up the granite walls. Fragrant roses meandered around the trellis work of the porch. It was altogether a pretty home. Vanda took a deep breath and rang the bell, which chimed merrily, belying the seriousness of her visit.

She heard someone approaching the door, which opened and a homely looking plump woman with salt and pepper hair tied up in a bun and wearing a flowered overall apron answered. "Yes?"

"Oh, hello. I have an appointment with Mr Thomas at 2:00. It's Vanda, Vanda Sullivan."

"Oh, yes. Melvyn is expecting you. Do come in." She ushered Vanda into a flagstone tiled hallway and closed the door. "I'm Melvyn's wife, Helen." Vanda nodded in acknowledgement. "He's in the study. Step this way." She led Vanda along a corridor to a room at the end and knocked on the old pine door before opening it. "Melvyn, Miss Sullivan is here to see you." She opened the door wider allowing Vanda to pass through and added, "I'll go and put the kettle on, I'm sure you'd like a cup of tea after your drive?"

"Thank you," accepted Vanda and stared at the roomy study with its dark grain mahogany furniture. One wall was lined completely with books ranging from esoteric literature, and numerous novels by various authors including some supernatural thrillers by Joe Talon and another by Dion Fortune. There was a glass cabinet containing a number of different Bibles, and prayer books and other biblical works. The window facing the garden had stained glass in the top pane and on the shelf beneath that, stood a large brass cross, which caught the rainbow lights of the glass. Either side were two ornately carved wooden candlesticks with cream candles that had dripped wax from much use that cascaded like flowing lava down the wood. Melvyn Thomas sat behind a heavy leather topped desk. He rose up to meet her and walked to the front of his desk and extended his hand. He was wearing a comfortable fawn lambs' wool cardigan with pockets, over a blue, small, check shirt and baggy brown corduroy trousers. He had a shock of brown hair with a broad streak of white at the front and thick bushy eyebrows that made him look like a mad professor.

"Ah, Miss Sullivan do sit down, please," and he indicated the seat in front of the desk in green leather, where she duly sat as he retreated to the other side of the desk and settled in a typical black leather office chair with a high back, and leaned back. "Now, what's this about The Children of Light?"

"Oh, it's not directly related to The Children of Light but regarding one of its members or maybe he was a spiritual leader, I am not sure. His name is Russell Draper."

Melvyn Thomas flinched at the name, and he shook his head vehemently. "Ah yes, Russell Draper. I haven't heard that name in a long while. A very handsome and charismatic man who had started out with true and good intentions of spreading the word of the Lord. He wanted to recompense for his misdeeds, failing in the priesthood and falling into sin with a young woman."

"What can you tell me about him?"

Melvyn shook his head. "A poor misguided soul who was seduced by that conniving witch woman."

Vanda looked up. "Do you mind if I record this?" She took out her voice activated Dictaphone.

"Not at all. But firstly, can you explain what your interest is, in this man?"

Vanda nodded and explained all that had transpired so far, including the events that Adam had related. Melvyn sighed and shook his head sadly. "You had better turn that machine on now. What I have to tell you is not only shocking but deeply disturbing. I had hoped never to come across that name again."

Vanda switched it on and asked politely, "Do you mean Russell Draper?"

He nodded slowly. "Russell Draper is a very sad case but the other name you mentioned, Leonard Shaitan. He is the devil incarnate."

Vanda stopped him. "Sorry, would you mind repeating all that you have told me?"

Melvyn nodded and repeated what he had already said and continued with Vanda asking various questions until the tape stopped and she had to turn it over. He described events as they had happened, concluding with, "So you see, Draper was a poor confused soul who was ripe for the taking. Shaitan is the embodiment of evil that corrupted the young flesh of the girls and corrupted Draper. I am convinced that somewhere inside Draper is that spark of good, a tiny flame of the essence of the man he once was."

"But I found no references to Shaitan in my research…"

"Nor will you. He is a very clever man. Somehow or another he managed to get away scot free. Whether it was bribery or sorcery I do not know but his involvement with the cult seemed to be wiped from everyone's mind except mine. No one would admit to knowing him. Draper took the rap for all of it. He escaped punishment as the girls admitted following him of their own free will so that no charges were made." Melvyn stopped and studied Vanda's face. "You are an attractive woman, Miss Sullivan. I would be very wary. Leonard

Shaitan has unworldly powers that can fool even the most educated amongst us. You are very much his type of conquest." Vanda shivered. "I would advise you to leave this business alone. Let the police deal with it."

"I can't. There are children involved, and young girls who have already died."

Melvyn encouraged her, "Then you had better tell me all of it."

Vance reached the police station in Brinkworth, parked outside, and admitted, "I've never been so spooked in all my life."

"Not even when the crows attacked us?" asked Adam.

"Well, that too. But this was just as scary, and you did warn me about it. It will certainly make me listen to anything you might have to say."

"Me, too," added Jacobs.

"Come on, let's get inside. Jacobs you take the car to the police car park."

Jacobs acknowledged as they all got out of the vehicle and stepped around to the driver's side. There was a whoosh of wings and Jacobs looked up. He saw the crow with the white tipped feather above his head and watched it as it flew across to a sycamore tree opposite the station and settled in its branches. "Those birds really unnerve me now."

"You're not the only one," said Vance. "Let's get inside."

"Wait," said Adam. "Isn't that the one from the woods?"

"Is it?"

"Look at the splash of white on its tail feathers."

Vance and Jacobs looked. "It can't be," said Jacobs incredulously.

"It certainly looks like it," agreed Vance. "Come on, forget the car for now. Hurry."

They ran up the steps into the station and made their way to Vance's office. Adam sat in the chair opposite Vance who was shuffling through a pile of messages and notes that had been left for him. Jacobs glanced at the window and stared as the crow arrived on the windowsill and peered in at them. It was the crow with white on its tail. "I don't like this," he muttered. "Why has the damn thing followed us?"

Adam looked at the creature. "I don't know. Maybe it's trying to give us some kind of message…"

"Or maybe it's after our blood," murmured Jacobs.

"Aren't they some kind of harbingers of death?" asked Vance.

"Along with ravens and vultures," said Adam.

"Thank goodness we don't have vultures here…" said Jacobs.

A feminine voice whispered in Adam's ear, "Careful what you say. It's listening to you."

Adam exclaimed, "It's watching us. Watching and listening."

Vance looked up sharply. "Are you sure about that, Adam?"

"It's what I've just been told."

"Then we had better be careful."

"And, I have to get back," said Adam. "I'll ring you later."

Vance nodded. "By which time, we should have worked out our next move."

Adam drove back to Black Head Ridge House and was surprised to see a yellow Vauxhall Astra parked outside. It was not one he recognised as belonging to a friend. He alighted quickly and looked up at the sky searching for signs of crows. There were none. He sighed in relief. The Astra driver's door opened, and a man got out. He was wearing a dog collar and had a shock of brown hair with a broad silver white streak at the front that almost looked as if it had been dyed. He wore a large gold cross around his neck and was carrying a file and a black leather bound Bible.

"Mr Barrie?"

"Yes?" Adam said questioningly.

"Melvyn Thomas." The name meant nothing to him. "Your friend Vanda Sullivan came to see me today."

"Yes?" Adam's voice was instantly more alert.

"Miss Sullivan said she would join us when you returned."

"Look, what's this about?"

"Sorry, let me introduce myself, I am the vicar at The Sacred Heart Church in Entwhistle." Adam remained silent and Melvyn continued, "Let me explain. Is it all right if I come in?"

"Where is Miss Sullivan?"

"I'll give her a call," said Melvyn.

"No," corrected Adam. "*I'll* give her a call." He took out his mobile phone and dialled her number, which was answered almost immediately. "Vanda?... There's a guy here says he's a vicar... Yes... Okay." Adam curtailed the call and addressed Melvyn. "Vanda said she'll be across. You had better come in." Adam crossed to the house and took out his keys, as he did so the wind chimes at the cottage tinkled in the air although there was hardly a breath of wind. They entered and Adam led the way to the sitting room. "Do sit down. Would you like a coffee or tea?"

"A glass of water would be good, thanks."

Adam nodded and went to the kitchen. He poured an ice cold glass of filtered water from his fridge and made himself an elderflower cordial and carried both into the lounge, where Melvyn was sitting in a wingback chair facing the double doors that led to the garden. As he passed the vicar his water he heard the front door latch and called out, "We're in here."

Vanda scurried in, acknowledged the vicar and gave Adam a swift peck on the cheek. She sat on the settee and turned to Melvyn. "Have you said anything?"

Melvyn shook his head. "Mr Barrie has only just returned. And anyway, I thought I'd wait for you."

Adam looked from one to the other. "Well, somebody tell me something."

Vanda nodded at Melvyn. "Tell Adam from the beginning."

"The Children of the Light was a cult that resided in the Peak District. I was a curate then at St. Margaret's Church in Wetton. The church committed to the safeguarding of children, young people as well as adults, but the main focus was children. They followed the House of Bishops' Guidance and had their own Parish Safeguarding Officers, PSOs. It was a wonderful parish until certain events occurred in Thor's Cave, Beeston Tor and in the abandoned house in Shining Cliff Woods. All of these places have otherworldly connections from the mischievous sprite that dwelled in Thor's Cave and would screech at night, and in haunted Shining Cliff Woods, which was inhabited by a malevolent stalker called Jeffers who was on the lookout for travellers that dared to enter his domain after nightfall. But I digress, the contour lines that link all these places make them powerfully attractive to spirits and it was this attraction that drew Lilith and other demons to the area." Adam and Vanda exchanged a look. "Russell Draper's looks and charisma, his Bohemian style of dress and his artistic talent made him a magnet to young girls, and he took advantage of this to enlighten children to come to God. As I said, originally, his presence was instructive and comforting but then something happened, and things took a sinister turn. A teenage boy died. It was claimed he fell through a hole in the roof of the abandoned house in the woods, but I know it was something else. Draper had a large following and he was their spiritual leader, but it was after a woman joined him and children disappeared. Others that were old enough, cut themselves off from their families and they would visit local towns and try to enrol as many people as they could, and the cult was truly born." Vanda shivered and Adam felt a drop in temperature. "One young lady, Fleur Henderson, became so caught up in everything, her parents contacted the church to see if we could help. Fleur had changed her name, as had other cult members, and she had picked the name Sabrina." Another look passed between Adam and Vanda. "She believed she was the chosen one to be with the Messiah as they called Draper. In the background of all this stood another man, Leonard Shaitan, who was the real driving force behind the cult, orchestrating things almost anonymously and he corrupted young Draper." Melvyn stopped and sighed.

"What happened?" asked Adam.

"I went in as a convert originally, to try and uncover the workings of the cult. They influenced and manipulated young, impressionable minds by using mind controlling drugs and hallucinogens."

Adam muttered, "I suspected as much. I'm sorry, please go on."

"The plan was to rescue Fleur with help from another two curates from neighbouring parishes. I would open the door of the cult premises to admit them. She didn't go quietly. She kicked and screamed and was slavering like a wild animal. The other two managed to drag her out to her father's waiting car and they drove away."

"So, in effect you kidnapped her?"

"I suppose so, yes. But I was left to take on Shaitan who had emerged from a basement in the property and faced me. There was no doubt in my mind that he was the embodiment of pure evil." Melvyn stopped as the memories of that night came flooding back to him. He had to catch his breath. "Events that happened that night left me with a permanent mark." He pointed to his stripe of white in his hair. "This happened overnight on that same night." His hand was shaking, and Adam was filled with compassion. He rose and crossed to him to reassure him. As he rested his hand on his shoulder a shock wave washed through his body and as Melvyn continued, Adam saw in flashback the terrifying events as they had happened.

He recoiled in horror at the appearance of Leonard Shaitan, whose handsome good looks changed dramatically after his eyes turned blood red. Half of his face was normal and the other half, fell away, dripping with wriggling maggots and a stench surrounded him emanating from his pores, which sprouted droplets of a vile black substance. His hands were heavily veined, and his thick nails resembled claws. He let out a screech and two hybrid wolf gargoyle-type creatures came up from the depths and flanked him. Melvyn lifted his Bible with one hand and began reciting from the Book of Prayer as with his other hand he held up his big brass cross making Shaitan hiss. Steam bubbled from Shaitan's mouth and he retreated back to the basement steps where Melvyn saw a swirling vortex that spun around and glowed until the thing that was Shaitan was sucked backwards and he shrieked blowing out a powerful blast of sulphurous air, which gusted across Melvyn's hair and forehead, turning it white. Adam's face had paled at what he had witnessed, and he sat with a bump on a chair, while Vanda looked on in puzzlement. She shook her head and went into the kitchen as Adam and Melvyn sat in an uncomfortable silence, which was broken by Vanda who returned with a pot of tea on a tray. No one spoke and Vanda looked from one to the other. She finally piped up, "So, what the hell just happened?"

"That's it," said Melvyn. "Hell."

Melvyn sat back in his chair and gratefully sipped his cup of tea, which Vanda had delivered. "Shaitan derived his power from a portal to evil that was a gateway to Hell made possible by the place where Ley lines were present allowing increased energy and spirit activity. It sounds to me as if Moss Woods is on a similar path of lines to Shining Cliff Woods, exacerbating the unearthly power that has manifested into a pit of evil."

Vanda and Adam were quiet as they digested all the information. Melvyn continued, "You cannot do this alone. You will need help."

"We have the police," said Vanda.

"That's not enough and they are not equipped to deal with such evil. You need the power of God to banish Shaitan back from whence he came and banish him for good."

"How do we do that?" asked Adam.

"I will help you."

LEONARD SHAITAN WAS PERFORMING A ritual in Moss Woods with his demon dogs at his side, now passive and sitting calmly. He had sliced into his arm and filled a chalice with his own blood. His injury was then sealed by Betty Buswell who knelt at his feet. He bade her to drink announcing, "My blood will mingle with yours, you are one more step closer to joining me in my kingdom." Betty took a mouthful, which dribbled down her chin. Shaitan smeared the residue across her face. Michelle now Sabrina was invited to do the same and last of all Lilith partook of the chalice and her eyes flamed red. "You now have the tools to defeat our enemies. Lilith will first visit Sergeant Jacobs and then go to Adam Barrie on the night of the next full moon and you, Sabrina, will steal Inspector Vance's seed. You will make him a slave to your passions and destroy him. Only then can we risk taking another child to refuel our power at the portal." Shaitan glanced across at Draper who looked concerned. "Something troubling you, brother?"

Draper floundered in his response. "Why do we need another child? Surely Lilith and Sabrina will be enough."

"You forget that to keep the portal open we need many innocent souls if we are to achieve our dominion on earth and all the earthly riches we desire. Does this trouble you, brother?"

Draper hesitated, "Er… No, Master. I just thought another missing child from the school would bring the police back here."

"Who said anything about the school?"

"Then... how?"

"There are villages around here with children. It's about time we spread our wings."

"Don't you think it's too soon?"

"Are you questioning me?" Shaitan's eyes turned a venomous black.

"No, Master. I just worry about discovery," murmured Draper.

"You do my will, obey my orders and we will soon achieve all our aims." Draper went quiet. He knew when not to press Shaitan. "Here!" Shaitan lifted a bowl. "Take and drink. It will calm your fears."

Draper was hesitant but knew he had to drink. He couldn't pretend to partake with Shaitan keeping him under such close scrutiny, so he took as small a draught as he dared and sat at the base of the hollow tree and waited for the substance to take effect. He knew how to react. Normally, the mixture would take away his will and increase his submission to all demands. And with those thoughts raging in his brain, he dropped his head as if falling into a glassy-eyed stupor. It was not safe to appear to rebel. He closed his eyes and waited.

A crow descended onto the bough of a tree that stood next to the police station. It had a white tipped feather at the base of its tail. From there it flew to the windowsill outside Vance's office. It stalked across the sill to the far edge and cocked its head as if listening to conversations in the room that filtered through the open window.

Vance was addressing his team. "We have to go back to the school and Moss Woods. Something very strange is going on there. We need to interview girls and staff. Jacobs contact Barrie, he can come with us. Arrange it for the end of the week."

Jacobs nodded. "Yes, sir," and he scribbled something in his notebook.

The crow on the ledge cawed and flew off in the direction from which it came. "Did you see that?" asked Vance.

Jacobs nodded. "Aye, sir. It was like it was listening." The other members of the team looked in amazement and disbelief at Jacobs and then back at Vance.

"Yes, I thought so, too. We will catch them off guard. It's Monday today. We will return Wednesday."

"Sorry, sir. Did you say you thought the creature was listening?" asked Harding.

"Yes, I did. I don't expect you to believe me but after Jacobs and my experience the other day, I don't doubt it." There was a hush in the room as the rest of the officers exchanged glances. "Now any questions?" One young officer raised his hand. "Yes, Warman?"

"Sir, if we are not going until Wednesday, what do we do until then?"

"I want everyone to do some more research, Jacobs can organise that at the end of this meeting." Jacobs nodded. "Divide it up. We need everything you can find out about Gilbert Bray School, its staff, financials, and the area. Also, the results are through on the residue of the milky substance that was found. It seems one of the main ingredients is shrooms otherwise known as magic mushrooms. I don't know if I can pronounce this properly but the main ingredient in the fungi is a hallucinogen called Psilocybin, which after ingestion turns into psilocin. I have a picture of them here." He held up a photograph of the fungi. "It grows in the wild and can cause nausea and vomiting but mainly makes people giggly and excited and causes confusion, distortion of sight and sound, setting off hallucinations. It can trigger a bad trip if the person taking it is in a bad place and it can be detected in the system for about eight hours, also the effects of the drugs last about five hours. It's often mixed with something else to make it more palatable. Okay, men, that's all for now."

The crow had flown back to Moss Woods and landed close to the hollow tree, where Shaitan still waited but alone. It croaked raucously and Shaitan lifted his head, his eyes were black, and he flicked his tongue around his lips. It was forked. The crow called again before flying off into the leaf canopy. Shaitan murmured aloud, "So that's their plan? To revisit at the end of the week. Well, I'll be ready. Thank you, Cawdor. You have been very useful." He rose up from the ground and disappeared inside the hollow tree and descended the leaf strewn path into the pit of the earth, where the temperature rose, and unusual sounds whispered. He moved onwards until he met a swirling pool of blue light that rotated in a turbulent pulsating vortex, and he vanished within it. There was a clamour of rasping voices, and a steady metronome drum beat that accelerated before being stilled into a cacophony of eerie wailing.

Russell Draper was in his quarters at the school and shaking as if gripped by some sort of ague. He was sweating profusely, and his face was unnaturally pale. He began to see all manner of deformed beasts and birds. He tried closing his eyes, but the images wouldn't leave him. He could smell their sulphurous breath and feel the proximity of their burning bodies and he shuddered.

Another gentle Welsh voice entered his thoughts, and his mind travelled into a spiral of memories of the Peak District and events that had happened there at the abandoned house in Shining Cliff Woods where the spirit of Jeffers that stalked there had sent a young boy crazy. He remembered Thor's Cave, Beeston Tor and The Children of the Light Cult that had ended so tragically.

Russell Draper sobbed for his soul that had once been pure and filled with love, and he yearned to be that man again. He rose unsteadily to his feet and stumbled to his chest of drawers. He wrenched open the bottom drawer and removed a pile of underwear, which he threw on the floor and stared at the leather bound Bible with its gold cross shining brightly almost glowing and went to pick it up, but it burnt his hand, and he dropped it. He took a handkerchief and wrapped it around his hand and lifted up the tome. Using his hankie, he turned the pages to the New Testament and began to read with tears streaming down his face. He fell to his knees, placed his hands together and for the first time in a long time he prayed.

Outside his window, Cawdor watched before flying back into Moss Woods.

Adam was busy chopping onions for the bolognaise sauce he was making for dinner that night, when he received an image of Russell Draper and heard a tortured cry for help. He stopped and wiped his brow. What was he seeing? And what could he smell?

Russell Draper was being dragged by shadowy misshapen beings into sulphurous depths. He cried out to God in anguish. The image dissipated into one of numerous crows landing in the clearing in Moss Woods. The crow with the white tipped feather, Cawdor, hopped onto a low branch of the hollow tree and appeared to address his gathering with a succession of raucous cries. The creatures flapped their oily looking, burnished, ragged wings and rose up into the canopy and flew off in different directions.

Adam shook his head. He hadn't a clue what the vision meant and tried to concentrate on the task in hand, but his face reflected his concern as Vanda breezed in.

"Mm something smells good," she indicated the bubbling pan and then glanced at his harried expression. "What's happened to you? What's wrong?"

"Nothing has happened to me yet. I just had a weird feeling come premonition."

"Well, what was it?"

Adam explained what he'd 'seen' and felt.

"Do you think there will be another attack of the crows?"

"I don't know. But what about Russell Draper?"

"If he's dragged away to Hell or wherever, isn't that a good thing?"

"But after what Melvyn said, I'm not so sure. If the man once had a good heart and was corrupted by Shaitan then maybe he can be reached. I don't know. But we definitely need Melvyn's help."

"Will you tell Vance?"

"I suppose I have to, especially with regard to the crows."

Vance was in his office trying to work out what had happened to Jacobs who looked as if he'd been out on the tiles all night. "For goodness' sake, man. What have you been doing? You look a mess."

"I feel as if I have been up all night. I don't know. I feel drained as if the life has been sucked out of me. It's hard to explain. And the dreams… I can't tell you all of them but there was a woman involved…"

"All right, Jacobs. We're not dealing in fantasy here but facts. Buck up."

"Yes, sir." Jacobs flopped into his seat looking defeated as if he had no will of his own.

The phone rang and Vance answered. "Adam? What can I do for you?"

Adam explained about his premonition and warned him, "I just thought you should know because…" He trailed off and Vanda looked across at him curiously. His eyes were moving rapidly, and he gasped.

"Adam?"

"Er, sorry. Is Jacobs with you?"

"Yes."

"Is he all right?"

If Vance was flummoxed by the question he didn't show it. He glanced at Jacobs still looking haggard. "Now that you mention it, no. He seems extra tired. Why?"

"Put him on the phone." Vance put it on speaker before passing it across to Jacobs, who looked up in surprise as he took it. "Hello?"

"Jacobs you need to be careful."

"Why?"

"Last night will be repeated. That woman… you must be aware… She is not a woman. She will try and enslave you."

"What? This is nonsense."

"No. Listen. She is a succubus."

"A what?"

"You're being visited by a demon lover who wants to steal your seed and drain your life from you."

"How do you know this?"

"I've seen it. And she will eventually cause your death unless you can stop it."

Vance interrupted, "But how? How can she be stopped?"

"He mustn't sleep alone."

"But my wife is in a separate room because of my snoring," protested Jacobs.

"Her name is Lilith, and her sexual passions and desire are lethal. If you don't resist or protect yourself, you will die. That is unless she falls in love with you."

Vance and Jacobs stared at each other in disbelief. Jacobs said, "How do I do that?"

"I will do my best to help you, but I have to call in a friend, a man of God. I'll get back to you. Don't go home tonight, stay in the station and we can take it in turns to sit with you. I have to go. Try and keep him occupied, Vance," urged Adam curtailing the call.

"You heard the man. Ring your wife and tell her you won't be home tonight, that it's to do with work."

"But…"

"No buts. Whatever is happening is dangerous and trying to stop us investigating murder."

Adam called Melvyn Thomas immediately, "Melvyn? Adam. We really do need your help urgently. Can you come to Black Head Ridge House and then on to the police station?"

"Why? What's happened?"

"Everything you feared and more. The police sergeant Jacobs has had a visit from Lilith." He paused slightly with a look to Vanda and added, "And I fear I am next."

Vanda's hand flew to her mouth, and she gasped. "Why do you say that?"

"My mother has just told me."

Melvyn had heard the interchange and exclaimed, "Adam!" There was a slight pause before he continued, "I'll be there as quickly as I can. I have to gather some things together. Don't leave the man on his own."

"We're not. He'll be staying at the station tonight. We'll take it in turns to keep watch."

"I'll be with you in around thirty minutes." Adam hung up the phone and turned to Vanda, "What have we got on the succubus? How can they be killed?"

Vanda pulled up what she had found in her research notes. "It says here that silver can be used against them…"

"What? Like a vampire?"

"It's not very specific, we can hardly chuck silver spoons at her…"

"I expect it means silver bullets or a silver knife."

"I've got a silver letter opener," said Adam.

"What else?"

"It says that Albasters are the sworn enemy of Succubi."

"What? The material that some figures and statues are made of?"

"No. An Albaster is a Fae species that feeds off sexual shame. Regarded as the natural enemy of the Succubus, Albasters siphon chi from their victims through their hands, by touching their victim."

"How does that help us? We're into the realm of fantasy here."

"I know, apparently a succubus can fight, but it definitely prefers not to, and certainly not when the odds are stacked against it."

"So, a bedroom full of people armed with silver weapons could overwhelm it?"

"Theoretically. But there would be nothing to stop it returning when it was safer to do so. It would just melt away into the shadows. It says here that they corrupt people in their dreams over time and only come to the mortal realm to drive their victims to the point of doing bad or otherwise evil deeds on their own. The victim's soul only belongs to a succubus after doing three evil acts, one each of thought, word, and deed. Once the victim's soul belongs to the succubus, the succubus kills their victim and sends their soul to the lower planes. The more 'good' a person is, the longer it takes, and the more pleasure the succubus gets from their downfall. You can bet that the more souls that are sent to the lower planes in the final days, the more power the succubus has."

"We need someone incorruptible, someone of faith, a Holy priest or nun."

"We definitely need Melvyn. He's been through this before and lives to tell the tale and he's on his way."

"Then all we can do is wait."

~ 6 ~

MELVYN THOMAS BUSIED HIMSELF PACKING a bag that he filled with some clothes, toiletries and a number of sacred items, a large brass cross, his Bible, a bottle of Holy water, a Catholic prayer book and his own prayer book. He wore his vicar's garb and hung a heavy gold crucifix around his neck. He hurried outside and picked a number of different herbs, and gathered a bunch of white sage, which he put into a bundle, which also went in the bag. He grabbed a drum of rock salt from the kitchen cupboard and an iron poker from the hearth before picking up his car keys and saying goodbye to his wife.

Melvyn sat in his car and started the engine as a crow landed on the fence outside his cottage and another began strutting around the garden. Another landed on the bonnet of the vehicle and Melvyn flinched. This wasn't right. He began to move down his drive with the crow still on his bonnet. The car picked up speed but the crow remained rooted in place until Melvyn opened his coat and lifted up his gold cross to the windscreen with one hand. The bird screeched and flew off the car. Melvyn drove as fast as he could, unaware that six crows were keeping pace with him flying directly above him in the sky.

He raced as fast as he dared along a quiet country road and skidded to a halt when he saw a shimmering haze that began to manifest in the road ahead. He shook his head realising that it was not of this world. He put his foot down on the accelerator and hurtled forward as the apparition of a child became more solid. He took a deep breath and ploughed on and into the 'child' who screamed. Melvyn didn't stop. He glanced in his rear view mirror and saw that there was nothing lying in the road behind him and heaving a sigh of relief he thundered on towards Brinkworth. He knew this was going to be bad and probably worse than he had experienced in the Peak District. He pressed on hoping that nothing else would try to stop him reaching his destination.

Melvyn gave a huge sigh of relief as he turned off the road to Brinkworth and made for Black Head Ridge House. As soon as he arrived outside the mansion, Adam opened the door ready to usher him in. He grabbed his bag, locked up his car, and heard a fluttering of wings making him look up and was shocked to see a number of crows land on the grass on the cliff path close to the house. He hurried inside the house and followed Adam to the kitchen where Vanda had just put the kettle on to boil.

Adam pointed at the bag, "What's in there?"

"Tools to help us defeat Shaitan. Let me explain." Melvyn opened the bag and took out the drum of rock salt. "Salt. We need to spread it on each threshold of doors that lead outside and on windowsills that have windows, which open to the outside."

"What does that do?" asked Vanda.

"It deters malevolent spirits from crossing into the house. Fresh garlic will also help but I didn't have any."

"We have some," said Vanda.

"Good. Place that around entrances, too. And we will need some for the police station, I'll probably need some more salt. This is a big house."

"Got that, too," offered Adam taking out a new cardboard container of rock salt from the cupboard, and some ordinary table salt.

"Not table salt. It must be rock salt." He waited until the table salt was returned to the cupboard. Next, Melvyn lifted out his bundle of white sage. "This must be lit, blown out and left to smoulder and the smoke wafted around the areas that need cleansing from ghosts or bad spirits. Ensure each corner of every affected room is treated. If you don't have white sage, garden sage will do just as well. It has a cleansing effect and will repel evil spirits. This must be done in the police station, too."

"This sounds more like witchcraft or pagan spells," observed Adam.

"I can get some more of that sage stuff from the Crystal shop in Brinkworth," murmured Vanda.

"I know it sounds crazy, but we need everything we can to throw at the demon that is Leonard Shaitan. Don't worry I have many Holy items, too." He looked at Vanda. "Do you have a cross you can wear?"

"I do. I have an ornate one and a rosary, which I can give Adam, and my crucifix that my parents bought me."

"Why would you have a rosary?" asked Adam.

"From a fancy dress party where I went as a nun. It's at home. You can wear it."

Adam threw her a look with a half-smile. "I'd like to see that."

Melvyn ignored the banter and held up some lavender. "This is used for protection against psychic attacks and has a soothing and calming effect. Dried lavender can also be burned but do it safely in a ceramic or metal bowl and place it in the centre of a room. It will certainly be needed after we repel him and Lilith."

"Why do you have an iron poker?" asked Adam.

"It must be pure iron not an alloy and not overworked wrought iron. If touching a demon with it, it can neutralise their power and weaken them. This poker is pure iron. Do you have anything similar?"

Adam shook his head. "Not that I know of."

"What about silver?" he queried.

"I have a silver letter opener."

"Good, bring it. I have some silver spoons."

"I have some colloidal silver," said Vanda. "I use it for simple infections and so on."

"Bring that, too."

"I'll go back to my house and pick these items up."

"Not while those crows are around," warned Melvyn. "They were at my house and followed me here. They are outside now."

"Then what do we do?" asked Vanda.

"Can we get to your house by car?"

"Yes, but it's a long way around. Adam and I just walk along the cliff path to visit each other."

"It's too risky. Let me run through the other items and then we'll see."

Vanda's face had drained of colour, and she was feeling decidedly ill at ease. She left the kitchen and peered through the sitting room window and could see six of the birds on the grass, not strutting around but unmoving as if waiting. She dashed back to the kitchen where Melvyn had now emptied all the contents of his bag.

"There's six of them outside just standing there, not moving." She shivered uncomfortably.

"Six. That's the devil's number from six, six, six – the mark of the beast. The Holy number is seven as seven overpowers six," said Melvyn.

"What is that?" asked Vanda pointing at a bunch of yellow star shaped flowers.

"Perforated St. John's Wort, a Christian plant that repels devils and demons. Its leaves can leave a red stain said to be the blood of St. John or Christ and the tiny holes in the leaves are the marks where Satan tried to destroy it. Demons are hurt if they touch it."

There was a pause as the trio reflected on the task ahead. Vanda broke the uncomfortable silence. "Can't we use something to help me get back to my house? Something to protect me?"

"I have some Holy water."

"Can we get any more?"

"If you have some bottles of purified water then I can bless and sanctify it," said Melvyn.

"I've got some bottles of mineral water in the fridge, will that do?"

"Perfect," said Melvyn. "Give them to me and I will transform them. First, pass me your rock salt. It is good that you have salt in a pure form. Do you have a bowl or vessel I can put it in?"

Adam took out a large cereal china bowl. "Will this do?"

"It will." Melvyn tipped some rock salt into the vessel. "You may join me in prayer as I consecrate it. Follow this prayer here." He opened the Catholic prayer book and found the page. Vanda and Adam joined in the ritual prayer with Melvyn, finishing with, "Through our Lord Jesus Christ, Thy Son, Who lives and reigns with Thee through the unity of the Holy Spirit, God forever and ever, Amen… Now pass me the water. And I need another vessel."

Adam found a large copper bottomed saucepan and set it on the table.

Vanda took the two bottles and removed their tops. "Good. They have tops like a spout that can be used as a water pistol," observed Melvyn as he poured the water into the pan and Melvyn began performing an exorcism over the water, inviting Vanda and Adam to join in as before in the prayer.

"Now we mix the two, any salt left over, keep, and label as Holy salt. Don't confuse it with your table salt. You may need it again." He picked up a handful of exorcised salt and sprinkled it into the water in the shape of a cross reciting the correct words as he did so concluding, "The Lord be with you," to which Adam and Vanda responded, "May he also be with you."

Melvyn blessed the water finishing with the sign of the cross and looked up. "It is done. Fortunately, there is a pouring lip on this pan. You may now refill the bottles. That's a litre, and with what I have, we should have more than enough. We will have to share with your police friends."

"And we have more Holy salt if we need to make more," said Vanda with a smile.

"We do indeed," replied Melvyn. "Go now and place a trail of salt on your thresholds and sills."

Adam took two receptacles and picked up the rock salt. He filled both bowls and passed one to Vanda. "Vanda, if you do the doors downstairs, I'll do all the windows upstairs. It will take me a while."

"I'll do the downstairs windows, too," added Vanda.

"And then we will have to get out to the car," said Melvyn.

Melvyn waited in the kitchen as Adam and Vanda went off to do the salt protection. He was shocked to hear a tapping on the kitchen window where the largest crow, Cawdor sat and rapped its beak against the glass. Melvyn flinched and muttered a prayer to himself. He heard a rumbling sound coming from another room. Puzzled he walked into the hallway and followed the sound of the noise, which led him to the sitting room. Soot and debris came tumbling down the chimney. Melvyn stopped and rushed back to the kitchen and grabbed some rock salt and sprinkled it on the hearth and the noise stopped. He called out up the stairs, "Don't forget the fireplaces, anywhere where something could gain access."

Melvyn returned to the kitchen where Cawdor sat, pecking at the glass. He hoped the glass wouldn't break as the bird was battering it with such force. Melvyn walked to the window brandishing his cross and the creature screeched painfully like something inhuman and flew away.

Adam was the first back. "Thanks for calling out about the fireplaces. All the bedrooms have them upstairs. The salt is quite depleted now."

"We will have to purchase more from the cook shop in Brinkworth," said Melvyn.

Moments later Vanda returned. "All done. Have we enough to do my place and the police station?"

"We've already decided we need more. We'll get some on the way. Now are you ready?"

Vanda nodded and asked, "How do we do this?"

"We'll travel in my car," said Melvyn. "Have you an umbrella?"

"In the hallstand," said Adam.

"I suggest you get it. Is there more than one?"

"I think there are a couple," Adam said his brow furrowed as he tried to remember.

"Right. I'll pack these away. Take a bottle of Holy water each. I have mine. Let's get out to my car. Put the brollies up as soon as the door is opened. Can you still lock up?" Melvyn asked Adam.

"I can just pull it to. It will lock automatically."

"Good. What about the house next door?"

"There's no one living there, yet," said Adam.

"I should keep it that way until this business is over," advised Melvyn. "Now, have we got everything?"

"Everything from here. We still have to get Vanda's stuff."

"We'll get to the car, use your brollies for protection. If a crow flies at you, squirt it with water and flap your brolly. Let's drive around to Vanda's." Melvyn crossed to the door. "On the count of three, open it and your brolly, and get to my car. Quickly as you can."

Adam counted, "One, two, three." He opened the door. Melvyn went first opening his brolly in the porch and holding his water bottle like a gunslinger about to do battle. He flapped his umbrella pushing it up and down until he got to his car and opened it when the first crow flew down from the rooftop. It ripped at the umbrella, but Melvyn managed to open the door and continued flapping the brolly until he was sitting and closing his protection when the same crow tried to get into the car. Melvyn squirted his water bottle saying a prayer of banishment and the bird screamed and flew off wildly, cawing a warning. Vanda came next, and following Melvyn's instructions reached the car without any of the creatures attacking her. Adam pulled his door closed and waited for the click of the lock before he ran to the car when five of the creatures dived down attempting to settle on the umbrella even though he was flapping it. One bird caught him on the hand with its sharp beak and Adam squirted it. The thing flew off cawing and taking the others with it. Adam sprinkled some Holy water on his cut hand. It appeared to ease the sting, and he made it to the car. Vanda opened the door for him, and he slipped inside, shuddering, and said, "These aren't ordinary crows, these are from the devil's realm."

"Yes," agreed Melvyn as he started the car. "Not normal crows." He turned his vehicle around and sped off following Vanda's directions by road to Cliff Head House.

They pulled up in her driveway and Vanda looked about her warily before alighting. "I'll be as quick as I can." Carrying her water bottle and brolly she scrambled out of the car, and she hurried to her house and entered.

"Should I go after her?" asked Adam half-opening the door.

Melvyn peered up into the sky. "No. I think she'll be okay. I can't see any of the critters, can you?"

Adam peered out. "No, the sky is clear at the moment. Shouldn't we salt all her entrances and windows?"

"Later. No time now. We must get to the station. She can stay with you, can't she? Until this is sorted?"

"I suppose," said Adam hesitantly. "But Vanda does like her own space as do I."

"It will only be until this is over."

"That's if it ever gets over," said Adam miserably.

Vanda had found her items and was now wearing her crucifix. She passed the ornate one to Adam who hung it around his neck. He murmured, "It makes me look like medallion man."

"Better safe than sorry," quipped Vanda before passing him the rosary.

"What do I do with this?"

"Wear it."

"Bit overkill, isn't it?"

"You can always give it to Vance or Jacobs to wear. I doubt that they'll have anything like this."

"Perhaps you're right," said Adam as Melvyn sped off to the main Brinkworth road. The rest of the journey passed in silence until they reached the cop shop and parked in the police's back car park. Adam checked around the car and looked in the sky before giving the others the go-ahead to get out of the vehicle. Keeping their wits about them they hurried to the front of the building and ran up the steps and into the station, where they were greeted at reception by one of the constables on duty. Adam breezed up to the young man who phoned upstairs announcing their arrival and they were told to proceed to the top floor.

Once in Vance's office, Adam introduced Melvyn, and he explained what needed to be done. He looked at Jacobs who was looking haggard and drained and advised, "While here, we will fix you up with some sort of safe sleeping arrangements." Melvyn glanced at Vance and nodded at him to continue.

"We have a room with facilities for those officers who have to remain on duty all night in extreme circumstances. This clearly is one such time," said Vance.

"Where is it and can we see it?"

Vance nodded. "Follow me." He trooped from his office followed by the rest of them and led them down a corridor to a room with a bunk bed, a bedside table with a clock, two easy chairs and ensuite.

Melvyn looked around. "This is fine. At no time must the sergeant be left alone and it is imperative that the person or persons watching him, don't fall asleep. We have a number of things to do to protect the station. Measures have been taken at Adam's home. We will do Vanda's when we get back. I suggest you Chief Inspector do the same procedures at your home."

"What do we need to do?"

Melvyn explained all that was required. He removed the rock salt from his bag. "Miss Sullivan here, will purchase more from the cook shop in town." He addressed Vanda. "Do you have the rosary?" She nodded. "Hold it and I will bless it then give it to Jacobs to wear around his neck. It will help."

Vance interrupted, "What are we protecting him from?"

"Jacobs has been visited by the primordial mother of demons, Lilith. She is no ordinary woman but a succubus."

"A what?"

"A ravishingly beautiful woman that comes in the night to seduce men and infiltrate their dreams and steal their seed, which the creatures need to survive. Have no doubt, she will enslave him and corrupt his soul. She will fill him with desire and cause her victim to commit the three betrayals of thought, word, and deed and then the victim's soul belongs to the fiend. Sometimes the victim dies immediately after the sexual encounter, sometimes it's drawn out, but it will seem that the victim died of natural causes like a heart attack. Only if the creature falls in love with you, will you survive."

"This is crazy," snorted Vance.

"No, it's not," affirmed Adam. "It's at the root of the paranormal activities at Gilbert Bray School. You must listen to him."

"Silver will melt their skin. I have here a silver spoon, Adam has a silver knife. I'm afraid we don't have any silver bullets. But they are a deterrent. We have Holy water and sacred emblems to repel the creature. Did you notice anything unusual about this woman?"

Jacobs stuttered, "She had… claw-like talons, otherwise she was just as you said. But all this sounds potty. I thought it was just a… you know… a wet dream."

Vanda interrupted, "But it's not and no matter what you think, can you afford to take the risk?"

"The talons are a sign, and sometimes she has a serpentine tail," added Melvyn.

"So, what's the plan?" asked Vance tetchily.

"We draw up a rota of who is to sit with Jacobs and when. We must have two people at all times watching him. Not only that we have to be prepared to be attacked by other demonic beings, like those crows," said Adam.

"And the dogs?" asked Vance.

"And the dogs," agreed Adam.

Melvyn turned to Vanda, "You must be especially careful. Leonard Shaitan could easily try and attach himself to you. He has the desires of an incubus. He will want to conquer you."

Vanda shivered. "Get your roster drawn up. What about protecting the room and the station?"

"Adam and I will do that. Chief Inspector, can you send someone to get the rock salt? I don't think it's safe to send Miss Sullivan." Vanda looked up sharply, aghast at this pronouncement.

"I'll send Harding. But we can't let this information get out to the people of Brinkworth or amongst the rest of the Force. We'll be laughed out of town."

"Tell Harding the salt is to deal with an ants' nest. It'll do for the moment," suggested Adam.

"And now," said Melvyn, "we prepare."

$$\sim 7 \sim$$

THE FLAMING RAYS OF THE sun had dipped and disappeared through the horizon emblazoning the sky a bloody red, which mixed with pinks and oranges that was nature's version of an artist's oil painting of a sunset. The pink hues would soon melt to dusk to wait for the approach of the cloak of night.

Salt had been sprinkled on all thresholds leading outside and on all windowsills, which opened to the night air. Melvyn had set up his large brass cross. He sat in one of the easy chairs, his gold crucifix around his neck, holding his heavy black leather bound Bible. His book of prayer was at his side together with his bottle of Holy water.

Jacobs sat on the edge of the bunk looking tired and uncomfortable. Vance sat in the other chair. He leafed through a magazine before tossing it aside with a sigh. "How long do we have to wait?"

"As long as it takes," replied Melvyn. "Adam will be relieving you soon. He's taking the graveyard shift, as we say. He is well equipped to deal with this, as am I."

"What about you?"

"I'll be here throughout. I can snatch sleep as long as my partner on watch remains vigilant and awake, and he rouses me when anything strange happens."

Vance grunted, "If I hadn't witnessed what I've experienced so far, I'd think this was a load of mumbo jumbo."

"That's what these entities rely on. Lack of belief. It makes their job much easier as folks don't properly prepare and succumb to their will in fright."

Vance fell silent, he had seen too much to doubt what was being said and in truth he was feeling both apprehensive about what was to come and nervous. The relief was apparent in his eyes as Adam entered. He signalled to Vance, who rose and walked to the door, and turned as Adam sat in his vacated chair. Adam watched Vance as he hesitated. "Vance, I'll see you in four hours. Now try and get some sleep." Vance nodded and left. Adam glanced at Melvyn. "You, too, Melvyn. I'm wide awake and feeling fresh. Take this opportunity to grab some shuteye. I'll be okay."

"Very well but keep an eye on him. If he falls asleep it may visit him in his dreams and not manifest before us. Watch his eyes and his breathing. It could be a sign."

Melvyn leaned back in his chair and closed his eyes. Moments later he was sound asleep. The room became oppressively quiet. All that could be heard was the deep rhythmic breathing of Melvyn. 'At least he doesn't snore,' thought Adam.

The metronome tick of the room's carriage clock seemed to steadily increase in volume and Adam looked about him warily.

Jacobs spoke, his voice was loud in the uncanny silence except for the ticking clock and Adam recoiled. "Adam… Sorry, I didn't mean to startle you."

"That's okay. I think we're all a bit jumpy."

"I was just going to say, I'm going to try and get my head down if that's all right?"

"Go for it. Think you'll need it."

Jacobs adjusted the pillow and stretched out on the bed with a sigh, pulling up the blanket to cover him, hiding the rosary from sight.

Time seemed to stand still as the temperature began to drop and Adam shivered. He could feel that strange sensation of the hairs on the back of his neck and arms beginning to prick up and stand to attention. Adam took a deep breath and leaned forward in his seat to carefully watch Jacobs. He stared hard at the figure of Jacobs convinced he could see a shimmering, translucent greenish mass hovering above him that appeared to float down and sit on his chest.

Jacobs struggled to move but it was apparent his chest was constricted as if trapped by constricting vines or the serpentine coils of a python. His breathing was becoming laboured as if the life was being sucked out of him. Adam stood and picked up his silver letter opener and slashed at the mystery emanation, which manifested into a woman who hissed in anger as the blade melted her skin where Adam had hacked at the form, which he couldn't physically see. He grabbed his Holy water and splashed some on the apparition who was now a physical being. The thing on Jacobs screeched in pain and dissolved before his eyes.

The agonised shriek woke Melvyn who rose, brandishing his cross and reciting a prayer. He crossed to Jacobs, blessing him with a prayer of purity and sprinkled Holy water over him and urged him to hold tightly to the rosary and leave it in visible sight on his chest.

Adam gasped, he had seen a woman with long flowing hair who was mesmerizingly beguiling and beautiful, but she had sharp claw-like talons for nails and he was sure he had seen a serpentine tail. He sighed her name, "Lilith, it must be." He turned to Melvyn, "What do we do?"

"She won't return tonight. Now she knows he has a support network she will be more careful."

"But we can't keep guard over him forever."

"No. And she knows that. She will wait and strike again."

"Then how do we get rid of her?"

"We will have to go to the portal and banish her in the name of God, the Holy Ghost and Jesus to the pits of Hell. But it will be dangerous and there are no guarantees."

Jacobs rose shakily and examined his chest, where he had felt searing pain. It was marked with claw marks that had drawn blood. His eyes looked wild as if defeated. And he slumped back down on the bed.

"But how did she get in?" queried Adam.

"She must have piggybacked on someone's shoulders…"

"How can she do that?"

"These creatures are cunning. They can't enter themselves as the salt will prevent them, but they can hitch a ride over the threshold by using an innocent soul, but that soul had better beware as they could find themselves a target for the succubus."

"Well, it can't be one of us, we have been here from the start."

"It could be anyone. It can ride in with that person again and that can provide a link between the two. You can be sure she will have chosen an attractive male that she can 'use' later."

"So, what do we do?" said Adam despairingly.

"We have to be vigilant and hope for the best. We can hardly furnish every copper with Holy items. You may be able to stay by the entrance and spot the victim, but it would mean I would be on my own here with Jacobs. I will need to sleep at some point."

"Then it's best we do as we're doing."

"Or take the step of visiting the portal." Melvyn left the sentence hanging in the air.

The velvet cloak of night enclosed Gilbert Bray School in its embrace. The girls who had remained at school were all dressed in loose white robes and Leonard Shaitan stood before them in his costume with a wolf's head. He was flanked by his two hybrid wolf dogs that sat at his side. A cauldron bubbled with some kind of liquid. Cawdor sat on the branch of a tree and watched. Betty Buswell knelt at his feet. She was swaying from side to side in some kind of trance. Shaitan stepped forward and commanded, "Lilith come forth." The leaves on the trees rustled and a whirling wind sprang up and danced around the clearing disturbing the leaf litter and detritus. Shaitan demanded again, "Lilith! I call on you to come forth."

A greenish haze flickered and glistened heralding the arrival of Lilith who began to manifest before them. The girls sighed and moaned in ecstasy as the full form of Lilith could be seen. As she appeared she hissed at Shaitan and showed him her arm where her skin had melted from the attack with the silver paperknife.

Shaitan insisted, "Whoever did this will suffer. He will be punished for hurting you and damaging your beautiful skin. Come let me heal you and make you whole again."

Shaitan began reciting in some strange language, "Keely mishwa, maragsha. Carridari Shalimar." He dropped some pasty coloured liquid onto her arm, which sizzled and fizzed. He rubbed the concoction into her skin before he called one dog to lick off the paste and miraculously underneath, the skin had been renewed. He praised and thanked Beelzebub, Lucifer, Moloch and Belial and the darkness around them intensified like syrupy molasses, and shining greenish emanations shimmered in the dark. A thousand voices whispered in the thickness and words could be partially heard and a demand grew. Shaitan raised his arms. He hushed the girls who swayed and wailed.

"He has spoken. We need another sacrifice, another life to be given up."

Michelle AKA Sabrina came forward. "Take me. I am become Sabrina, my life for immortality to be Lilith's sister, to serve you and defeat our enemies."

Shaitan shook his head. "It is not yet time. We must find another and not from our nest. To the cauldron, now."

The assembled girls rose and clasped hands encircling the cauldron as Shaitan raised his arms as if in supplication and called on his lord Satan to reveal truths to him. The surface of the bubbling cauldron ceased its jubilant bubbling and became still like a mirror. Shaitan waved his hand across the top and saw inside the police station and what had transpired. He noted the target Jacobs, and Adam watching over him. Shaitan took a sharp intake of breath as he saw Melvyn Thomas settled back on another bunk and his eyes turned a murderous red.

He waved his hand again, commanding the elements to reveal suitable children who could be taken from the surrounding area. The cauldron bubbled again before reverting to a pond-like stillness where a children's playground came into view. A pretty golden haired five or six-year-old sat on a swing stretching out her feet and leaning back and forth pumping her legs to rise higher on the swing. There were a number of kiddies playing on the roundabout, slide and see-saw. But Shaitan was fixated on this child, his eyes pulsed and he felt a craving. He asked his demon lords where this playground was situated.

The liquid in the cauldron rippled and changed and the name of the village on the village sign shimmered into view. It read 'Pengarran'. He almost sighed the village name, "Pengarran." He turned to Betty Buswell who was wild-eyed and almost seemed out of it. "Do you know where that is?"

Betty nodded and threw her head back in abandonment, looked at him and licked her lips lasciviously before answering, "Just down the road. About fifteen miles away."

"So, not too far away, but far away enough not to implicate the school." Shaitan looked back at the steaming cauldron, where the village sign was fading. "Show me the child again," Shaitan ordered, and the picture reverted back to the playground and the little girl happily playing with a little red-headed child on the slide. The selected child had an aura, which Shaitan studied. "I see... An Indigo child." He continued, "These children are believed to possess special, unusual, and sometimes supernatural traits or abilities. Perfect."

Shaitan closed his eyes, held his arms aloft and the girls remained holding hands and swaying as Shaitan intoned in a low voice. His words were unintelligible as he spoke in some strange tongue. The only distinguishable words were Russell Draper. Minutes later the art teacher appeared in the clearing and Shaitan alerted him to the next job in hand. He beckoned him across and using the water in the cauldron showed him what he had seen. "That little girl in Pengarran, she is special. Our master will be pleased. Where does this girl live?" Almost, as if in answer to his question, the mother came to the slide and helped her daughter up from the bottom. Her face puckered and her lips pouted. She clearly didn't want to go. The mother opened her bag and took out a lollipop, which she passed to her and content with that the youngster popped it in her mouth and began to suck it before waving to her friends. She held her mother's hand and they left the park, which Shaitan saw was Somersby Park. Shaitan watched as mother and child walked down the avenue and turned into Greenfield Road. He continued to watch until they walked up the drive to number 59. He had his answer.

"So, Russell, are you ready? Ready to embrace your future? Ready to appease me and our master for your lapse to the unmentionable as Cawdor has told me." Russell's eyes filled with alarm, and he looked down as if in submission and nodded. "Good. It is good. You must prove yourself. You are chosen to find her and bring her to me."

Russell looked up sharply. "You mean kidnap her?"

"But of course. How else are we to bring her soul to our master and lead her into his dominion?" Russell remained silent. Shaitan continued, "You cannot walk away now. You must fulfil your obligations. Then and only then will you have glory on earth, enjoy earthly pleasures and become untouchable. It's a small price to pay."

Draper nodded and sighed, it was clear he was reluctant to go. Betty Buswell spoke up, "Surely, it would be easier for me to collect the child. A child will more readily go with a woman than a man."

Shaitan pondered this and agreed. "You may be right. A woman will be more anonymous. The child will be more trusting of a woman. But mark this, you, Russell Draper, your loyalty is to be tested. I note your reluctance to do the task. You and Betty will do it together. Now go, make your plans. I must have the girl by the night of the full moon. You have three days." Shaitan raised his arms again, intoned an incantation and dismissed all the girls, who ran back through the woods in wild abandonment, giggling and laughing. Shaitan called his dogs, and they trooped off towards the hollow tree.

Draper and Buswell traipsed back to the school and stopped as the girls ran past them bubbling with excitement. Draper stopped. He turned to Betty, "Are you happy about this?"

She answered quickly, "Of course. If we are to have dominion on earth we must fulfil his wishes. It is a means to an end. I cannot wait for his kingdom to come, and we will be blessed with all that we desire."

Russell could see the feral light in her dark eyes and her commitment to the darkest of humanity and said no more. Betty turned to him. "I suggest we go before the night of the full moon. If we go too soon, it will be hard to keep her hidden." Draper nodded as he and Betty went their separate ways.

Draper retreated to his quarters his mind in turmoil. Yes, he had been promised a lot and it all sounded wonderful but to take a small child from her home and mother did not sit well with him. In fact, much of what Shaitan was doing didn't sit right with him. He felt that while under the influence of Shaitan's administered mind controlling drugs he had been brainwashed into doing Shaitan's will. But now... now he had resisted taking the offered mixture; he'd just pretended to drink it and had not been discovered, and now he was filled with deep remorse and shame, as he remembered all in which he had been involved. There was no talking to Betty who was besotted with Shaitan, nor could he reason with Shaitan. He was stuck but then... he thought... there just might be a chance. He needed to get in touch with Adam Barrie and soon.

The little blonde haired child, Marissa, sat at the tea table as her mother was preparing the evening meal. There was a clatter of pots and pans, and steam rose from bubbling water where vegetables cooked.

Marissa was smiling and giggling happily. She held her knife and fork and banged on the table in time with the music playing on the radio and the cacophony of kitchen sounds. Cawdor flew down and landed on the windowsill of the kitchen diner and peered in through the window. His malevolent beady eyes focused on the little girl, and he tapped on the window with his beak.

Marissa turned her head and stared at the crow. She frowned and her gaze became more penetrating. Cawdor croaked raucously and his eyes turned red. Marissa burst out in her small but clear voice, "Go away! You bad bird. Go."

Cawdor shook himself and flapped off the sill and away. The little girl settled back in her seat and smiled. It was a strange, all knowing smile that quickly vanished as her mother spoke to her. "What is it, Marissa?"

"There was a big, black bird, a bad bird."

"Where?" Marissa pointed her little finger at the window and her mother glanced across to the window. "Well, it's gone now. It was probably looking at its reflection in the glass. Nothing to worry about."

"What's flection?"

"Reflection." Marissa's mother lifted her up and took her into the hall. She stopped at the hall mirror. "Look, what do you see?"

"Mummy and me," said Marissa.

"Yes and the crow sees itself in the glass and thinks it's another crow and they're very territorial. They don't like strange crows on their home ground. Like I said, nothing to worry about."

"Well, I don't like them. That bird was bad."

"How do you know?"

"I just do."

"Well, it's gone now. Come on let's get back and have our tea." But the expression on Marissa's face showed she didn't believe it.

Adam Barrie sat up with a jolt. It had been his turn to sleep, but he had a strange feeling, and images of a little blonde girl popped into his head, followed by the same vision he had experienced about Russell Draper being dragged into some kind of vortex. He rubbed his eyes as his mother's voice filled his head.

"Adam, you need Russell Draper. Don't let him be taken."

Adam hadn't a clue what that meant but now he was wide awake. Jacobs still slumbered peacefully. The strain on the man's face was clear for anyone to see. He looked exhausted and drained. He tapped Melvyn on the shoulder who was dozing. Melvyn soon shook off the remnants of his half-sleep state.

"Melvyn, I need to get home for a shower and change of clothes. Will you be all right?"

"Vance should be here soon. You go. How long will you be?"

"An hour or two. No longer. I'll bring back something for you to eat. Tell me, do you believe Russell Draper is a threat?"

"He was, but I still feel that spark of goodness in him can be reached. He is not all bad and was once a man of God. Why?"

"Oh, nothing. Just a feeling." Adam didn't say anymore. He nodded at Melvyn and left the room.

ADAM STOOD IN THE KITCHEN at Black Head Ridge House making some sandwiches. He was freshly showered and changed. He turned to Vanda. "I was beginning not to like my own company."

"Go on with you."

"No really. I don't like sitting in the same clothes for two days."

"I thought you'd taken a bag?"

"I did. But I didn't fancy wearing anything I took. Not enough choice."

"You sound like some sort of glamour boy," said Vanda with a laugh. "If I didn't know you better…"

The doorbell rang and the wind chimes next door tinkled. "Who can that be?" said Adam.

Vanda shrugged, "How would I know? You're the psychic," she said teasingly. Adam made a face at her and left the kitchen. He walked to the front door and opened it. He was more than shocked when he saw Russell Draper standing there. He almost shut the door in the man's face.

"No wait! Please hear me out. You have to stop Shaitan." Adam looked at him questioningly. "Can I come in?" Adam shook his head. "Please. I have a lot to say to you and we can't risk Cawdor hearing us."

"Cawdor?"

"The crow with white tipped feathers."

Adam looked up at the sky and around the cliff top to see if the crows were evident. He opened the door and admitted Draper, who followed Adam inside to the kitchen. Vanda turned as they entered and looked at Adam completely stunned. "Are you out of your mind?"

"No, please hear me out. Both of you. You need to hear this."

Vanda's face remained frozen, her body language defiant. Adam gestured for Draper to sit, whilst he continued to prepare his sandwiches, but Draper insisted, "You need to stop." He indicated the sandwich making. "Please listen, I cannot be away for too long."

Reluctantly, Adam put down his knife and sat with a sigh. Russell continued, "I know you are deeply suspicious and with good reason, but you need to help me stop the death of a little girl."

Adam and Vanda exchanged a look and Adam said, "I'm listening."

Russell Draper was hesitant to begin with as he detailed his background but as time ticked on he grew more confident, and his words flooded out. He told them what they already knew so Adam became more prepared to listen and when Draper outlined Shaitan's plan to kidnap and sacrifice a little girl in order to achieve his end, Adam was full of questions.

"How and when is this to be done?"

"He has planned the ritual for the night of the full moon and instructed Betty to go with me to abduct the child."

"Betty?"

"The school secretary and receptionist."

Adam nodded. "I know her. We met her when we visited the school. But how am I to know that this isn't some ploy to make us leave Jacobs for his succubus to suck the life from him?"

"You know about Lilith?"

Adam nodded. "I do."

"That is not my concern. Her actions are out of my hands but a small child…"

"Tell me."

"I cannot reconcile taking a little one from its mother, especially one as gifted as her."

"Gifted?"

Draper nodded. "Yes, she is an Indigo child with special abilities. Shaitan has specially selected her for his master."

"Indigo child?" asked Vanda.

"Very special children, with psychic abilities and powers."

"How did you get involved in all this?"

Draper sighed. "To begin with, it all seemed a bit of fun, a cult that revered love and sex. We met at the school where I was teaching art. We got on immediately, he's a very charismatic man… we had a connection. It gave us what we desired, I am ashamed to say, compliant willing girls."

"Underage girls," said Vanda.

Draper shook his head. "Not me. Shaitan, yes. I prefer, young women not children." Draper coloured up. "I'm not proud of any of it. But I was being fed various narcotics and literally brainwashed into doing his will."

"So, what changed?"

"I stopped drinking the ritual liquid, I would pretend to drink and let the fluid run down my chin. I learned how to field the pills, pop them in the cheek of my mouth and retrieve and dispose of them without taking them or being caught. But he is getting suspicious. He has sent Cawdor to watch me, and Cawdor watched me pray."

There was a short silence while they digested this and then Adam asked, "Tell me more about Cawdor?"

"His demon crow that can listen at windows and report back. It is a vile creature."

Adam nodded. "Yes, I know. I have come across it."

Vanda intervened, "What do you want us to do?"

"Stop him. Stop him from taking that little girl. Stop us from abducting her. And be warned, on the night of the full moon, Lilith will pay you a visit in the dead of night. It has been ordered."

"What is Shaitan's ultimate aim?"

"To bring Satan's dominion on earth and to keep the portal open."

"Portal?" asked Vanda.

"The gateway between this earth and the netherworld. With enough innocent souls sacrificed the portal would remain open for eternity allowing all manner of beasts and demons to walk freely amongst us leading the world as you know it into chaos."

Vanda and Adam sat back in stunned silence. If Draper was to be believed, this was far worse than either of them envisaged.

"What do you want me to do?" Adam said after a long pause.

"Will you help me?"

"How?"

"I will give you the address and tell you when Betty and I will be there. You have to stop us. I cannot have another innocent's blood on my conscience. And you …" he stared hard at Adam, "You must be very careful. Watch your back." He turned to Vanda. "Watch over him and you must be careful yourself. If Shaitan sees you he will want you."

Vanda shivered. "I keep hearing that."

"I must go. I can't be missed for too long."

"How will you explain your absence?"

"I'll visit the gallery in Brinkworth. Pick up some paintings to use in class."

Adam nodded. "Before you go, I have to tell you something, too." Draper looked surprised. "I had a vision, a premonition of you being dragged by shadowy misshapen beings into sulphurous depths through some kind of vortex. But I also know that we need you to defeat this evil. I can't let that happen to you."

Draper spoke again. "What are you? Some kind of wizard?"

"No, not a wizard but I have certain gifts, and I try to use that ability for good. I also know that you will call on Jesus to help and save you and that is a good thing. You must reach inside you for your spiritual truth."

Draper nodded. "I believe you, but I would rather be taken to Hell than to take that little girl's life."

Adam and Draper locked eyes. They understood each other and more importantly, Adam believed him.

"Here," he passed Adam a piece of paper with a couple of addresses. "This is where the child lives, and this is where she goes to school. The children's playground is in Somersby Park. She goes there frequently as it is close to her house. I don't know where the abduction will take place but it's imperative it's stopped. She mustn't be taken."

Adam took the paper, and scribbled a number on another and passed it to Draper. "This is my phone number. It may be better if you memorise it." Draper nodded. "One more thing, I saw crows landing in the clearing in Moss Woods. The crow with the white tipped feather that you call Cawdor, hopped onto a low branch of the hollow tree and appeared to address his gathering with a succession of raucous cries. The creatures flapped their oily wings and rose up into the canopy and flew off in different directions."

"They will be watching and listening. I must go, now." The urgency in his voice was apparent.

He moved out into the hall and Adam followed when Vanda called out, "Wait!" They stopped. "It may be too late."

"Why?"

"There's a crow on the windowsill and it's tapping at the window with its beak."

"How long has it been there?"

"It's just landed."

"Good, maybe it doesn't know I'm here," said Draper.

"Is there just one?" asked Adam.

"As far as I can see."

"Take a good look."

Vanda crossed to the window and the bird stared at her as she peered through the glass. She couldn't see any others. Vanda banged on the windowpane and the bird flew off and circled before returning to its perch staring in the kitchen. Vanda walked into the hall. "There seems to be just one. It doesn't have any white tipped tail feathers."

"We need to get you out of here without being seen," said Adam.

"If it's come here, perhaps it's come to watch you," murmured Draper.

Vanda returned to the hall and added, "We need to disguise you in some way, so you won't be recognised and then I have an idea."

Russell Draper was kitted out in Adam's trench-coat, his flaxen hair tucked under a hat, with the brim pulled down. A pair of sunglasses completed the picture. Vanda studied him. "It doesn't look like you so we may get away with it."

"What now?" asked Draper.

"Adam will go into the kitchen and busy himself with the sandwiches so the bird should be occupied. It is clearly watching Adam. You and I will get out into the annexe and garden. In the shed there is an underground passage, which will take you to a cave on the beach, from there you can walk up the cliff path into Cliff House, my home. The door's unlocked, go in and wait. Give me your car keys." Draper handed them across. "I will drive your car around to my property. The creature will see me not you. Once there, you can drop your disguise, get in the car and drive away."

"You make it sound so simple." Draper hesitated, "… what if more of those creatures arrive?"

"I can't answer that. But you wait here. Adam, come on into the kitchen." Vanda and Adam went back in the kitchen and ignored the bird still sitting on the sill. He finished making the sandwiches as if nothing had happened. Vanda sidled up beside him and put her arms around his neck. They kissed and the crow pecked at the windowpane. Vanda announced, "Just going to take a shower and then I'll be popping out for a moment. Won't be long."

Vanda escaped Adam's arms and dashed back to Draper in the hall. They left quietly and quickly and entered the annexed cottage's garden. There was no sign of any birds. They scrambled through the overgrown wilderness and into the shed where Vanda pulled up the rug revealing the trapdoor. Draper looked at Vanda. "Tell me this isn't for real?"

"Oh, but it is. Follow me. I never thought I'd go down these steps again." Vanda shrugged off the memories of her sister and how she and Adam had discovered her sister's body in a refrigerated chest in the cave. Taking a deep breath, they descended the steps through the rocky cavern to the cave. "See the entrance to this cave?" Draper nodded. "Walk along the beach to the rocks at the far end and there's a path that leads to my place. Keep your head down and go inside to wait. My cat won't bother you. Her name's Elsa. Now go."

She watched as Draper traversed the beach staying close to the cliff face and then she made her way back through the cave, and tunnel and tried to still the trembling that had manifested. Once back in the garden, she felt better. She slipped out through the side gate of the cottage and got into Draper's car. She started the engine and turned the vehicle around to travel the back roads to her house.

Vanda was pleased that Draper's car was an automatic, which suited her. She hadn't driven a stick shift, manual for some time. She raced along the back roads. There were no crows in sight and heaving a sigh of relief she turned into the small single track road that led to Cliff House. She parked, leaving the engine running and dashed inside where Draper was waiting. He divested himself of the coat and hat, which Vanda donned. Once Draper had driven away, Vanda walked along the cliff path back to the house at Black Head Ridge.

She rang the bell, the door opened almost immediately, and she dived in, closing the door behind her and removed Adam's hat and coat.

"How did it go?" queried Adam in a whisper.

"It seemed to be all right. I didn't spot any crows." She, too, spoke in hushed tones.

"That's something, then. The one that was pecking at the window is still there. Hopefully, that's a good sign."

"So, what's next?"

"Back to the station and relieve Melvyn. See how Jacobs is."

"Are you telling Vance?"

"Of course. We will need help in stopping this. Wait here." Adam returned to the kitchen and packed a small rucksack with his sandwiches, fruit and a few other items and made his way back to the hall. "Did you lock up your house?"

"Yes, once Draper had left."

"What do you think?"

"About Draper?"

"Yes."

"I was very wary at first but after listening to him... I believe him. He's definitely ashamed of his past and remorseful. I don't think it's a trap. Do you?"

"No, I believe you're right. But that's no guarantee. If this Shaitan is as Draper's described it's going to be tough. Who's to say he won't manipulate or drug Draper again?"

Draper had reached Brinkworth and found his way to the gallery. He was studying the paintings and prints on display. He selected a few to take to the till and was horrified to see through the open door, another crow strutting outside the entrance. He stopped. Was this one of Shaitan's creatures or something not so sinister? He passed the artwork to John Grey, the gallery owner. John looked up surprised. "We've met before, haven't we?"

"Have we?"

"Yes. I never forget a face." John snapped his fingers. "Caroline Mitchell's memorial. We had quite a chat. Hang on... your name will come to me in a moment. I know... it's Draper and you teach art at a posh school."

Draper laughed. "Guilty as charged. Of course, I remember now." They chatted for a few moments longer while John packed up the art. Draper indicated the crow outside. "Friend of yours?"

John laughed. "No. He's been hanging around for months now. He shoplifts in the supermarket opposite and then brings his spoils to eat outside my gallery."

"Shoplift?"

"Yes, he will sneak in and pinch a packet of crisps off the bottom shelf and then cross the road to eat them outside my shop."

Draper laughed. "Quite a character then."

"Yes, I call him Chutney. He answers to it, now and I feed him the odd titbit."

Draper paid for his pictures and left, saying he would be back. He looked suspiciously at the crow that took absolutely no notice of him. Feeling relieved he made his way back to his car and drove off towards Penmyron and the school.

The afternoon promised to be warm and sunny, and Adam enjoyed his drive to the police station in spite of the fact he was aware of the crow following him. He parked in the police car park and went into reception. The copper on duty, greeted him like an old friend and Adam was allowed to go up the stairs to Vance's office, where he relayed everything that had been said by Russell Draper.

Vance was more than alarmed at the news of the planned abduction and sacrifice of the small child. "When is this supposed to happen?"

"Night of the full moon, although they will take the child before that."

"Then, we must be vigilant. I'll send Harding with a couple of other detectives, out on surveillance. Perhaps Jacobs can watch the house with Harding and me. The other two can keep an eye on the school and woods."

"Won't that look bad? Two men watching a school?"

"Not if they're not noticed."

"What about the playground?" asked Adam. "Can't have blokes watching a kiddies' playground."

"I'll send a man and a woman. I know this place. There's a pub opposite, think it's called The George and Dragon, they do a good pint there and home-cooked food. They can sit outside and watch from there."

Adam nodded. "I can do that, with Melvyn and maybe Vanda, saves getting more people involved than necessary."

The suggestion seemed to satisfy Vance who nodded. Adam retreated to the room where Melvyn was on watch over Paul Jacobs. "Am I glad to see you," said Melvyn. "I can feel my eyelids drooping." Adam said nothing. "Are you all right?" Melvyn questioned.

"Something's happened. It's about Draper."

Melvyn sat up. "Tell me." And Adam recounted Draper's visit and all that was said. Melvyn sat forward and whistled through his teeth. "That's some story. Did you believe him?"

"I did. He had no reason to search me out and warn us. You were right, there has to be a spark of goodness within him."

"So, what's the plan?"

"Vance has got a couple of men to watch the school and Moss Woods and another with him, keeping tabs on the house."

"Who is watching the playground?"

"That's down to us."

"Yes, we need someone there, too. It will be an easy place to cause a distraction and take a child."

"So, that's you and me," said Adam with a nod.

"But, what about Jacobs?" queried Melvyn. "He must be kept safe. So far it's just the one visitation where she succeeded. I don't doubt there'll be another, especially as the last attempt failed."

"I think Vance has something up his sleeve regarding Jacobs. But we can't stay here indefinitely. And Jacobs will have to go home at some point."

"Defeat Shaitan and it should all go away."

"Easier said than done."

~ 9 ~

PENGARRAN WAS CURRENTLY SHROUDED IN mist stealing away the warmth of the sun, making everything seem dull and gloomy. Occasionally, the sun broke through the stubborn cloud cover but it didn't seem to smile down as usual. The rays from the golden disc dissipated into the ever-increasing leaden atmosphere.

Little Marissa sat on her mother's lap who was reading her a story and Marissa was engrossed in the yarn. They were just getting to an exciting part of the tale where the night witch, Sclarvete, was battling the master of the dwellers of the inner earth, Manovra, a great wizard.

Marissa's face became solemn, and she looked up at her mother. "Is this where the bad men want to take me? To the inner earth?"

"Why Marissa, whatever are you talking about?" exclaimed her mother, Janine Porter.

"Mummy, I know they are coming for me. They want to take me into the woods and…" She stopped.

"Where is this coming from?" said Janine her tone becoming anxious. "Has someone said something to you?"

"No."

"Then how?"

"I just know. I've been told."

"Who by?"

The little girl shrugged. "I don't know. It's just a voice in my head that speaks to me."

Janine was trying not to upset her daughter and attempted to pacify her. "It's possibly part of a leftover dream, a bad dream."

"No," Marissa insisted. "I wasn't asleep. I heard it now."

Janine closed the book. "Perhaps it's the story, after all the little girl, Suki gets taken away and ended up a prisoner of an old witch, called Grushka."

Marissa eyed her mother. "I want to get down now." She scrambled off her mother's lap and ran to the window where a crow pecked at the glass outside. "Why does it do that?" she asked.

"It's reacting to its reflection. They don't like other crows invading their space."

"No, it's listening to us," insisted Marissa.

Janine had to admit it did look like the crow was listening to their conversation, popping its head on one side and peering at them through the glass. She shivered and forced a smile before reassuring her daughter. "It probably liked the story we were reading. That's all."

"I don't think so. And who is Adam?"

Janine shook her head. "I don't know anyone called Adam."

"He's nice, Mummy. He will help us."

Janine was even more confused and believed her daughter's fertile imagination had concocted some sort of story. And now...

Marissa's voice broke into her thoughts.

"Mummy, when can we go to Fort William?"

It was then Janine remembered when Marissa was very small, about two and a half, that she had insisted she needed to see her other parents and her husband as they were missing her. Janine and her husband, Don, had thought it was all make-believe. But Marissa was forward in her speech for one so young and they tried to humour her, believing it was all some sort of game, until she gave them the place where they lived in Scotland, Fort William. Janine explained they couldn't go all the way to Scotland as it was at the other end of the country but maybe when she was older. Marissa seemed to have accepted this and forgotten all about it, so they put it down to a child's imaginings. But now, now she was mentioning it again. And how did she know of Fort William? It didn't make any sense.

"We have to go soon as they're moving to Wick."

Janine was stunned and felt very unsettled.

Adam was talking with Vance and trying to keep his voice as low as possible. He didn't want anyone else overhearing him. "So, what do we do? Jacobs can't be left but if this little girl is to be saved it will take all of us to watch over her."

"There's only one thing for it. As I said before... Jacobs will have to be part of the team."

"Is that wise?"

"Have you any other suggestions?" Vance paused, and then continued, "I know he's drained and exhausted but he's better off with us. This creature isn't going to attack again in company. She'll wait until he's alone. We can keep an eye on him."

Adam nodded, he had nothing more to offer and returned to Melvyn who watched as Jacobs slept.

"Well?"

"Vance is making Jacobs part of the team," and he explained why.

Melvyn was sceptical. "I'm not convinced. The man's already exhausted. I will pray for the Lord's strength to protect and bless him."

Adam suddenly swayed and put his hand out to steady himself.

"What? What is it?" asked Melvyn suddenly alert.

"I'm not sure..." said Adam. "I felt as if someone was touching my shoulder and neck, caressing it."

"Oh, my Lord, no!" Melvyn stood and began to incant a prayer and held out his cross, demanding all demons leave. Adam's knees buckled and faint feminine mocking laughter could be heard. Melvyn stared hard, he could swear that he saw some shadowy entity behind Adam, waving her arms about as if trying to enter his body. Melvyn held out his cross and tossed Holy water on Adam, which sizzled and smoked before a shriek was heard. Adam crumpled to his knees and Melvyn helped a dazed Adam to a seat.

"I don't understand. What happened?" murmured Adam.

Melvyn was uncertain how much to say, when he had a thought. He walked to the window. There was no sign of the rock salt they had sprinkled. He dashed from the room and ran down the stairs to the front entrance. There was no salt there either.

He saw Vance remonstrating with someone and a female cleaner shouting back. "No one told me. I saw a mess and cleared it up. There was salt everywhere!" Vance's face was almost apoplectic.

Melvyn was not given to swearing but swear he did, under his breath. He dashed back to Adam. "The protection has gone. The salt has been cleaned up."

"What?"

"Vance is dealing with it. It seems odd that no one told the cleaner. Do we have any more rock salt?"

"I'm not sure. I can ask Vanda to get some."

Melvyn nodded. "Yes. Do that. It's safe for her to do so now. In the meanwhile, we need to get out there and protect this little girl."

Adam didn't ask any more questions.

Russell Draper and Betty Buswell were driving towards Pengarran. Draper tried to involve Betty in some sensible conversation. "Doesn't it bother you that we're about to abduct an innocent little girl?"

Betty turned her huge china blue eyes on Draper. "Does it bother you?"

Draper squirmed in his seat uncertain what to say. "… I suppose it does on some level. I would hate for it to be my daughter, niece or granddaughter."

"Well, it's not," snapped Betty. "We have been promised so much. It's worth the loss of one small child surely?" Draper shrugged. "Not getting cold feet are you? That would not please the master. It wouldn't please him at all."

"No…" Draper spoke carefully, "I just thought a little girl with her life before her…"

He trailed off as he felt Betty's eyes boring into him. "I mean, she is a special one. An Indigo child."

Betty looked at him suspiciously. "So? What's it to us?"

"Do you have any children?"

"Yes. Three."

"Would you be willing for one of them or their offspring to be taken?"

"But it's not."

"No…" Draper's voice was measured. "It just makes me think that's all."

Betty's expression softened. "No. I wouldn't want one of mine taken. But you had better be careful. Speaking like that will get us into trouble with the master, and that thought terrifies me. We just do our job and get her out of here."

"If we can manage it."

"What do you mean?"

"It's broad daylight and we have no plan."

"Then we had better make one," said Betty. "Where do we go first?"

"The playground. It will be easier. Have you got any pictures on your phone of puppies or kittens?"

"No. But I can easily pull some up."

"Good. Find some and then we can lure her with a promise of taking her to see the pups or kittens."

Betty nodded and began trawling through her phone until she found what she wanted. "Here. Will these do?" She showed the picture on her phone to Draper.

"Perfect. I can engage her mother in conversation and distract her, while you talk to the little girl. Do we know the child's name?"

"Marissa," said Betty confidently. "Pretty name."

"Yes, it is." Draper fell silent and no more was said as he wondered how he could avert the abduction of the child.

Adam suddenly shivered, as in his head, he heard a child scream. The sound was fading as an image of a woman swirled in his mind showing her taking the hand of a small child. A clock chimed out the hour and he counted the strikes. Adam swayed but he felt a flood of warmth flow through his body calming him and he somehow knew his mother and grandmother had wrapped their arms around him.

"Are you all right?" asked Vanda looking curiously at him as she walked into the police station with more rock salt, which she passed to Vance.

"Er... yes, I think so." He turned to Melvyn. "We have to go." He felt a little nudge in his back. There was no one behind him. "And Vanda, you must come, too."

"Really? Why? I thought you wanted me here."

"I have a feeling we will need you. You can travel with us." He nodded at Melvyn.

Vance announced, "Let Melvyn bless the salt then I'll see that it's spread and follow with Harding and Jacobs. Go and get ready." Adam could hear the urgency in Vance's voice.

Melvyn consecrated the salt quickly and blessed it in prayer before hurrying after Adam.

The motley crew made their way outside to the car park. There was no sign of any crows and Adam heaved a sigh of relief. They climbed into Adam's car and set off. Adam could see Vance exiting the station with the others as he drove off.

"If you don't mind, I'll take a nap and get some sleep. You don't need me to drive?"

"No rest your eyes. They say a catnap of twenty minutes is as refreshing as a good sleep."

"I don't know about that. But I'll give it a go."

No more was said on the rest of the journey.

The day was bright but cloudy and when the clouds stole away the warmth of the sun it made Vanda shiver, she felt it was a portent of what was to come, and a feeling of unease rolled over her. Melvyn slept the whole way to The George and Dragon, where Adam was able to park at the back of the pub. Vanda nudged Melvyn who stretched and yawned noisily. "Oh, excuse me. That was just what I needed. Where are we?"

"Car park of The George and Dragon. We need to find a table at the front of the pub where we can see the playground."

"Good, we can get some lunch," said Melvyn. "I'm starved." He picked up his bag of accoutrements and left the car. Vanda and Adam did likewise, and they walked around to the front of the pub. Melvyn and Vanda settled at a table for four and Adam went in to order drinks and pick up some menus.

He was soon back with a tray carrying a large glass of iced spring water with the remainder in the bottle. Vanda had ordered an elderflower cordial and Adam had a zero alcohol beer. None of them wanted an alcoholic drink when they had a job to do. Time enough for that when the job was over.

They soon perused the menu with Melvyn opting for lasagne, Vanda decided on sea bass and Adam ordered good old fish and chips. They kept their eyes on the playground where a number of children ran around having turns on all the different apparatus. Mothers sat on benches, chatting with each other happily as they watched their children.

"I can't see any little blonde girl yet," murmured Vanda.

"And they may not arrive," said Adam, but he felt a strange prickling sensation like iced water trickling down his spine and he knew he was wrong. Something was going to happen.

"Wait! Look over there," exclaimed Vanda. "Isn't that Draper and that Buswell woman?"

They all looked where Vanda had indicated, and sure enough Draper and Betty Buswell were approaching the area. They appeared to be deep in an intense conversation and walked towards a wooden bench just outside the perimeter of the playground where they sat and continued talking like any other ordinary couple.

They perused the kiddies that were playing but were unable to see anyone that could be Marissa anywhere. Betty indicated a small child aged between three and four who was toddling towards the slide. They bent their heads together as if coming to some agreement as Adam and his companions watched. "It looks as though they have selected a substitute if Marissa doesn't show."

Vanda nodded. "Or they could head for her house."

"True," said Melvyn. "But the house is being watched, isn't it?"

"It is. But the abductors are here. We will sit tight and wait."

Marissa was tugging on her mother's skirt and pleading, "Please, Mummy. Can we? Please." She drew out the last please in a wheedling tone.

Eventually, her mother seemed to give in. "Oh, all right. But you must eat your tea first."

Marissa nodded and smiled in agreement as she dashed to sit up at the table and began to nibble at her sandwiches. Her mother, Janine, smiled fondly at her little girl and poured her a glass of apple juice. The child chattered happily as they finished their tea.

"When we come back from the park, I want to do a picture for Daddy."

"Of course, I think he'll love that. Okay, now drink up your juice and we can have ice cream when we get back."

Marissa beamed, scrambled off her chair and ran into the hall. She tugged at her red coat on the stand but couldn't get it off the peg. "Mummy, I want to wear the red one it makes me feel special."

Janine laughed, took off the coat and handed it to her daughter who put it on, but Janine started to laugh as Marissa got into a muddle with her buttons. "Here, let me help you with that."

"But I want to do it."

"I know. You can try again next time." Marissa nodded solemnly and they left the house together. Marissa dropped her mother's hand and skipped happily in front of her. Anyone watching them could see that Marissa was a miniature version of her mother in her looks and bubbly personality.

Vance and Harding were watching. Jacobs was not quite with it. He looked as if he hadn't slept for a week, but he came to as his boss spoke. "They're on the move. Come on, we must follow them."

"I thought we were watching the house?" said Harding.

"We were, but it's the child we need to save."

"Shouldn't one of us stay, in case someone infiltrates the house or plants some sort of trap?"

Vance thought for a moment. "Okay, Jacobs, you come with me. Harding, you keep an eye on the property. You've got your phone?" Harding nodded. "If anything transpires, call me."

Vance and Jacobs stepped out from the shrubbery where they had been hiding. Harding took off his mackintosh, laid it on the ground, and sat, keeping his eyes on the Porter home.

Vance and Jacobs stumbled after the mother and child towards the playground and made their way across the road to The George and Dragon. They sat at another table within nodding distance of Adam, Melvyn and Vanda. All had their eyes on Marissa who seemed oblivious to the interest in her. She bounced towards the swings and begged her mother to push her.

Harding sat on his mac in the shrubbery and began to yawn. It was as if a spell had been woven over him. He tried to blink himself awake and sit upright but a strange tiredness was enveloping him. He found himself closing his eyes and stretching out on his mac. A black crow with white tipped tail feathers flew down and landed next to him. It eyed him beadily and cawed before retreating back to the bush to watch.

His eyes flickered open as a shimmering green mass began to manifest into the figure of an extraordinarily beautiful woman with long lustrous ebony locks. She had full pouting moist lips with a perfect cupid's bow and appeared in a tight fitting outfit that clung to her skin. She sat astride him, and her skirt began riding up her toned thighs, revealing her lack of underwear. She sighed and leaned forward and whispered in Harding's ear before wriggling her tongue inside his ear canal and around his earlobe.

Unable to move, as if paralysed, and unable to help himself, Harding could feel himself responding to her touch and her caresses. His trousers began to bulge, and she gently released him, straddled him and rode him until he was spent. She threw back her head and continued to tease and arouse him to full wakefulness once more and rode him again, kissing his neck and tweaking his nipples through his shirt, which she then ripped open with her claws. He groaned in the height of ecstasy, his eyelids fluttered, and his head fell back. Harding was helpless and as she lifted herself off him she laughed crazily, and her physical body dissolved into a shimmering emerald mass once more and vanished.

Cawdor hopped down from the branch where he rested and cawed four times and as if being granted permission he pecked at Harding's eyes, devouring them before flying off towards Moss Woods.

Janine Porter sat with two other mothers she knew to have a chat, once her daughter was off the swings and playing on other pieces of playground equipment. Janine was feeling quite relaxed until a terrible scream erupted, and Marissa shouted at the top of her voice, "Bad man, bad, bad man." Everyone turned to look where Marissa pointed, and her finger rested on Russell Draper who acted surprised and denied any wrongdoing. Some mothers called their children and Marissa continued to point.

Betty Buswell hurried across to the other child she had pointed out earlier who was just coming down the slide for the umpteenth time. Her mother had gone into the ladies' toilets and Betty Buswell had taken her chance. She took the little one's hand and hurried the toddler away from the park, scooped her up in her arms and rushed towards her car as the mother came out from the toilets and searched around for her child.

Adam, Vanda, Jacobs and Vance hurried across from The George and Dragon to the chaotic scene. Marissa ran towards Adam holding out her arms and called to her mother, "Mummy, this is Adam. He will save us." The little girl jumped into his arms much to the shock of her mother.

Mothers dashed to their offspring and gathered them up leaving one mother, Yvonne Sinclair, searching and crying madly for her daughter Sophie, who was now nowhere to be seen. Vanda had seen where Sophie was being taken, and she ran after Betty Buswell. Finding sprinting power from somewhere she chased down Betty Buswell who had put Sophie down and was half dragging the frightened child. Betty reached the car and talked soothingly to the little girl promising she was going to take her to find her mother. She opened the passenger door and helped Sophie inside. This gave enough time for Vanda to catch up and she yelled out, "Stop! The police are here," before she flew at Betty, rugby tackling her to the ground. They rolled over at the side of the car; Betty, like a wild cat was scratching, kicking and biting. She pulled at Vanda's hair and tugged out a handful, which made Vanda scream. Betty rolled over on top of Vanda and socked her in the face knocking her out cold. The little girl watched through the window her face full of fear. Betty dived into the driver's seat and without a thought of Russell she started the car and drove away at speed spewing small stones from the tyres.

Vance was attempting to calm the mothers down and explaining that he was a police officer, which seemed to satisfy some mothers who continued to let their children play on. Vance tried to enlighten them on why he was there and that they had a tip-off that something was going to happen at the playground and so they had come out to observe for safety purposes.

Marissa was hanging on to Adam's legs and still pointing at Russell Draper, who was now in conversation with Melvyn and feeling calmer. Vance alerted Jacobs to contact Harding and get him across to the playground. Jacobs tried calling, all to no avail. "He's not answering, sir," said Jacobs who was now looking and feeling much better.

Vance ordered, "Jacobs with me. Let's get Harding. Where's Vanda?"

Marissa said, "She ran after that lady. The lady who took Sophie." Marissa looked up at Adam. "She'll be all right. They just had a fight." Adam gasped, how did the little girl know this? But then, she was an Indigo child and he knew they needed to talk.

Draper called out, "We have to follow Betty and get that child back. I don't like to think about what will happen if we don't."

Vance ordered, Adam, "Go after her, find Vanda and bring back that child. Take Draper with you. Jacobs and I will see Marissa and Mrs Porter safely home and get Harding. Hurry now, go!"

Marissa reluctantly let go of Adam who told her, "Don't worry. I will come back, and we will talk. I promise." This seemed to satisfy the child, and she went happily with her mother and the police. A tearful Yvonne Sinclair was persuaded to go with them with the promise that her daughter would be found and returned to her. Adam, Draper and Melvyn hurried to their car, where they found Vanda just coming around who relayed what had happened.

Draper urged them, "We must hurry. The light is fading and Shaitan will be preparing for the sacrifice. Please. Step on it."

Vance and Jacobs had finally settled Mrs Porter and her daughter, Marissa, who was now happily drawing a picture for her father, James, who was due home soon. He left Jacobs to take a statement from Yvonne Sinclair and gather all her details, while he went across to the shrubbery to find Harding.

What Vance found was like something from a Hammer horror film. Harding's apparently dead body gazed up at him with empty eye sockets and blood all over his face. His clothes were in disarray as if he had been sexually attacked with claw marks and bite marks on his body similar to the ones Jacobs had suffered. "No, no, NO!" He got on his knees to check Harding's pulse and to see if he was breathing. He wasn't. Undeterred, he called the emergency services and began performing cardiopulmonary resuscitation. He was still attempting to start the heart when the ambulance arrived, and the paramedics took over CPR before whisking Harding away to the hospital.

With heavy steps Vance returned to the Porters. Jacobs looked questioningly and Vance shook his head as Jacobs suppressed a yelp.

Harding had been his friend.

10

SHAITAN HAD GATHERED THE GIRLS in his cult together and they stood outside the hollow tree in Moss Woods dressed in their white robes and headdresses. Shaitan had his demon dogs beside him and their eyes glowed red. The ritual had begun, and the children were drinking the milky fluid to intoxicate them and sap their will.

Betty had taken the little girl, Sophie to the school and prepared her in a snow white dress. The child had begun to complain, "Where's my mummy? I want to go home."

"And so you will, as soon as you have been to our little party. There will be lots of other girls there. It will be very grown up and lots of fun," soothed Betty.

"I don't want a party," said Sophie obstinately. "I want to go home."

A hint of ice crept into Betty's tone. "And you will but first a little drink to help calm you down. Here." She thrust a cup of milky liquid at her. "Drink this. It will make you feel better. I promise." The child started to weep and dashed the cup to the floor making Betty swear and she slapped the toddler across the face, making her cry even more.

Betty tried once more to placate and cajole her. Sophie was now snivelling and insistent. "I want my mummy."

"Sophie, Mummy said you were to come with me to be safe. She filled another cup with the drug filled liquid and Sophie stared wide-eyed at her with her eyes brimming with tears. "Your mummy is going to come to the party, too.

You don't want her to be cross with you, do you?" The little girl shook her head sorrowfully. "That's a good girl. Now drink up and dry your eyes. We're going to a party."

Sophie allowed Betty to dry her eyes and freshen up her face. She took the cup of milky liquid and drank, and Betty encouraged her to drink it all up with the promise of a chocolate bar when it was finished. "Come on now, that's a good girl. Is it all gone?" Sophie turned the cup upside down to show it was empty and Betty handed Sophie a small chocolate bar, which the child gratefully accepted and began to eat.

"Will mummy be there now?"

Betty nodded. "Yes, I am sure she will have arrived. Let's go." She took Sophie's tiny hand, and they began to walk towards the woods. Sophie stumbled and fell before fainting clean away. Betty scooped her up in her arms and Draper's voice reverberated into her mind as she looked down on the child's sleeping face remembering her own children and grandchildren. *"Would you be willing for one of them or their offspring to be taken?"* She was suddenly flooded with guilt and then remonstrated with herself, "Too late now, Betty Buswell. Too late now."

A makeshift altar had been erected outside the pentacle and Shaitan stood behind it as the girls chanted on his instruction. They swayed as they sang and Shaitan lifted his arms in supplication to his demon master, the horned god. Betty entered the clearing carrying the child, and laid the little one on the altar. Shaitan turned on her, "This is the wrong child."

"I know. It was impossible to kidnap her. There were too many people around and …" she hesitated, "I am sure the police were there."

"Police?"

"A woman chased after me, she yelled that the police were there. I had to knock her out."

"Where's Draper?"

"I had to leave him. The other child pointed him out as a bad man and kept shouting it out. It was chaos."

Shaitan's eyes narrowed and turned from red to black. "So, Draper is with the police. Then we had better be quick. The moon will soon be fully up."

Adam, Vanda, Melvyn and Draper raced on towards the school and Moss Woods. Adam asked again, "Tell me what is supposed to happen. How long have we got?"

"The ceremony will have started. The girls will be incapacitated."

"Drugged?"

Draper nodded. "Yes. There are a number of ritual elements that have to be observed as soon as they are done the sacrifice will take place and then it can't be stopped. It will be end of days, for all of us."

Vanda murmured, "Surely Betty will have some conscience? She's taken that little one to her death."

"No. She's totally taken in by Shaitan, brainwashed and the drugs compel her to do his bidding. The girls and her, need to see him as he really is. They think he's some kind of attractive messiah who will bring them riches and joy. The girls just believe it's a lot of fun, in a secret society like it's some whacky game."

"Put your foot down, Adam," called Melvyn. "I can make them see the man as he really is in all his putrid glory."

Adam pressed his foot on the accelerator pedal pushing it flat to the floor and they roared on.

Shaitan raised his arms and intoned in another language from the old world, Sumerian. The words had no meaning for the girls, but they followed the ceremony blindly, following Michelle as Sabrina, chanting answers in English when Shaitan paused. "Kaku u alap shame."

"Great emissary!"

"Re'u kinu shame utu'ame rabutti."

"Viper."

"Zibantium, akrabu, pabilsag, Gula."

"Ravening dogs of scorpion man like a hurricane bring in the horned beast."

The chant was repeated over and over again and Shaitan cut his arm and dripped his blood into a vessel filled with milky liquid for the girls to come up to drink one by one. Betty was first. The bloodied mixture ran down her chin and dripped on the sedated child who murmured softly.

Draper appeared in the clearing and Shaitan turned on him. "You have betrayed me. But it is too late now. You cannot stop the inevitable, but I can stop you." Shaitan shouted to the demon dogs who curled their lips and snarled. They loped towards Draper and stopped him coming further into the clearing.

The girls swayed and hummed as if to some inner tune and the sound of a Tanbou drum could be heard coming from the hollow tree. Shaitan called out, "Humbaba, come with the shadows and take your prize away."

Two ghostly entities like murky shapeless dark shadows with little substance emerged with a misshapen beast, the guardian of the forest, sporting horns and a scaly spiked back. He had three massive claws at the end of his arms and a spiked tail. The shadows grabbed Draper and forced him towards the hollow tree. He screamed in terror and the girls continued to sway and chant. The dogs followed slavering at the mouth.

Melvyn and Adam rushed into the clearing, both were holding out a cross in front of them. Still the girls writhed and swayed murmuring strange words. Melvyn ran forward but Shaitan stretched out his arm, and held out his hand in a stop motion and Melvyn's feet became stuck to the ground as if sinking in oozing, clinging, mud. Melvyn cried out to Draper. "Draper! Call on God in the name of Jesus and repent."

A brisk wind blew up and began whirling around the clearing. Some of the girls became disturbed by this wind that blew in their faces and tore at their robes. One or two began to cry as they gazed about them in bewilderment.

Shaitan laughed cruelly and exclaimed, "His god can't help him now."

But Melvyn persisted, and called above the rising wind, "Draper, Russell, do as I ask." He turned to Shaitan, brandishing his cross. "In the name of God the Father and in Jesus Christ his only son, our Lord, and the Holy Ghost let the scales fall from these children's eyes. Let them see the devil as he is, in all his putrid hideousness. Save the souls of these children and heal them. Take back your power and condemn Leonard Shaitan to the pits of Hell where he belongs." Melvyn took his bottle of Holy water in his other hand and pulled the cork out with his teeth. He threw the liquid over Shaitan who screamed in agony and thrashed his arms around as if warding off the will of God.

The girls stopped their chanting and swaying and stared at their 'master' whose facial good looks faded into that of a diseased corpse with a multitude of wriggling maggots that dropped as he tried to prevent Melvyn's Godly onslaught of Holy words.

The girls caught sight of Shaitan's evil altered looks and one by one they began to point and scream at his changed appearance. Some broke free of the pentacle and ran for their lives, back through the woods towards the school. Betty Buswell, fell to the floor in a shivering fit and began to froth at the mouth. More girls shrieked and ran away escaping the clearing. Michelle as Sabrina fainted clean away.

Shaitan bellowed, "You will not defy me. I will have my kingdom on earth," and his eyes began to drip blood as Melvyn continued to recite the Holy scriptures intent on returning him to the realm of demons. Prayers of exorcism and banishment of evil dropped from his lips as Adam looked on in shocked amazement. Vanda arrived in the glade, ran to the altar and picked up the little girl, Sophie, and took her to the edge of the clearing. She was still unconscious.

Inside the hollow tree, a strange blue swirling light pervaded the night and Draper's voice was clearly heard. "Dearest Lord Jesus, save me from this infernal Hell. I repent all I have done wrong, and I beg you; please, Jesus forgive me my sins. Please show me mercy. I give myself to thee to do the Lord's work."

The light in the tree grew brighter and a phantasmagoria of illusionary images spiralled into a kaleidoscope of colours at the heart of which, was a beating, pulsing, crimson bubbling liquid fire. There was an explosion resembling a fireball and the two dogs, now looking like ordinary, domesticated animals, ran out with their tails between their legs and hurried to Melvyn's side and lay down panting. Draper too was forcibly expelled from the portal and landed at Melvyn's feet. Shaitan struggled against an invisible force that was pulling him back into the tree. He was sucked inside and the portal swallowed him up.

"We are not yet finished," announced Melvyn. "We need to banish Lilith from the earth and into the portal with Shaitan." He raised his Bible and held his cross out calling, "Lilith, you who is the temptress of men, I order you in the name of God and in Jesus Christ our Lord with the Holy Spirit to appear now."

Lightning flashed. There was a rumble of thunder and the crows that had adorned the branches flew off into the canopy. An iridescent emerald-green mist began to take form and the demon known as Lilith began to appear. Her eyes lit on Adam, and she began to walk seductively towards him. Adam's eyes widened and Melvyn shouted, "Adam protect yourself."

She continued to sashay towards him licking her pouting lips. She ran a clawed hand over her breasts and began to tease down the front of her skin-tight body suit revealing an ample cleavage. Her eyes fixed on him, and he was unable to avert his eyes. Draper stepped in front of Adam, took his bottle of Holy water from his hand and brandished his New Testament, taken from his pocket. He spun around to face Lilith who hissed in anger at the sight of the Holy book. Draper called out, "In the name of our Lord Jesus Christ who died for our sins I order you back to Hell and to leave this place." Draper squirted the bottle of water over Lilith who shrieked in pain.

Melvyn yelled at Adam, "Adam! Your silver paper knife. Use it now."

Vanda urged him, "Adam. Do as he says."

Vanda's voice seemed to wake Adam from his stupor. He took his paper knife from his belt as Draper stepped aside and Adam threw it at Lilith's chest and the creature began to shrivel before a powerful tornado-like wind blew up from the vortex and drew Lilith back into the tree. The silver knife dropped from her body. The portal began to swirl crazily and snapped shut with a metallic finality and vanished. Draper fell to the floor.

Betty stopped her spasmodic trembling and seemed to recover from her seizure. She looked about her, unable to work out where she was and murmured, "Who are you? What's happened? Why am I here?" Her mind seemed to have been wiped clean of all memories. Michelle came forward and helped her to her feet.

Adam finally spoke. "Is everyone okay?"

Melvyn nodded and dropped to his knees where the dogs frenziedly licked his face. He smiled. Michelle and Betty looked about them bewildered.

Adam opened his arms to Vanda who walked forward still holding the child. "Let me take her. Come on, let's get back to the car."

"What about the dogs?" asked Vanda looking at two docile friendly animals.

Draper got to his feet. "I'll take them. They can come with me." He turned to Adam and whispered his thanks. "Without you my soul would have been damned to Hell for eternity. How can I ever thank you?"

Adam gave Draper his hand and pulled him up. "And I have to thank you… You saved my life, protected me from Lilith… You will have to work out what to say to those young girls because no one will believe the truth of what we've just witnessed."

"And what can I write?" said Vanda. "My scoop exposé - No one will believe what we have all seen tonight."

"I think we can work out something acceptable but without telling the whole story," said Adam.

"What about Shaitan? How do we explain his disappearance?"

"He will be your story," said Adam. "A man who started a cult in a girls' school and has escaped justice and vanished after being discovered for who he really was."

"You mean for me to say he's done a runner?" said Vanda.

"Yes, he can be put on a most wanted list and if he ever finds his way back to our world again he will be arrested and picked up."

"That's if he can get back, which I pray he won't," said Melvyn staggering to his feet. "But I know this evil, and I fear that one day…" He stopped.

Adam turned to look at him. "Melvyn…" he said looking shocked.

"What?"

"Your hair."

"What about it?"

Everyone turned to stare and there on the other side of his head was another streak of white to match the first. "Come on let's get back to the car and call Vance."

"What about this tree?" asked Draper. "I know the portal has gone... but..."

"Burn it," said Melvyn decisively. "It may serve your purpose, with the girls," he said looking at Draper.

"How?"

"I'm not sure how much they will remember or *if* they will remember but if there was a fire in Moss Woods, it could explain their shocked state."

"That could work," said Draper in agreement. "You, all of you, get back and take that little one to her mother. I'll deal with this. I'll be in touch. I have your number." He turned to Melvyn. "And thank you. Thank you for believing in me that I could be saved."

"Don't thank me. Thank God."

"I intend to. Thank you, all of you."

Adam, Melvyn and Vanda made their way out of the clearing and returned to the car just as Sophie was starting to come around from her sedation.

"Where's Mummy?"

"We're going there right now. You don't have to worry anymore, poppet."

Adam got in the vehicle and started the car as there was a loud crackling bang like two gunshots. Adam looked back at Moss Woods and could see flames rising from the woods, lighting up the sky. It looked as if Draper was carrying out Melvyn's instructions.

Sophie's mother was at Janine's house and Marissa was comforting her. "It will be all right. Adam will bring her back. I promise. He is a good man and then he will help me."

Janine looked at her child, puzzled. "You don't know that, darling but we hope and pray that you're right."

"I am. And we should all pray. Pray all together to God to thank him for saving us."

Janine turned apologetically to Sophie's mother. "I don't know where all this is coming from. We are not even a religious household."

"Well, I am praying in my heart and head and if Marissa is right I will continue to thank and praise him. I will do whatever it takes." She took Marissa's hand and held it. "Okay, Marissa, let us pray. We will pray together." Janine looked at them both and she, too, joined hands with them.

In the car, Vanda asked quietly, "Do you really think this is over?"

Adam shook his head. "I don't know. Melvyn, you have had more experience in this, than me. Is it over?"

"For the moment. But I cannot say forever. We were lucky."

"It didn't feel like it," said Vanda.

"No. These are powerful forces. Who knows when they will be back and in which part of the country?" murmured Adam.

"Yes... Who knows? Shaitan is quite likely to gather his band of demons and make more plans. The only thing that's certain is he won't be able to use Moss Woods for more of his evil acts," said Melvyn.

Little Sophie was cuddled up to Vanda and she had nodded off to sleep with the movement of the car. "So, what do we tell Vance?" whispered Vanda not wanting to wake the child.

"The truth," said Adam. "I've learnt that lesson. He can decide how much he puts out to the press. He still needs to explain the death of Parkes and Melanie. They can all be put at Shaitan's door." They drove on in silence until they reached the Porters' house. As they parked, little Sophie awoke.

Outside in the shrubbery was a forensic tent and police cars with their lights flashing. "What's going on?" murmured Vanda.

Adam received a jolt of electricity that made his body tingle and images of Harding flooded his mind. He recoiled in horror.

Vance and Jacobs came out from the house with Sophie's mother, Yvonne Sinclair, Marissa and Janine Porter. Sophie fled to her mother's arms who was crying in relief as she hugged her daughter to her.

Adam looked about him questioningly. "Where's Harding?" Vance shook his head, sorrowfully. "No! How?"

Vance looked at the others. "I'll explain later. Can you come into the station on the way back?"

Adam nodded. "For sure. I just need to have a chat with Marissa and her family as I promised." Marissa tugged on Adam's hand, and he went inside with the little girl as Vance offered Melvyn a lift back to collect his car, which was at Black Head Ridge House.

11

ADAM SAT AT THE KITCHEN table with Marissa and her mother Janine, and Vanda. Janine attempted to reprimand Marissa for taking up Adam and Vanda's time, but Adam stopped her. "No, please let her speak. I promised to listen, and I will."

Janine blustered and fussed, "But it's all nonsense. Something from her imagination, when she was a toddler."

Adam spoke gently to Janine, "I know this might be tough for you, but I really feel that she has something important to say. Your little girl knew my name and knew we were here to help. How could she have known that?"

Janine went quiet for a moment. "I am just afraid that I might lose her…"

"That won't happen, Mummy. I just need to set things straight, that's all. You are my mummy and daddy now."

Tears filled Janine's eyes, and she nodded. "Very well. Go on, Marissa."

Marissa smiled brightly and turned to Adam. "When I was very little I had pictures in my head and voices of my other mummy and daddy and the man I married at age eighteen. I knew they all missed me. I told my mummy and daddy here and they just thought I was imagining things and told me to forget about it."

"Okay," said Adam slowly. "Where do this other family live?"

"They were in Fort William as is my husband, Christopher, but my parents are moving to somewhere called Wick, and Christopher is getting married again." Marissa was very precise. "I know you can help me. Will you? There are things my old family and Chris need to know, before they move."

"Like what?"

Marissa looked around. "I'd rather not say, now. I'll tell you later when we visit."

"Right." He looked up at Vanda. "It looks like we might be taking a trip to Scotland."

Vance had dropped Melvyn off at Black Head Ridge House to recover his vehicle and he followed Vance back to the police station.

Vance was pacing, and railing at anyone who would listen. "We have three murders, little Melanie Parker, Leonard Parkes and now Harding. We have one suspect, Leonard Shaitan, who has disappeared. We need to put out a warrant for the apprehension of this man. Press releases, crime stoppers and more. It will mean bad publicity for Gilbert Bray School... And Harding's family still have to be contacted. Fortunately, he doesn't have a wife and kids but it's still a horrible death. His family will be devastated."

Vance dropped into his seat with a thump. He dropped his head in his hands and sighed heavily. "No one, but no one would believe the truth."

Melvyn sat at the table. "My fear is that Shaitan could reappear somewhere else. This is the second time I've had to deal with him. I thought we had won last time. He'll pop up again but probably in another part of the country. But it won't be immediately... Don't forget we're dealing with a demon."

Vance looked up and raked his fingers through his hair. "Don't let anyone hear you say that, please." Vance looked around him. "We need to bury this as best we can, or we'll be a laughing-stock."

Vanda and Adam made their way back from Marissa's house. She pressed him again, "So what sort of a scoop can I write on this? There must be something."

"Vance won't let you write anything on the paranormal events. Take the straight story, a chemistry teacher using drugs and other nefarious means, who started a cult in an all-girls school... a charismatic man who lured in youngsters who promised them earthly riches if they followed him..."

"Go on..."

"The man escaped after trying to hide his acts and detract attention by burning down a part of Moss Woods."

Vanda's tone revealed she was uncertain. "What about the murders?"

"Melanie Parker was his first victim... he was afraid of what she'd discovered, Leonard Parkes was suspicious of him and after Shaitan witnessed him talking to investigative reporters... he was killed to silence him..."

"And Harding?"

"That may be trickier... Maybe a heart attack and then crows did the rest... I don't know."

"It won't make such a good story."

"Maybe not. But it would be the truth with a number of omissions."

"It would make a great book."

"Yes, that, too."

"Now the next question..."

Adam groaned. "What?"

"The little girl, Marissa. What have you learned?"

"You were there. You heard what she had to say."

"Yes, I recorded it all." She removed her Dictaphone from her jacket pocket. "It's all on there. Do you really believe that there is such a thing as reincarnation?"

"After what I've witnessed, I don't see why not. We have to check this child's story and see if it pans out."

"How do we do that?"

"We see Marissa again and then a trip to Scotland I think."

"You know she'll want to come with us?"

"I don't think so. Her mother won't let her out of her sight, I'm sure. I think with technology we can use FaceTime or Skype or something, to do a video call and Marissa can interact with them... the other parents."

"And her husband?"

"Him, too."

"That's if the people agree."

"If the people agree..." confirmed Adam.

They continued on in silence until they finally reached the police station where Vance was waiting.

"You can't print or report any of this," said Vance to Vanda who shot a look at Adam.

Adam then related what he and Vanda had talked about in the car. "There are bound to be a lot of questions. You will have to satisfy the public."

"But not with the truth."

"Not the whole truth just with some omissions."

"Like Shaitan was a demon."

"Yes," said Adam resolutely. "Have Shaitan's private quarters at the school been searched yet?"

"It's been sealed off as a crime scene. We will do a full search there and at his chemistry lab. There is bound to be something."

"I'm sure you will discover more than you bargained for."

"What do you mean?"

"Shaitan was not just a demon but a scientist, chemist and an alchemist. He used mind controlling drugs including Rohypnol to brainwash the children. There will be evidence of this. It should make your case easier and to get Shaitan onto the most wanted list. If he ever reappears in human form again with this name, you will know about it. If he doesn't, all well and good."

"There will be many questions and Draper might be implicated. After all he tipped you off."

"I'm sure it's nothing you can't sort out," said Adam confidently. He suddenly shivered as if a cold breeze had entered the room.

"What? What is it?" asked Vance.

"You will be giving a press conference soon. Be careful. One tenacious reporter will spot that there is more to this story than is being said. Be prepared for any question and answer with confidence and authority… that's all I can tell you, for now."

"If you think of anything else…"

"Don't worry, I'll be in touch and now I really must speak to Melvyn."

Melvyn stepped forward. "I'm all yours. Then I must get back. Helen will be concerned. She remembers what happened last time."

The two men went outside. Melvyn opened his car door and set his bag of Holy items on the back seat. "Get in. We'll talk inside."

Adam clambered into the passenger seat. He turned and studied Melvyn's face. "You don't think this is over, do you?"

Melvyn shook his head. "No. It was too easy. Last time it took me over a week to rid the world of his evil. Yes, Shaitan was sucked back to his own domain to plot again. The portal is closed for now, but he will want retribution. He will want revenge on Draper, and he won't be the only one in his sights. I believe you and me, we will be high on his list."

"What about Vanda?"

"Her too, she's just his type."

"So you have said," said Adam wryly. "So, if he's coming back what do we do?"

Melvyn shrugged. "I don't know. I don't know how, when or where but he will be back. But that's not what you wanted to talk to me about, was it?"

"No," said Adam slowly. "Marissa."

"Ah, the special one. Shaitan would like to get his hands on her, too."

"That's a horrifying thought."

"It is…"

"What do you know about reincarnation?"

"I know the Church doesn't believe in it. It's not mentioned in the Bible. There are only references to rebirth in Christ."

"What do you think?"

"I've seen enough in my time not to discount anything. I have an open mind. Why?"

"Marissa remembers her previous family in Scotland. She wants me to check it out."

"She said that?" said Melvyn in disbelief.

"Not exactly. I think she wants to visit them to prove it to her parents. I thought maybe using technology to speak to her other family…"

"Be careful. You never know what doors that might open."

"I can't imagine that would be dangerous…"

"Maybe not. Just keep your wits about you."

"How did the child die?"

"I don't know. I haven't asked her yet."

"Get as much information as you can. Remember the strange case of the Pollock sisters?"

"Can't say I do."

"Google it… you may find it enlightening. Or the story of a mother called Mary."

Adam shrugged. "Now you've just confused me."

"Jenny Cockell. Formerly Mary. It's on You Tube on True Lives introduced by Michael Aspel."

"I don't know who that is…"

"Aspel must be about 91 now, he was a well-known TV presenter. Check it out, it may prepare and enlighten you."

"How do you know all this?"

"Let's just say, I had my own odd memories when I was a child. And now I must go."

"Can I call on you again, if I need to?"

"You have my number."

Adam opened the door and left the car. He strolled across to Vanda sitting in his vehicle and got in. He looked across at Vanda, who exclaimed, "I know that look. Spill."

So, Adam explained as best he could on the journey back to Black Head Ridge House.

Vanda listened carefully in shocked disbelief. "Do you believe in reincarnation? It all sounds so farfetched."

"I don't not believe it. Tell me, would you have believed in demons and succubae if you hadn't experienced what went on with Leonard Shaitan?"

"No, I suppose not. And it could be an interesting story."

"That's if the families allow you to print it?"

"Do you think they'd refuse?"

"I don't know. You will have to find out… Don't forget, you have to write the story about the school, yet. Something that Vance agrees with."

Vanda's face puckered as she thought. "Yes, I don't think the world is ready yet for accounts of demons, sacrifices and portals to Hell… I'll work something out. In fact, I may even use it as a basis to write a novel. It's one hell of a story."

Adam nodded as he turned into the road leading to Black Head Ridge. "It is. Are you coming in?"

Vanda nodded. "Yes, I don't relish being in the house alone after everything that's happened. I'll go and feed Elsa and come straight back. We don't know if that Lilith has been destroyed and, we know you are on her radar. Think we'd best stick together at night for the time being."

"Is that the only reason?"

"No," she said chirpily. "I'd like it, too."

Adam smiled and mused, "So would I."

Back at the station Vance was talking quietly to Jacobs. "Not a word of what happened to you or to us during this investigation. Our report will have to be sanitised. We still have to prepare a press release regarding the murder of Harding, Parkes, and the schoolgirl Melanie Parker." Adam's words came rushing into his mind. "The press conference. I've got to know what I am saying, be prepared, and confident."

"What do you want me to do?"

"You can accompany me to the Parkers. We will go there first, then to Harding's parents and finally to the groundsman's home. That will help us to get all the details right. We can decide what we need to say and be consistent with our story en route. Are you ready?"

"What, now?"

"Now."

Jacobs nodded and Vance left instructions with his team to carry on as normal, while they dealt with the aftermath of Harding's death. There were a lot of raised eyebrows and as soon as the DCI and his sergeant had left, there was a rush of whispering as the remaining police force speculated about what was really going on. Most agreed that things had been exceptionally weird since the discovery of the child's body in the boot of that car. And what was the deal with all that salt? There was much shaking of heads and mutterings.

Vance and Jacobs were on their way to the Parkers' house in St. Keverne. Jacobs looked out of the window. "No crows about, are there?"

"Not seen any. I'll never look at those birds in the same way again," said Vance.

"No. Nor me. I never minded crows. Always thought they were very intelligent."

"They are. But those weren't normal crows. Think I'll be just as wary as you." He paused. "Okay, how much further?" asked Vance.

Jacobs looked at the map. "It's about 57 miles. Think we'll be gone most of the day."

"Best sort out the most direct route," advised Vance.

"Where is it that Harding's parents live? Have they been informed yet?" asked Jacobs.

"No. No names were mentioned in the first police report on South West news, only that a policeman had suffered a heart attack on duty and the family had yet to be informed."

"The address, I've got, says they live in Helston," said Jacobs studying a sheet of paper.

Vance pressed on assertively. "Change of plan. We'll go there first as it's on the way."

Jacobs nodded. "Makes sense," and he entered the postcode into the Sat Nav system whose directions they obeyed.

They followed the route into a housing estate behind the main High Street and shopping centre, close to a children's play area. They travelled along the road to a modest bungalow that looked well-kept and overlooked the town. Vance took a deep breath as he alighted and knocked on the door. Jacobs stood at his side.

A fair haired plump lady in her sixties opened the door and looked in surprise at Vance who showed her his warrant card. "Yes? Can I help you?"

"Mrs Harding?" The woman nodded. "DCI Vance and Sergeant Jacobs, may we come in? It's about your son, Andrew."

She opened the door wider to admit them and they stepped inside. "What's all this about, Chief Inspector? Is Andrew all right?"

She led them into a comfortable sitting room with a chintz covered suite and indicated they sit. Mr Harding, Andrew's father was sitting in a wing back chair reading the local paper. He looked up curiously.

"David, these men are from the police. It's about Andrew."

David rustled his paper as he folded it up. "Yes?" He was instantly alert. Vance could see the resemblance between Andrew and his father. "It's not about the policeman who died, is it? We saw it on the news."

Myra Harding's hand flew to her throat and she sat down with a bump onto the settee.

"I'm afraid so." Vance continued on gently, using the cover story he had concocted for the press. He ended with, "He was an excellent officer and valued member of the Force. There was no record of any heart problems in his medical records, so it was a huge shock to us, too."

"He was also my friend," added Jacobs. "I will miss him enormously. My kids loved him, too."

"Yes," sniffed Mrs Harding. "Andrew talked about you a lot. You would work together at getting questions sorted for the local pub quiz."

"That's right," said Jacobs. "I will miss him in so many ways."

"Can we see him?" asked Harding's father.

"He's in the mortuary at Brinkworth General but you best be warned. Whilst he was on surveillance and collapsed, he was attacked by wildlife."

"Wildlife?"

"We think it was some big birds... I don't know how to say this... But the creatures pecked out his eyes." Myra began to cry as Vance continued. "I'm so sorry, Mrs Harding. Andrew was a good man."

"Isn't that unusual behaviour?" quizzed Mr Harding.

"Well, in some ways, yes. But birds like crows and buzzards have been known to devour the eyes of young lambs and other baby critters. Andrew was just lying in the shrubbery and not able to defend himself, so it is unusual but understandable."

Vance and Jacobs remained with Harding's family for some time before finally moving on. They both heaved a sigh of relief when they returned to their car.

"At least Andrew wasn't an only child. That would have been even worse," said Vance.

"It was bad enough," added Jacobs. "Especially, hearing about the plans his siblings and family were planning for his fortieth birthday party."

"Yes, well we mustn't dwell on it for too long. Just hope we can get that bastard Shaitan at some point."

"You think?"

"I have to believe in some kind of justice. Or I will go mad. Why the heck are we in the Force?"

Vanda and Adam were researching stories regarding reincarnation. They had watched three videos on You Tube and were in awe of what they had learned. Vanda eventually spoke. "Do you believe it, or do you think it's something else?"

"I think it's a wonderful possibility."

"But you're not certain?"

"Who can be certain about anything?" Adam left his words hanging in the air.

He jumped up suddenly. "Right then, I'm off to Marissa's house. I am going to learn as much as I can. Coming?"

Vanda smiled, saying, "Try and stop me. But first I must make sure Elsa is okay."

THE AFTERNOON SUN POOLED IN through the kitchen window where Adam and Vanda sat with Mrs Janine Porter and Marissa. The conversation was polite but stilted as they drank a cup of tea and Marissa had a glass of milk. It was Marissa who broke the awkwardness by speaking determinedly. "Adam, I need to know, are you going to help me?"

Adam raised his eyebrows at the directness of her question. "That depends."

"On what?" asked Marissa popping her fingers to her lips.

Adam looked at Janine. "I need to know that you are in agreement with this? That you support Marissa and give me consent to investigate on your behalf?"

Janine bit her lip. "My husband and I have talked about this and agree that Marissa needs to know but I have to admit I am more than a little scared. I am worried."

"Why?" asked Marissa.

"I'm scared that you will want to be with your other parents and want to leave us."

"That won't happen," said Marissa. Her language and the way she spoke made her seem much older than her five, soon to be six years of age.

Adam glanced at Vanda who looked meaningfully at him willing him to ask the important question. "Mrs Porter, Marissa, we will be happy to investigate but…"

"But…?"

"Will you be willing for my partner here to document this case?"

"You mean write about it? … I am not sure…"

"It would be dealt with carefully and truthfully, not sensationalised. I promise you it will give hope to many people and could open the door to others coming forward with their own stories," said Vanda.

Janine considered the proposal and finally said, "As long as my husband agrees then it's fine by me."

"Then I am happy too, but now, I need to ask Marissa a number of questions, Vanda here will take notes."

"Yes, do you object to me recording this? I don't want to get anything wrong," asked Vanda.

Janine Porter shrugged. "It's okay by me."

Vanda smiled and removed her Dictaphone and set it on the kitchen table. Adam lowered his voice and spoke gently to Marissa. "Now, Marissa, I want you to tell me everything that you remember, and I will be asking you about some things you might find uncomfortable. Okay?" The little girl nodded her head vigorously. "Good," then we'll make a start. "You said you lived in Fort William, can you tell me where?"

"In Oban Terrace number 24." Marissa's voice was assured and positive.

"What was your name?"

"Mrs Maria Campbell." As she said her name a hint of a Scottish accent came through those words. Her next words were spoken in her usual tones. "I was trying to get used to it I had always been a MacDonald before I was wed."

"And how old were you when you passed?"

Marissa screwed up her face as she thought. "I was eighteen, nearly nineteen. I got married young and had to get my parents' permission."

"Do you know how it happened?"

Marissa nodded, and as she spoke her voice seemed more mature and her language more eloquent. It was hard to believe she was only coming up to six years of age. Janine was looking at her daughter amazed. "My Uncle Ian was driving me from Inverlochy primary school, where my mother taught, I had been shadowing her. I was going to Lochaber High School for the morning to see where I was to be a teaching assistant and meet the teachers I would be supporting. I was excited, going to see my new workplace. It was raining heavily. A truck was coming in the opposite direction it skidded in the wet and was sliding towards us and Uncle Ian swerved hard. We mounted the pavement, went through a fence barrier and hit a brick wall."

"Do you remember what happened next?"

Marissa screwed up her face and thought. "I remember jumping out and looking at the mess the car was in. Uncle Ian had his face in a white bag. He wasn't moving, people came out to look and I was shouting at them to help my uncle. He was so still but no one took any notice of me. They just ignored me."

Adam continued, "Go on."

"I looked in the car as people were yelling to hurry and get out the young woman that was in there as the car was starting to smoulder. I kept saying I was all right, but no one would listen but then, I looked again and saw myself all crumpled up and blood all around my head."

Janine and Vanda exchanged glances. It was clear that Janine was very unnerved by what she was hearing.

Marissa took a mouthful of her milk and looked around. She said chirpily, "It's all right I wasn't hurt."

"Can you remember what happened next?" said Adam soothingly.

"An ambulance came and took us to Belford hospital. That was after the firemen got us out of the car."

"Yes?"

"I sat in the back with my uncle next to me. I couldn't understand why I was in a bag and all zipped up. It was weird. I didn't realise I was dead."

"What happened then?"

"My mummy and daddy... my other mummy and daddy were standing around me in this room. They were sobbing. I tried to make them hear that I was fine, but they didn't take any notice of me. Then my husband arrived, and he was in bits and crying, too."

"Can you tell me something about your parents and family?"

Marissa screwed up her face. "Daddy's name was Peter and mummy was Charlotte. Everyone used to call her Charlie."

"Anything else?"

"Daddy had a nickname for her. It was Squeak."

"Squeak?"

"Yes, she used to laugh silently and then it would come out as a squeak. My brother used to say it was because she laughed like a mouse."

"Who was your brother?"

"He was older than me, twenty, I think. His name was Trevor. I had much younger sisters, too, Alice and Anna. They were twins and my age now. Daddy used to say they were a happy accident."

The conversation continued and Adam managed to get more information about the MacDonald family and the Campbells.

Janine Porter stopped them. "No, this is ridiculous. Just childhood fantasy."

"But Mummy, it's not. Please, Mummy they need to know I'm all right."

Adam intervened, "Please, Mrs Porter. Let us check this out and see if we can verify everything in Marissa's story. But firstly," he turned to Marissa. "Is there anything else, something that only you and your family would know or even something that they wouldn't, and you could tell us. And your husband?"

Marissa nodded. "My piggy bank."

"Yes?"

"I used to hide it when I was small because Trevor would raid it. I had a special hiding place in my room, where he couldn't get to it. I left it there when I got married and I was going to get it and give it to my first baby as a surprise. I also had a book of poems that I had written about my husband. We'd only been married three months, that's in my home with Christopher."

Adam smiled. "Thanks, Marissa you've done well."

"Is that it? Can I go and play now?"

Janine nodded. "Of course. Off you go."

Marissa scrambled down and sped off into the garden to play in the sand pit.

"Mrs Porter, I know this is difficult for you, but Marissa is quite unique, and I really feel we should follow through on this."

Janine Porter sighed and nodded. "I understand, but I have to admit that I am apprehensive and more than a little frightened."

They continued to talk together and discuss how the investigation should proceed, and no one noticed Marissa return from the garden and stand listening at the door. She overheard Adam saying, "Vanda and I can go to Scotland and visit the Campbells, with their permission of course. If they are agreeable we can do a zoom call with them and with you and Marissa here. I am not sure how we approach her husband."

Marissa burst in. "NO! I want to go to Scotland with you. I want to see them properly not on a screen. Then everything will be fine."

Janine was shocked. "But Marissa, it's the other end of the country. I just can't let you do it. I'm sorry."

Marissa burst into tears and ran to Adam. "Please, Adam, make her understand. Please."

Adam let the little girl climb on his lap and said quietly, "Look, I know how tough this is for both of you… How about we all go? Vanda, Marissa and you, Mrs Porter, with me?"

Janine Porter blushed. "I'm sorry. I don't know if I can afford to do something like that."

Adam exchanged a glance with Vanda who nodded encouragingly. "Mrs Porter. It will be at my expense. Mine and Vanda's. It won't cost you a penny. It will be my pleasure. What do you say?"

"Please, Mummy."

"I don't know what to say." Janine had tears streaming down her cheek.

"Say, yes, Mummy. Please."

Vance and Jacobs were now travelling towards Melanie Parker's home address in St. Keverne. They had been quiet for most of the journey since leaving the Hardings' house. It was as if a dark cloud had settled on their shoulders.

Vance jumped as Jacobs broke the silence. "Over there. We've just passed Mr Retallack the butchers. Not far now. Through the square and it looks as though we will soon be at Trythance. Vance followed the directions, and the cultured female voice said, "You have arrived at your destination."

"I'm not looking forward to this," murmured Vance as he parked the car.

Jacobs just nodded. There was no more to be said. It was always a difficult job to confirm the details surrounding the death of a family member, let alone when that victim was a young child. But Vance had promised the Parkers answers, and he knew he had to fulfil his promise.

Mr and Mrs Parker were huddled together on a comfortable looking sofa. Vance had already confirmed to them that the body they had discovered belonged to Melanie. But what was even more difficult was trying to explain events surrounding it.

Mrs Parker sat elegantly with her ankles crossed. She was dabbing at her eyes with a white lace hankie and clinging on tightly to her husband's arm with the other hand. She looked as if she had been weeping for a month.

When Mr Parker spoke, his voice was quietly restrained and cultured. "So, you're telling us that Melanie's chemistry teacher, this Leonard Shaitan, is the one responsible and now he has disappeared?"

"Yes. He started a cult in the school in the guise of an after school club, Children of the Light. But it seems Melanie was suspicious of him and the drinks he was plying to the students in the 'club' plus the fact he was intimately involved with an older girl in the school. Melanie became too curious and with what she found out about his actions she challenged him and threatened to report him. His response was to get rid of her before she revealed the truth about his murky dealings."

"Why didn't the school know about his activities?"

"No one informed against him. It was only Melanie that had suspicions that he was drugging students."

"And this Shaitan has gone, absconded?"

"Don't worry, he is on a most wanted list, and we will eventually catch him, and he will pay for his terrible crimes. It is almost certain he has left the area."

"Almost?"

"The police are doing everything they can to find him. I have a meeting with the headmaster next week and the school is hoping to hold a memorial service for Melanie once back after the holidays. They are as shocked as the rest of the community. I dare say, it will have a profound effect on their reputation and future boarders."

Mr Parker looked none too convinced. "You will keep me updated on your investigation?"

"Of course."

"Then there is no more to say. Thank you for explaining it to us."

It was a polite dismissal. Vance nodded and rose. "We'll see ourselves out."

Vance sat behind the wheel and loosened his tie. "That was awkward."

Jacobs murmured consolingly, "It wasn't that bad. You said what you had to say. I think they accepted it."

"Maybe, maybe not. But it was all we could say." He turned to Jacobs. "Are you up to driving?"

Paul Jacobs nodded. "Yes. About time I got back into the swim, so to speak. And I am feeling better, not so drained."

"You will still have to be very careful. This Lilith woman got her hooks into you, she could come back."

"I will be sleeping with my wife, and I assure you I will be wearing that cross and have Holy water to hand. I'm not going through that again."

Vance and Jacobs alighted and swapped places. "Right! Where to next?"

"Back the way we came to the groundsman's house and then the school."

"Okay. Set the Sat Nav." Jacobs started the engine.

Adam and Vanda had left the Porters' house after reaching a tentative agreement with Janine and her husband, who had returned from work and was reluctant at first but then relented at Marissa's pleas, plus Adam's assurances that the need Marissa had inside for closure would settle her down. The Porters would confirm this after further discussion together. They were returning to Black Head Ridge to pack some items, source flights to Inverness, car hire, and somewhere they could all stay for a few days. They needed to be prepared. Adam knew he needed to speak to Marissa's other family as this could be a huge shock for them as well. As they drove in comparative silence Adam felt a wave of something washing over him, like pinpricks of electricity that tingled down his arms and legs as he drove, and he swerved suddenly.

"What is it?" asked Vanda.

Adam pulled in at the side of the road and stopped the car. "I don't know. It's a weird feeling like something is going to happen."

"What?"

"That's it. I don't know."

"Isn't that unusual?"

"It is. But I can't explain it." As the feeling began to wane Adam started the car again and moved off towards Black Head Ridge.

The day had turned overcast, and the gloomy weather had tipped Adam into something of a melancholic state. As Adam pulled into the yard in front of his house the wind chimes were tinkling although there wasn't a breath of wind. Strains of Beethoven's Moonlight Sonata filled his head. He was taken aback when Vanda murmured, "Where's that music coming from?"

"You can hear it, too?"

"Beethoven's Moonlight Sonata, seems to be coming from your hallway."

They left the car and Adam gingerly moved towards the front door but once the key was in the lock the music stopped and then all Adam could hear was a child crying. He pushed open the door. He couldn't be certain, but he thought he saw two small girls of about eleven in school uniform, wearing kilts with white blouses and dark green ties, who scurried along the corridor.

Adam strode off down the corridor leaving Vanda looking puzzled. "Adam?"

He called back, "Won't be a mo…" He ran towards the study, there was a rush of wind, and the study door banged shut in his face. This time he heard two little girls laughing. He tried the door. It wouldn't budge. As Vanda appeared behind him he tried again and this time the door opened easily. Adam stepped inside and a white feather floated down onto the desk.

"Oh, no," muttered Vanda. "Not again."

Vance and Jacobs had arrived at Kenneth Parkes' house. Lola, Ken's wife had admitted them, and they sat in her cosy sitting room politely enjoying a cup of tea. "I know they said Ken's death was inconclusive and most likely he suffered a heart attack while in the throes of some nightmare."

"But what about the scratches and bitemarks?"

Lola shrugged. "The coroner said they had to be self-inflicted, that he'd scratched and bruised himself thrashing around in bed."

"What about the bitemarks?"

Lola coloured up. "They said it was likely to be from some energetic lovemaking. But Ken wasn't like that. He wasn't rough. He was gentle and kind. It's been written off by everyone as something unusual but not abnormal. But I know differently." She began to cry.

"Mrs Parkes, we don't believe it's natural."

"What else could it be?"

"Until we find any more evidence that is how it will stay, but I am not giving up and I believe that it's something that's been orchestrated by Leonard Shaitan. You know he's disappeared?"

"Leonard Shaitan? Never liked that man and I know Ken thought he was a wrong 'un. He suspected him of being a kiddie fiddler, you know? He tried to report it and for that he got the sack."

"Rest assured, Mrs Parkes we will continue to look into it. And if we discover anything I will be in touch. Leonard Shaitan is a wanted man now. If he turns up anywhere we'll find him."

"Thank you, Chief Inspector. I appreciate that."

"If you think of anything else, anything at all you have my number," and Vance passed her his card.

He and Jacobs rose and left the house feeling subdued. Once in the car, Paul Jacobs turned to Vance and said, "That could have been me."

More strange things were happening at Black Head Ridge House. Adam had closed the door on the night as he and Vanda went into the sitting room for a nightcap when the wind chimes tinkled. They were both instantly alert.

A tune on the piano in the hallway morphed into a full rendition of Beethoven's Moonlight Sonata. "What is this?" murmured Vanda. "We have swapped Portishead for Beethoven?"

"You can hear it?" whispered Adam.

"I hear it," she replied. "Come." Vanda pulled Adam up from the settee and tentatively moved towards the door leading to the hall. They both stepped out cautiously and both saw the black and white piano keys playing on their own. As soon as their presence was felt the music stopped and the lid of the Steinway banged shut followed by a peal of girlish laughter.

Adam walked to the piano and gently stroked the wood and as he did so, he felt a small hand on his back that traced up and down his spine and he shivered. The temperature had dropped dramatically.

He heard his mother's voice. She was reprimanding two girls who were giggling, "Lucy, Margaret, enough of this teasing."

"Lucy Ward? Margaret Lake?" Adam asked. These were the names of two girls that had previously gone missing from the school.

The temperature dropped still further, and fronds of ice shot across the hall window. Adam asked again, "Show yourselves, please. I am not here to hurt you, only to help."

The frosty air in front of him began to shimmer and two small girls in kilts and white blouses started to manifest. Vanda caught hold of Adam's arm and she gasped as she could see them, too.

Adam persisted, "I am here to help you move on. So that you can rest in peace."

One child spoke, "We can't, not until we're found."

"Where are you? Tell me. I can help you."

The other leaned her head from side to side mechanically and murmured, "Ding, dong, bell."

Vanda whispered, "What does that mean?"

The two girls laughed, but the laughter turned to tears and crying. The sound disintegrated into vibrations like tinkling bells, and they vanished from view.

Adam called out, "Don't go! Let me help you."

"You have to find us first…" The word, 'first' echoed around the room before dissipating into a final wail of sadness and all was still once more.

Vanda let go of Adam and looked about her. "What does that mean?"

"It means we have to find their bodies."

"And just how do we do that? Ding, dong, bell. It's not much of a clue."

"No," said Adam, raking his fingers through his hair. "But we have to find the answers, somehow."

MARISSA WAS EXCITED. HER FATHER, James had given her the final okay to travel with her mother, Adam and Vanda to Scotland. James persuaded his wife, "Don't you see? If she does this, it will stop there. No more speculation. Marissa herself said she just wants to visit the once. I believe, as Adam said that it will give her some sort of closure."

"But what if she wants to stay with her other families?" questioned Janine.

"Don't worry. A six-year-old can't be married and she would be too much for older parents. She will want to come home and live this life with us. It's as Adam has said, she is a special little girl."

"I wish I could be as sure as you."

"Look, I'll be scared, too. But somehow I feel this is right. This is what we need to do, once and for all."

Janine nodded her head reluctantly. "I hope you're right. I'll ring Adam now."

Adam and Vanda were searching the internet for places in the vicinity of the school within a fifty mile radius that had a bell tower or bells. They were numerous from St. Mary's to St. Buryan, and many more. "This is hopeless," said Vanda. "There are far too many for us to check out every church in the diocese. How do we even know if it's a church? It could be anything. There's even a bell tower at a block of flats in Penzance. How would we know where to look?"

Adam scratched his head. "Until we have more information, it's all we've got."

The phone rang interrupting them. Adam sighed and stretched before rising to answer it. He listened to whoever was on the other line and said, "That's great. I'll fix it up now and get back to you."

Vanda looked quizzically at him. He smiled. "Pack a bag, we're going to Scotland. The Porters have agreed."

"What about our research?" she asked.

"It'll have to wait. One thing at a time. We can continue when we get back. Now we need to finalise hotels and flights to Inverness and car hire."

Vanda groaned. "Okay, boss! I'll look up flights. You do the hotels and car hire. When are we planning on going?"

"As soon as…"

"Thought as much." She cleared her current searches and pulled up flights to Inverness from the South West. "There's nothing from Plymouth and the Exeter flights are two stops and take hours. We can go from Bristol that gives us more choice…"

"I trust you. Book it. Check what time we land, and I'll sort out car hire."

Marissa was sitting in the front room, coat on, looking out of the window. She was very excited. Her mother Janine smiled to herself as she walked in. "Sitting staring out of the window won't make Adam get here any quicker."

"I know. But I want to be ready when he does."

"And so you are!"

"Yes, I understand that."

Janine sighed. "Is there anything else you want to take?"

Marissa screwed up her face as she thought. "Ooh, Polar, I've forgotten Polar."

"Then go and get him, they'll be here soon."

Marissa scrambled off her seat and ran back up the stairs. She soon returned cuddling a soft, fluffy polar bear stuffed toy. She gave him a kiss on his nose. "Sorry, Polar. I almost forgot you. Can't leave you behind."

"No. You won't sleep."

"I know." Marissa plonked herself back on the window seat and exclaimed excitedly, "They're here! Here's Adam, now." She jumped off the seat and ran to her front door ready to welcome him in.

Adam and Vanda alighted and walked up to the front door. He smiled when he saw the little girl. "Are you all set?"

Marissa beamed, "Yes, we're ready. Aren't we, Mummy?"

"Then we had better get your luggage in the car and head for Bristol."

"I've never been on a plane before. It's like…" She searched for a word. "Thrilling."

"Let's hope this trip will settle all your fears," said Adam with a grin.

"It will. I promise," said Marissa with a huge smile on her face.

They loaded the car and pulled away leaving Marissa waving frantically to her dad standing on the doorstep. They waved until neither of them could see each other anymore and with all the excitement and movement of the car, Marissa fell asleep hugging Polar.

Things went smoothly at Bristol airport and the flight to Inverness took off on time. Marissa could hardly contain her enthusiasm, she was like a shaken up bottle of bubbly champagne effervescing everywhere. Vanda had to admit her enjoyment of the flight was made much more pleasurable by Marissa's joy at experiencing something that was new to her. She oohed and aahed at the view from her window seat and studied the clouds below the plane's flight path and commented that it was always sunny in the sky above the clouds. She added that she wished she could fly all the time.

Once they had left the plane Adam looked for the shuttle bus that would take them directly to Arnold Clark's car hire where they would pick up their vehicle. Marissa's lively enthusiasm seemed to wane, and she went very quiet. Vanda tried to coax her out of her solemn state. "Come on, Marissa, cheer up. Aren't you excited?"

"Yes, but I am also worried."

"What about?"

"That they won't believe me."

"I'm sure you will be able to tell them enough that they will believe you. Don't worry about that now. Look, here comes Adam. He's waving to us to come. He must have found the shuttle bus."

Marissa half-smiled and pursed her lips saying, "We'll see." But she perked up and followed Vanda and her mother to where Adam stood waiting.

They soon got on the bus and made their way to Arnold Clark's car hire and compound, where a vehicle waited. Adam had hired a four by four Range Rover that was comfortable and large enough to take everyone's luggage. They set off for Fort William commenting on the spectacular scenery as they travelled.

As they hit the outskirts of Fort William Marissa jumped up in her seat, excited. "I know where we are!" She began shouting out directions. "Follow this road and go across the lights to the bottom. Take a right and go as far as you can and then fork left."

Janine exclaimed, in astonishment, "I can't believe her language is so developed... I mean right... and left? I've not taught her that."

Adam nodded. "I know, but I'll follow what she says, and we'll see what happens." He continued to follow the child's instructions.

"There!" she shouted excitedly. "The white house with green shutters and the copper beech tree in the front garden. The house is called 'Beech Trees'. There's another beech tree in the back garden. That's where my husband lived with me when we were together." Her face crumpled. "He won't know me now. He thinks I'm dead."

They pulled up outside the house and saw the sign on the wall, which did indeed say, 'Beech Trees'. Vanda exchanged a look with Adam. The house name could not be seen from the top of the road, but Marissa was right. It was called 'Beech Trees'.

Marissa struggled to get out of her seat belt harness. Janine helped her and as soon as she was free she opened the car door and went to run up the path. Janine tried to prevent her, but Adam shook his head and stopped her.

"Let her go."

Marissa skipped up the path and ran to the front door. She opened the letterbox flap and fished inside pulling out a long string. On the end of the string was a key. This time it was Janine's turn to stare. "Marissa don't!" she called out as the child stood on tiptoes to try and insert the key in the lock but she was too small.

Adam and Janine hurried up the path to the child's side just as the door opened. "Hey, what is this?" said a young man as he saw the child with the key on the string and the two adults. Vanda watched curiously from the end of the driveway.

Marissa flung her arms around the man's legs and hugged him. "Christopher, it's so good to see you again."

The young man flinched. "How do you know my name?"

Marissa smiled and said, "You are Christopher Campbell, and I was your wife, Maria."

"Is this some sort of joke?" said the man. "What *is* this?"

Adam stepped forward. "Sorry, let me explain." Adam explained as best he could how and why he was helping Marissa. He concluded, "In fact, Marissa led us here."

Marissa pleaded, "Please, Chris, let us in. I can show you that what I'm saying is true."

The bewildered young man opened the door wider and they stepped into his house. Marissa ran into the hall. "There look!" she pointed at a group of small black framed pictures. "See the one with the smiling ginger kitty on? That was a card I had from you when we had been going out together for a month and I loved it so much I framed it."

Chris' jaw dropped. "I don't understand… at least, I do… but I can't get my head around it."

"There's more," said Marissa and she ran along the small passageway to the kitchen and opened a small closet. There was a piece of plywood that appeared to be the actual back of the cupboard, but Marissa pushed it hard at the bottom and the plywood popped forward and she asked Chris to remove it. Once he took it away there was a small metal box. He took it out and Marissa opened it.

Inside was a building society passbook and a small notebook. She passed them both to Chris. The passbook was in the name of Maria Campbell and Christopher Campbell. There was almost a thousand pounds saved.

"I was saving in secret for a long time. You will need that getting married again."

"But how...?"

"Just take it. It's yours. My wedding gift to you." Janine and Adam looked on amazed. "Look at the book."

Chris opened it and exclaimed, "Maria's handwriting. I'd know it anywhere." His eyes filled with tears.

"Don't cry. It's a book of poems, all about you. I always liked to write poetry, and you were my... I forget the word."

"Inspiration," suggested Adam.

"Yes, when you look at them and read them you will always know how much I loved you." She turned to her mother. "Okay, Mummy. We can go now."

"Wait!" said Chris. He stooped down and took Marissa by her shoulders and looked into her face. "You have Maria's eyes. I can see her soul inside you, you are Maria." Tears began to trickle down his face.

"Don't cry. You have a new love now. I just want you to be happy. Who knows we may meet again in another lifetime."

Chris' knees buckled, and he studied the little girl in astonishment. Marissa took her mother's hand. "We have to move onto Oban Terrace now."

Chris gasped. "You'll have to hurry. They are moving today or tomorrow. I'm not sure which."

Marissa tugged at her mother's hand. "Please, Mummy. We must be quick."

Chris followed them to the front door. "I'll phone Peter, sort of prepare the way for you."

Marissa stopped and turned back. "If they haven't left the house yet, tell them to go to my room and there is a loose floorboard under what was my bed. If he pulls it up, underneath, he will find my piggy bank that my brother used to raid, so I hid it. I meant it to be for any child we had together, a bit of fun."

"Well, okay. I will and I will give you their number."

"Thank you," murmured Adam still stunned by all that had happened.

Chris scribbled a number on a pad and tore off the page for Adam. "Let me speak to him first. It will all come as a hell of a shock."

Adam nodded. "I know. I'm finding it hard to believe myself." Adam took the paper and pocketed it. "Vanda's not going to believe this."

Marissa stopped and turned. She let go of her mother's hand and ran back to Chris and gave him one last hug. "Always remember, you will be my boofy and I your Cinders."

Adam looked at Chris whose mouth was agape again. He explained, "We went walking in the highlands and Maria lost her shoe in a bog, it was sucked clean off her. I called her Cinders after that."

Adam looked puzzled and then appeared to twig. "Ah, I see… Cinderella losing a shoe."

Chris nodded unable to speak. He had become choked up again. He watched Marissa let go of her mother's hand and run down to Vanda who opened the car door for her. She turned back and gave Chris a final wave before climbing in the back of the vehicle. Adam and Janine walked silently back to the car in stunned incredulity.

Once settled in the Premier Inn, Adam rang the MacDonalds only to learn that they had already set off for Wick shortly after Christopher's call. Adam didn't want to get into lengthy explanations and agreed to ring again the following day after they had all arrived in Wick.

The following morning the sun had vanished from the sky to be replaced by a leaden bubble wrap of slate coloured clouds. The wind was brisk, and the temperature had dropped so much so, that the grass, shrubbery, leaves and other plants looked as if they were shivering in the breeze such was the change in temperature.

They piled into the car from the Premier Inn where they had stayed the night and set off for Wick. Vanda had called ahead and booked an apartment attached to Mackay's Hotel close to the centre. They would all be more comfortable there and they could eat at the hotel, which boasted an excellent menu.

The journey was beautiful, driving through glens with towering mountains on either side of the road and passed along stretches of water and lochs. Marissa seemed mesmerised by the scenery outside. Even her mother, Janine was exclaiming, "Wow!" as she took in the sights.

On the approach to Wick the roads deteriorated badly. Most of the main highways were exceptional to travel on, but as soon as they hit towns and villages there were potholes and crumbling roads. They could see why many had installed a twenty mile an hour speed limit.

However, they managed to find the hotel, which was in Ebenezer Place, designated as the world's shortest street. The hotel was an interesting shape coming to a head where Union Street met River Street and where one entrance was situated, the main entrance being in Union Street.

Adam parked the car, and they piled into the main entrance lobby and spoke to a charming woman, Fiona Ablett, behind the reception desk. She was more than helpful and recommended they went to the bar while they waited for their apartment to be ready. They ordered coffee and a soft drink for Marissa and sat down to wait. Marissa was fascinated by all the photographs of the hotel's owner posing with best of show breed bulls and asked lots of questions.

Adam took advantage of the time to call Peter MacDonald, Marissa's other 'father'. They had already spoken the previous evening and he admitted that he had been quite dismissive and disbelieving at first, but after following up on the information from Christopher and the discovery of the piggy bank this had encouraged him to listen to all that Adam had to say. "So you see, in Marissa's mind seeing you and your wife would give her closure and she can live her life happily with her mother and father in Cornwall."

"You've come all that way with her?"

"Yes. She gave us a lot of information, that you called your wife, Charlie, Squeak. It was all to do with the way she laughed." There was silence on the other end of the phone. "Mr MacDonald? Peter?"

"Yes, yes... I am still here." He sounded shaken. There was another pause. "Then, you'd better come here. I have to warn you – we moved yesterday, the house is full of boxes, and we are in something of a mess..."

"Don't worry about that." Peter gave him the address, which Adam scribbled down. "We'll be with you late afternoon sometime. I'll ring you as we leave." Peter acknowledged this and curtailed the call. Adam turned to everyone in the apartment. "Listen up, everyone. I've arranged to visit the MacDonalds late afternoon. We'll have lunch first and I'll call him when we are on our way."

"Have you got the address?" asked Vanda.

"Yep."

"Then we'd best look it up and see whereabouts it is." She took out her iPad and searched the postcode that Adam gave her. "Here it is." She passed it to Adam who studied it.

"Fairwinds. It looks nice, overlooks the sea."

Marissa ran up and peered at the picture. "Peter always wanted to live by the sea. It was his dream."

Adam studied the little girl whose speech was remarkably mature for one so young. It was almost as if an older spirit had entered her body and taken her over. "What did your other mummy and daddy do for a living, Marissa?"

"Daddy was a teacher in Business Management and Mummy was a teacher in Primary School." It was hard to believe the sentences were spoken by a six-year-old.

"Well, you are soon to see them again. Come on. Let's go for lunch."

A seagull flew towards the apartment window and landed on the ledge. It tapped at the glass with its beak. Marissa watched fascinated.

"What is it?" asked Vanda.

"Is this bird like the bad birds?"

"I don't think so, why?"

"It's tapping the glass."

"It can see its reflection, that's all."

Marissa walked up to the window and put her hand against the glass. The gull put its head on one side and then the other, and with a chuckling call flew back to the top of the lamppost on the opposite side of the road. Marissa smiled. "No, it's not bad. It's just a gull."

Vanda smiled and held out her hand. "Come on. Let's go."

Marissa snatched up Polar and took Vanda's hand. They left the apartment and went down the curving staircase to the Victorian tiled hall and went out into the street.

~ 1 4 ~

MARISSA STARED OUT OF THE window at the azure-blue sky with a few fluffy white cumulous clouds and studied the wild beauty of the landscape as they travelled through the countryside towards Fairwinds. The smell of salt was in the air and the breeze had picked up bowing the trees down to them as if in obeisance and honour as they passed. They were soon driving up to the coast road and on towards the house on the cliff that overlooked the sea, Fairwinds.

The house was magnificent with huge, tall glass windows that had outstanding views of the water. It looked spacious and impressive, and Adam felt a similarity in its position to his own house at Black Head Ridge.

They arrived and all four exited the car and walked up the paved path to the front door. Marissa hugged her cuddly polar bear as she walked. Adam rang the bell. They waited until footsteps were heard and Marissa's 'other father', Peter opened the door. "Come in." He looked down at Marissa who beamed at him. "You must be Marissa."

She nodded vigorously and added, "Hello, Daddy. This looks a nice house. You always wanted to live by the sea."

Peter opened the door wider as he invited them in. They all trooped into the sitting room, where Marissa's other mother sat waiting. Her eyes filled with tears as she saw Marissa. "So, you were once our Maria?" Marissa nodded and smiled. "You have Maria's eyes and smile, and…" She pointed at the bear she was cuddling. "Maria had a bear like that, too."

"I know," said Maria confidently. "And I called this one the same name."

"And what would that be?" asked her mother, Charlie.

"Polar," answered Marissa simply. "Does Daddy still call you Squeak?"

"He does," said Charlie with a sigh. "And we have something of yours." Charlie nodded meaningfully at her husband, and he vanished from the room and returned with a box.

"This box holds all the things you left at home including your money box. It also has baby memorabilia and some photo albums you might care to look at."

"And Polar," added Charlie. "Don't forget Polar."

Peter set the box on the floor and Marissa scrambled down and sat on the carpet and began to browse through the items. She picked up the piggy bank. "Maybe Alice or Anna would like this?"

Peter replied, "It was yours and we feel that you should have it."

Charlie nodded. "Yes, it was yours, go on, take it. We have already agreed it should be yours."

Marissa smiled and nodded. "Thank you. Yes." She pulled out another cuddly polar bear stuffed toy. "Polar... my first Polar. They could be twins!"

Charlie got up and sat on the floor with Marissa. She dived into the box and pulled out a photograph album. "These are all of Maria when she was born. You might like to look at them, too." Charlie nodded at Janine, who joined them on the floor. They all studied the album together.

Adam and Vanda watched closely hardly believing what was happening. Another album came out showing Maria as a toddler. Charlie pointed at one with Maria sitting on her foot and holding her hands as if riding. "You always liked that nursery rhyme. Remember? This is the way the ladies ride..."

Marissa nodded. "Yes, and the old man... hobble gee, hobble gee and down into a ditch, but my favourite was Ding Dong Bell."

Vanda and Adam exchanged a glance. Adam interrupted them, "Remind me of that one again."

Marissa duly obliged with, "Ding dong bell, Pussy's in the well. Who put her in? Little Tommy Thin. Who pulled her out? Little Tommy Stout. Oh, what a naughty boy was that to try and drown poor pussycat. Ding dong bell."

"You always used to add ding dong bell at the end," laughed Charlie.

"Because it finished it off." Marissa turned to Adam. "Isn't that what you wanted to know?"

Adam's jaw dropped and his eyes lit on Vanda who looked equally amazed then back at Marissa. She scrambled up from the floor and ran to Adam. "It is what you needed, isn't it?"

Adam nodded. "Indeed it is."

Marissa smiled and added, "I can help… with the girls… they'll talk to me." She then padded back to the floor and continued to look through the photo albums.

Janine looked curiously at Adam. "What's all this talk about ding, dong bell?"

"I'll explain later. Now then, how are we doing, Marissa?"

Marissa was then calling out in glee. She pointed at a picture of her holding hands with her mother and father. "I used to do tumble toss with you like this when we walked."

Marissa's actual mother, Janine's eyes filled with tears. "Then you really are Maria. I half hoped… but never mind."

Peter dropped onto the floor with them and put his arm around his wife, whose eyes had also filled up. "This is good, Squeak. It means life goes on. Maria is all right and is living again."

Janine murmured, "It's just so hard to take it all in. It's like some weird Sci-fi or fantasy movie and I'm in it."

Charlie nodded. "I know. It's all very difficult to take in but… there is no other explanation, Marissa was Maria and has been reborn. We have to believe and if I'm totally honest, it's very comforting to know that life goes on. That the energy that is us survives death."

The rest of the afternoon drifted into evening and Peter and Charlie reminisced with Marissa about various things. Some memories were cloudy, and others couldn't be recalled but many were, much to the amazement of Janine, Adam and Vanda, who made copious notes. She asked, "Do you mind if I document this strange case?"

Charlie replied, "It doesn't bother me. Peter?"

"No. I think, as you said, it could give people hope. So yes, you have my permission to write this story."

Marissa suddenly scrambled up. "You were a good mummy and daddy. But it's time for us to go now."

Janine rose with her daughter and asked, "Are you sure?"

"Yes, Mummy. I needed them to know I was okay, and I needed to see them one last time."

Charlie stood up with Peter. "Will we ever see you again?"

Marissa shook her head. "I don't think so. But if I ever grow up and get married, we could ask you to the wedding, couldn't we, Mummy?"

Janine looked surprised again and muttered, "I suppose so."

"Good. Then let's go. We can tell Daddy all about it."

Vanda and Adam rose and thanked the MacDonalds. They said their goodbyes and Marissa ran down the path and back to the car. She had both polar bears with her and cuddled them tightly in her arms.

"Well, I would never have believed it, if I hadn't heard and seen it with my own eyes," said Vanda with a sigh.

"Nor I," said Adam. They gave a final wave to the MacDonalds before getting back in the car and setting off back to Wick and Mackay's Hotel.

In the car conversations were muted while everyone digested what had transpired that afternoon. It was then Adam spoke up. "Marissa?"

The little girl looked up. "Yes?"

"You said you could help me. Is that true?"

She nodded vigorously. "Yes. As long as Mummy will let me." She looked at her mother. "Can I, Mummy? Please…"

Janine looked doubtful. Vanda tried to squash her fears. "She won't be in any danger, and it could help us a lot."

"What do you expect of her?"

"You can come with her and see. It is only to Black Head Ridge House, where I live. Marissa can help us with some unusual activity. You will be there, too," said Vanda eying Janine carefully.

"When would this be?"

"Preferably, as soon as she is able," answered Adam. "As you are aware, Marissa is very special, and her talents could give two young girls peace."

"Mummy?"

Janine was thoroughly bewildered but inclined her head. "Very well. But, if anything upsets her I will take her home, immediately. Understood?"

"Understood and thank you."

As soon as Janine had given her permission, Marissa snuggled up to her mother and her head began to nod. By the time they reached the hotel, Marissa was fast asleep. Once they reached the apartment, as Janine took Marissa off to bed, Adam switched on the TV, which was on the local news and the reporter was warning of a road closure caused by a landslip. One family home had been engulfed by the deluge of earth and vegetation caused by an excess of rainfall the previous month. They learned the Brora coalfield, now closed, was where the landslide had occurred, and it was only about forty-seven miles away. Adam's knees buckled and voices swam in his head.

"Is everything okay?" asked Vanda.

Adam shook his head. "I don't know. I think the excitement of the day has been a bit much. I could do with a drink."

"Me, too. Let's go to the hotel bar. Leave a note for Janine. She can join us later if she wants to and Marissa is awake."

Adam nodded in agreement, and scribbled a note to Janine and they left the apartment quietly.

Once in the bar, Adam began to feel better, and the life came back into his eyes.

They finished one drink and were enjoying another and began talking about the time spent in Fort William and Wick. "I know I've already said it but, if I hadn't heard or seen it with my own eyes, I would never have believed it. It's really made me think," said Vanda. "What an amazing story."

Adam had to agree. "I've always known there was something more. That our energy, the essence of us went on. Never doubted it. But remembering past lives is really thought provoking. And why do some people remember and others not?"

"I shall have to do more research. Find others that remember their past lives. It will make a great story. I'd love to know my own past life or lives, wouldn't you?"

"Don't know if I would. This life is enough to deal with."

Just then, the television above the bar flashed up with breaking news of severe weather warnings and floods followed by several other natural disasters around the world, mud slides in Hungary, hurricanes and tornados in the United States, earthquakes in Brazil and other South American countries. Adam was caught up in the report and a strange expression came over his face. He grabbed the bar to keep his balance as his knees began to give way. His eyes began to move rapidly from side to side as if he was watching something quickly unfolding before him. He could see himself, but it wasn't him as he was now. He was dressed in a rough cotton shirt, leather jerkin and breeches. He was rushing through the litter strewn, dusty and dirty back streets of London towards the docks. He passed sick people whimpering and crying out for help.

Adam was physically sickened by the sight of a poor mother and her baby collapsed on the ground. Their faces and hands were covered in suppurating pustules. She raised her hand imploringly, weakly pleading for help. Adam turned away guiltily he could not stop to help anyone. He avoided all contact with the beggars who frantically searched for food in the rubbish heaps piled up at the corner of alleys.

A ship's foghorn hooted nearby. The air had become misty, almost foggy, and wreaked of urine, faeces, and human sweat. Adam gulped as the acrid smell hit his throat. Vanda watched him and asked him what was wrong, but he didn't hear her and couldn't answer he was so caught up in his plight.

Adam's breathing was laboured and his heart thumped as he approached the docks on the bank of the Thames. Mists from the water, rose up, writhed and coiled inland. The ship sounded its horn again. Adam looked wildly about him and dropped down behind some crates and watched a Dutch sailing vessel preparing to leave.

He jumped as a rat leapt down from the crate followed by a dozen others.

Their sharp quick claws scratched as they scurried by. Adam moved hurriedly out of the way with a wailing yelp, and he crumpled to the floor.

Vanda immediately was at his side helping him up and ushering him into a seat. Her face was full of concern. "What is it? What's happened?"

Adam groaned, "I don't know. It was like nothing I've ever experienced before… Oh, man!"

Vanda went back to the bar and ordered a brandy. She took it across to him. "Here, sip this. You've had a shock it will help. Perhaps you can tell me what just happened?"

"It was like no other vision I've ever had," and he started to relate what he had seen. He ended with, "I know it was me, but it didn't exactly look like me. I was dressed in old fashioned clothes from another era."

"If you were seeing sick people on the street, you could have been back in the middle ages in the fourteenth century when the Black Death was rife, or in the second wave that happened in the mid-1600s when London was again in the grip of the bubonic plague."

"I don't know what I was seeing. But it was most unpleasant. And the rats… I've always had a thing about rats. Can't bear the creatures. I have a real phobia."

"I never knew that," murmured Vanda. "I'm not so keen on them myself… Come on, drink up. I think you need an early night especially as we have a long journey back to Black Head Ridge, tomorrow."

Adam sighed. "Perhaps, you're right. I just wish I understood what I was seeing."

That night, Adam woke with a cry, rousing Vanda. He was covered in sweat. "Are you all right?" she asked sleepily.

"Just go back to sleep. I had a bit of a bad dream, that's all. I'll try and settle back down."

"Sure?" she murmured.

"Positive." Adam tried to clear his head and relax but couldn't get comfortable or chase away the remnants of the dream, which replicated his vision earlier. He pummelled his pillow, twisted and turned, and closed his eyes firmly, willing sleep to come. It wouldn't. And when Vanda made a complaining sound at his movements he made up his mind. He looked at the bedside clock's luminous dial, which read 3:15 a.m. Wearily, but quietly, he swung his legs out of bed and padded out of the bedroom in his boxer shorts. He closed the bedroom door quietly.

He stood and listened outside Janine and Marissa's room. He could hear Janine breathing deeply as he waited at their door, and he tiptoed towards the sitting room and kitchen silently. He gingerly shut the door and trying not to make any noise he filled the kettle and switched it on to boil and made himself a cup of tea. He took it into the sitting room and switched on the television keeping the volume low and watched the news channel. The reporter was highlighting global warming as the reason behind all the terrible disasters around the world. Volcanic ash was being expelled from volcanoes in Iceland, horrendous flooding in many other parts of the UK, and in India and Pakistan. Hurricanes and tropical storms in North America, wildfires in California, earthquakes in New Zealand, fiery volcanic lava flowing in Maui, toxic mud slides in Hungary, avalanches in the Himalayas. Newsreel footage of more catastrophes swam across the screen, oil seepage disasters in the Gulf, impending war in the Middle East, continued conflict in Eastern Europe... it went on and on. Finally, the latest tragedy in Death Valley where a meteorite had crashed beneath the mountains leaving an enormous crater.

The picture returned to the studio and a female presenter talked with a climate change expert and finally said, "Is this all down to global warming and climate change or is the acceleration of these deadly events somehow linked? Maybe, Nostradamus' prophesy of Armageddon really is at hand." Adam rolled his eyes and switched to another channel covering the meteorite crash. The journalist was in discussion with a scientist in the UK on Dartmoor, where a sinkhole had appeared unexpectedly. They talked about possible abandoned mineshafts as a cause, before moving on to a male reporter with a mic in hand who was interviewing a local resident farmer in Princetown.

"So, we can see first-hand that strange things are happening as far afield as Vegas and in many other countries. But here in the South West of England more bizarre tales are coming to light."

Adam switched off the television. He picked up Vanda's notebook and pen from the coffee table and made notes. These disasters were something he felt he seriously needed to consider, something that would have repercussions in his own life. But, first, there was the question of two spirits needing closure to move on. Somehow he knew Marissa would be able to help. But now, now he needed to sleep.

Adam crept back to bed where Vanda was sleeping and breathing easily. He slipped into bed beside her and placed his arm around her waist and she turned in her sleep towards him with a sigh of satisfaction.

The next day saw the sun rise in a brilliant blue sky without a cloud to be seen. The air smelt clean and fresh. It was the kind of day that it felt good to be alive. They checked out of Mackay's after breakfast and loaded up the hire car and headed for Inverness. Marissa was much calmer and seemed serene now she had revisited her old life. She turned to her mother and said, "I don't ever have to go back there again, and I won't mention it again either. I know it upsets you and Daddy."

"That's all right," said Janine with a smile, fondly stroking Marissa's blonde hair. "And when the time comes, and you get married yourself we will think about inviting them to your wedding."

Marissa snuggled in tighter to her mother and whispered, "Mummy, you're the best." With that she turned her face to the window to admire the spectacular scenery.

The journey home was uneventful, the plane was on time, and the roads from the airport were not overly busy. Even so, after leaving Marissa and Janine safely at their house, Adam was more than relieved to turn off the road towards Black Head Ridge. Vanda was keen to see her cat, Elsa, that Jake, the postman, had volunteered to feed and water in her absence.

"If you can drop me off at Cliff House I will call you later. I can't wait to see Elsa and I want a long soak in a luxurious warm bath to have time to think and sort out my thoughts."

"Fair enough," said Adam swinging the car around to follow the back road to Vanda's home. They both alighted and Adam took Vanda's cases in and gave her a swift kiss as Elsa came hurtling down the stairs and wrapped herself around Vanda's legs. Vanda scooped up the cat that nuzzled her neck and hair, purring contentedly.

Adam laughed. "I'll let you and Elsa get reacquainted. Speak later?"

"For sure," said Vanda with a grin.

Adam stroked Elsa's head and left. He was also anxious to get home.

~ 1 5 ~

As soon as Adam got out of the car, he heard the music filtering through the breeze that gently whispered across the cliff. He heard words murmured through the heathers and tinkling laughter that turned to the plaintive sound of children crying. They sounded miserable and alone, forgotten voices in despair. He strained to listen. "Ding dong bell…"

Adam was in no hurry to open his door. He took out his small travel bag and locked his car, not that he felt it needed locking all the way out here. But best to be sure with mischievous spirits about. He walked to the edge of the cliff and looked across at Cliff House that stood tall against a background of trees. He gazed out at sea, drinking in the salty air and stared down at the sand where the tide was lapping flirtatiously, running in and running back out in a teasing manner. There was no one around. He half expected footsteps in the sand that would vanish as they were made, as they had with Caroline Mitchell. Adam turned and faced the lighthouse standing tall, its beacon warning ships not to sail too close to the treacherous rocks below. He saw a battered Land Rover driving up, which parked at the base of the lighthouse. So, they had found someone to replace Ted Johnson, the serial killer that had preyed on women in the local area. Adam wondered who it was and watched curiously and was surprised to see a young woman alight and mount the ladder steps to the little door, which she unlocked and disappeared inside. He decided he would make her acquaintance at some point if she was to tend the equipment and keep everything working. Also, he was interested to know if Ted's stuffed creatures still decorated the inside of the structure. But now, now he needed to get inside and relax.

He strolled to his front door, words drifting in and out of his head. The piano music was still vividly clear but as soon as he put his key in the lock all sounds stopped. He opened his door and stepped into the hall. The piano near the staircase had its lid up, his grandfather's portrait was askew and the doors to all the rooms were wide open. He moved to close the lid, and a white feather floated down gently coming to rest on his hand. He placed it in his pocket and sighed wearily. He was tired but glad to be home even though he knew he had the strange company of lost souls wandering around his house and up to mischief.

As if his mind was being read, one of Caroline Mitchell's paintings crashed to the floor in the hall. It wasn't damaged, the glass was intact. Nor was the picture cord frayed or broken. Adam picked it up to rehang and a child laughed as another picture slipped from its hangings and slid down the wall. Adam looked about him. He saw the two young girls in their Gilbert Bray school uniform and addressed them, "Margaret, Lucy don't do this. You might destroy the artwork. Please."

Lucy stepped forward, she pointed at Adam and blood appeared to fall from her eyes rather than tears. He heard her voice clearly in his head although her mouth didn't appear to move. "Then help us. Find us."

"Tell me how," insisted Adam.

"Ding, dong, bell," murmured Margaret and repeated, "ding, dong, bell."

"Do you mean the nursery rhyme?"

Lucy spoke again. This time her voice could be heard. "Yes. But we can't say more. We will be cursed forever if we do. You have to work out where and only then can we find peace."

The children faded from view and footsteps were heard running up the stairs. More laughter followed. Adam shook his head as if to clear it. This was something new to him. Was it a riddle? How could he find the well? Had the children given him any clues? He didn't think so. He left his bags in the hall and went into the kitchen to make a hot drink. He sat down at the kitchen table and opened his laptop. He searched for locations of wells in the surrounding areas.

Time ticked on and the house was now quiet and still. Night was stretching its tendrils of darkness to weave into a heavy cloth that would envelop the house and cliff. He glanced at the clock. It was now nine thirty. The nearly full moon was up in the clear night sky revealing thousands of stars. Either the spirit entities had decided to rest or were elsewhere. He thought about what the girls had said. He felt strongly that Marissa would be able to help and telephoned Janine. "Janine? It's Adam."

"Hello?" her voice was measured.

"Can you bring Marissa across tomorrow?"

"So soon?"

"Please. I really feel she can help me. Tell me, how was she when she came home?"

"She was fine. It's almost as if she's put her other family out of her head. She told me I could tell James all about it and she could then let go and be our daughter solely. It was weird, like talking to someone else."

"That's good. I understood that's how it would work. If she had been older it may have been a different story. It was certainly a strange experience." He paused. "So, will you bring her across?"

Janine murmured reluctantly, "Yes, all right. Are you sure she'll be safe?"

"Positive."

"Then okay. Will eleven o'clock suit?"

"Perfect. We'll talk more then." Adam curtailed the call. He replaced the receiver thoughtfully. It was only then he realised that he hadn't spoken to Vanda. He stood up, left the kitchen and opened the front door. He looked out at the night and the myriad of stars that graced the heavens and across at Cliff House, which was shrouded in darkness. He thought she must be asleep, and he was not going to disturb her. He would call her in the morning and anyway, he needed to get to bed himself. It had been a long drive from Bristol, and he was whacked. He knew he needed to get up early and do some more research before Marissa was due to arrive. He yawned and closed the front door, picked up his bags and ascended the stairs. He could hardly wait to get into bed deciding he would shower in the morning. He fell asleep immediately, but his dreams were filled with alarming images. He found himself back on the docks hiding behind a crate watching a Dutch ship preparing to set sail with some people fleeing from the slums of the East End and trying to escape the pestilence that was sweeping through the city. A heavily pregnant woman was pleading with a Dutch sailor who shook his head sadly and turned her away. The woman collapsed on the ground and sobbed in despair. There was something familiar about her and he was about to come out of hiding when a rat disturbed by sailors made its escape and headed straight towards Adam who shuddered and leapt out of the way sending the crate tumbling.

Adam awoke with a start. He was covered in sweat and his heart was pounding. He was feeling quite breathless as his chest felt constricted. He pushed back the covers, climbed out of bed and moved to the window. He pulled back the drapes and stared out at the sea with the lighthouse standing tall on the cliff its bright warning beam shining out to sea. The now full moon reflected on the water creating a silver ribbon path across the salty brine. There was something magical about the velvet night and strains of haunting piano music filtered through the cool air and played in his head. He sighed, and a sob escaped his lips as he was filled with a rush of emotion, and he didn't know why.

He heard children's voices singing a nursery rhyme, "Ring a ring of roses, a pocket full of posies, a-tishoo, a-tishoo, we all fall down." Adam shivered. Somewhere in the back of his mind he remembered reading about the Great Plague of 1665 or the Black Death that ravished the country. The ring of roses was the first sign of the rosy rash that heralded the beginning of the infection. The posies were carried and used to try and mask the horrific stench that the Black Death produced. The sneezing being another symptom that resulted in death as they all fell down. Why were the children singing this? Could they read his dreams? Adam was confused. He tried to put those thoughts out of his head and go to sleep. But sleep was a long time coming. He tried to make sense of things and eventually drifted away back into another time where a woman struggled to give birth to a child. The midwife was encouraging her to push and as the woman strained and screamed she lifted her head, and her long sweat soaked hair fell back from her face, and he saw her face clearly. It was Vanda. He knew it was Vanda but then the picture dissolved. Adam woke again. This time there was no going back. Was he going mad? Had something finally tipped him over the edge? No. He wouldn't accept that thought.

Adam threw back the covers, rose and went into his shower. He felt as if he needed to scrub himself clean. Once the hot water coursed down his body he felt a cleansing as if the physical act of washing was somehow revitalising him and refreshing his mind. In the background of the sound of the water, nursery rhymes could still be heard. Children sang ring a ring of roses, which segued into ding dong bell. Adam knew it was the two missing children Margaret Lake and Lucy Ward. He turned off the shower and vigorously rubbed himself dry and dressed after which he felt somewhat better and less jumpy.

Adam returned to his bedroom and pulled open the drapes. He gazed out at the calm sea and the beach below. There on the sand where Caroline Mitchel had stood before were the two schoolgirls and three other children all holding hands and dancing in a circle. The children fell down at the end only to jump up and start again. Suddenly, they stopped and stood in a line and gazed up at his bedroom window. They seemed to look accusingly at him and chanted, "Ding dong bell."

Adam suppressed a cry. He dashed down the stairs and into the hall. His mother's voice filled his mind, "Adam, no! Don't go out. They will lead you into danger, please."

He stopped. "Why would they do that? They want me to help them."

"Yes, but there is more to this than you know or understand. Find them and find the well."

Adam hesitated but heeded his mother's advice and went into the kitchen. He needed a coffee, a strong one, something that would bolster him up. He set the kettle to boil and took out a cafetiere and selected a strong rich roast coffee that would suffice. Once it was made he took it to the countertop where his laptop waited. He opened it up and did a search for working and obsolete wells in the area. There were over two hundred. How was he expected to find the correct one?

His mother's voice filled his head again. "Use a pendulum, Adam." Adam didn't have a pendulum. His mother's voice came again. "In the study, in a drawer." Her last word stretched out into a breath and vanished in the air.

Adam left his laptop and marched to the study. He pulled out the drawers of the desk and once all of them were open, a hidden secret drawer popped out revealing itself that Adam didn't know existed. In that concealed drawer was a small brass pendulum shaped like a teardrop on a gilt chain. Adam picked it up curiously. He closed the other drawers and held the pendulum by the end of the chain. He felt a strange connection with the object and a weird feeling rippled up his arm. He had never used one before. He knew about them, but they had never entered his life. Somehow, he knew this was important and taking the object he returned to the kitchen.

Adam pulled up a map of the wells in Cornwall on his laptop, enlarged it and set it to print. Once that was done he stared at it. Cornwall was smothered in wells all over the county. How could the pendulum help him pinpoint the exact one? He did another search. This time on how to use it.

Adam studied everything he could find as he sipped his strong coffee. It was somewhat bitter. He grimaced but was determined to drink it down. He practised holding the chain, took a few deep breaths to ground himself and asked aloud for guidance and honest answers, practising first over his hand asking simple questions he knew the answers to in order to determine which way the pendulum swung for 'yes' and 'no'.

Once he felt confident, he walked to the map and held the pendulum a few inches over the map ensuring it was absolutely still. He asked the pendulum to indicate when he was close to the area where the well was situated. He reached the Hayle area on the north coast of Cornwall and it began twitching and jumping about as if it was alive. He stilled the pendulum and asked if the well was close to Hayle and the pendulum rotated in a clockwise direction. He looked at the names of the surrounding villages and asked, "Is it in Angarrick?" The pendulum reversed, circling in an anticlockwise direction categorically stating 'no'. "Is it in Phillack?" The pendulum went crazy, and settled into a circular clockwise motion... So, the well was in Phillack.

Adam thanked his pendulum and went back to his research. He knew nothing about Phillack and needed to know the exact location of Phillack Holy well. He scribbled down the coordinates, SW 5650 3838, which would show him how to travel there. It was also known as St. Piala's Well. History revealed that the church was dedicated to St. Piala and St. Felicitas. The Irish princess, Princess Piala, was martyred in the church in the 6th century. The story of her life and the life of her brother Prince Fingar (called Gwinear after his conversion) was apparently available in the church.

However, the site of the church was Christian for more than a century before the arrival of the Irish saints. Above the porch door was a chiro stone lozenge found on site in the 1860s which dated from 350 – 400 AD. The Christian faith had been there for more than 1600 years! There were also two gravestones dating from the 5th and 6th century plus a wonderful 10th century stone cross portraying the crucified Christ.

From the description there were bits of the Norman build incorporated into the present church which was reconstructed in the 15th century and again in the 1860s. Adam let out a huge intake of breath. It was just the sort of site that Shaitan and his followers would love. There were a number of religious houses in line with this one, which would be a magnet for heightened spirit activity that could be abused for Shaitan's evil designs. Or it could even be another portal. That thought alone filled Adam with dread.

Adam knew that once he had met with Marissa and sought her help he would fix a date to drive to Phillack and see for himself. He returned to the reading of the history surrounding this ancient well. Apparently the well was restored in 1993 long before he had been born. According to the Historic Environmental Records the original Phillack Holy well was situated a few yards away from an extant pump and had a flight of steps leading down to it. It was covered over when the well water was diverted to the pump. A story was told that a Sheriff of Cornwall washed his mangy dog in the well and as a result suffered great misfortune and eventually death. 'This,' thought Adam ' is entirely in keeping with what I have already learned about these mystical happenings. So, there is the current well, which can be visited but the original one, which I think is the right one, will have been covered over and more than probably, nature will have taken control.'

He needed to find that well and hoped that Marissa would be able to help. Adam changed his search and hunted for directions to Phillack, which he found and printed off. Adam glanced at the clock and couldn't believe it was now approaching nine thirty. Time had marched on. The spirit girls in the house had behaved and been quiet for a few hours now. Maybe they were pleased that he was finally getting close. He heard the front door open and the sound of Vanda's footsteps approaching the kitchen. He looked at his clothes - he was still in his bath robe. She breezed in. "Have you only just got up?"

"No. Actually I've been up for hours. I had trouble sleeping," he said sheepishly. "I better get dressed."

"Mmm, need any help?" she said cheekily.

"Another time, yes but Marissa and Janine are coming so I better get ready now."

"Spoilsport!" said Vanda with a laugh.

"Don't worry, I will take up your offer another time soon." Vanda giggled and Adam kissed her. He jerked his head towards the toaster. "You can put some toast on, if you like, I haven't had breakfast yet and I am feeling ravenous."

Vanda nodded and said, "Good idea. I could do with a slice or two."

"Help yourself. I won't be long." Adam dashed from the kitchen and started up the stairs. Halfway up he swayed as voices filled his mind. None that made any sense and he struggled to rid himself of the sounds. It was as if he had been caught in a tide of thick swirling mud, and everything seemed to slow down. Again, he was transported back to the 1600s and the time of the Great Plague. He was there; he could smell the stench of death in the creeping rising fog at the docks. He shuddered as a rat jumped past and stopped, its whiskers twitching. The rat proceeded to wash its face and oily coat before scurrying away at the sounds of heavy footsteps approaching.

Adam struggled to steady himself. He knew he wasn't asleep and dreaming. He was awake and yet these visions were incredibly vivid and real. He could no longer doubt. He had been there at that time but why... why was he remembering that now?

Adam appeared to wake from his stupor and slowly continued up the stairs. He needed time to recover his thoughts, which were running away with him. He could feel a knotting twisting in his stomach akin to fear. His mother's voice came into his mind, calming and soothing him and a warmth of love and peace washed over him. But there was a word of warning, "Take care, my son. Make sure you protect yourself."

Adam showered and dressed hurriedly putting a question in the air. "What do I need protecting from?"

The temperature dropped dramatically. Adam felt his spine tingle. "Soon you will know." His mother's voice faded, and the girlish laughter of Lucy Ward and Margaret Lake became more prominent as the girls sang, "Ring a ring of roses..." Adam shivered and hurried back downstairs where the aroma of toast greeted him.

Marissa and her mother arrived at Black Head Ridge House as expected, at eleven o'clock. Marissa gazed at the view and then the outside of the house before Adam opened up to let them in. Marissa gazed about her in wonder at the house. She was drawn to the artwork of Caroline Mitchell and announced, "That was done by Vanda's sister, wasn't it? She was the first one you helped move on." Adam just nodded. "And out there, the lighthouse. The bad man lived there, didn't he?" Adam nodded again before ushering them into the sitting room where Marissa bounced onto the settee.

As they gathered there, Janine looked around uncomfortably as strains of Beethoven's Moonlight Sonata could be heard playing. Marissa ran into the hall and watched the piano keys going up and down. She spoke, "Hello. I'm Marissa. Who are you?"

She appeared to listen and said, "Thank you," before running back into the sitting room. A glissando was played on the piano as small hands ran their fingers down all the notes. She scrambled onto Adam's lap. "What do you want me to do?"

"Have you seen the girls, Marissa?"

"You mean Lucy and Margaret?"

"Yes," said Adam surprised at how much Marissa already knew.

There was a crash outside in the hall as the piano lid was slammed shut, lifted and slammed again. Marissa climbed off Adam's lap and went out to see followed by Adam.

The children laughed in glee and ran up the stairs to the first landing. Margaret pushed over a large ornamental Chinese looking vase, which stood on a plinth and went tumbling down the stairs. Adam just managed to catch it as it rolled, and he placed it safely behind the piano.

Marissa reprimanded them, "If you want Adam to help you, you must stop doing this." The children responded with a number of rude noises followed by giggling. Marissa continued, "Adam is a good man he helped me, and he will help you."

There was silence and then Lucy spoke. "He needs to find us to release us but in discovering us there is grave danger. We are cursed and forbidden to say why. We can only try and help with clues. I can't say anymore." The two girls vanished but their footsteps could still be heard running around upstairs where they played on the ship's wheel that drew and closed the drapes in Adam's room. Laughter followed. The curtains billowed slightly as the top of the window appeared to slide open a little.

Marissa and Adam returned to the sitting room. Janine and Vanda looked up expectantly. Adam shrugged. "I don't know what to say. The girls want to be found but they can't explain why there would be danger."

Marissa spoke. "Can I go upstairs and play with them?"

Janine looked horrified and was about to say, 'no' when Vanda intervened. "She won't be in any danger, and she may learn more without any of us present."

"Well, I don't like it," said Janine.

"And I don't want Marissa to be used by these two," said Adam.

Marissa pleaded again, "Please, Mummy, Adam. Vanda's right they won't hurt me, but they might just tell me more."

"Well, I think I should take you home, now."

Janine rose but Marissa stamped her foot. "No. I know I can help. Please, Mummy." With that she ran from the room and bounded up the stairs. Janine made a move to go after her.

"Please, Janine. Let her go, just for a short while. I promise you that if we hear anything untoward I will go and fetch her myself. Please," said Vanda.

Adam was silent.

Janine reluctantly sat down. "Very well. But I am not bringing her again. No matter what you say."

"Janine, Marissa is a very special little girl," said Adam.

"So you say."

"She has amazing gifts and insight."

"But that's not how it should be," said Janine her eyes filling with tears. "I am afraid for her and what if this man, this Shaitan comes back to find her?"

For that Adam had no answer.

MARISSA HAD FOUND ADAM'S BEDROOM and watched the children playing on the ship's wheel and she, too, giggled. She watched as the salt by the window blew off the sill and scattered on the floor. "Can I have a go?" she asked.

Margaret stopped and looked at her. "Who are you? Why can you see us?"

"I'm Marissa. I don't know how I can see you, but I can." Margaret stepped back allowing Marissa to take the ship's wheel. She squealed in delight as she spun the wheel and the curtains flew open. She spun it the other way and they closed. She beamed happily and smiled. "So, you're Lucy and you're Margaret. What happened to you?"

The two girls looked at each other. Lucy answered, "We were part of a very secret club."

Margaret piped up, "It was fun until other things started happening and we decided to tell."

"What sort of things?"

"You wouldn't understand," said Lucy. "But it wasn't nice."

"And before we could say anything or get away we were taken to another place, a hidden place," said Margaret.

"And we can't say anymore," insisted Lucy. "If we do our families will be cursed like us."

"What's a curse?" asked Marissa.

Lucy spoke solemnly, "It's like a very serious prayer type plea that instructs and calls on a supernatural power to inflict harm and punishment on someone.

That's what's been done to us. If we say anymore the same will happen to our families. We can't tell you."

"And we won't," added Margaret. "But..."

"But...?" questioned Marissa.

"Let's play," said Lucy. The two girls held hands and Marissa joined them. They danced in a circle singing, "Ring a ring of roses..."

"Why do you keep saying this nursery rhyme?"

"That's for you to find out and Adam to remember. That's enough for now. Adam needs to protect himself."

The girls dissolved and vanished from sight leaving the words of the nursery rhyme lingering in the air. Marissa stared about the room. She spun the wheel once more and the drapes pulled open again. Marissa walked to the window and looked out. There on the beach were the two girls playing in the sand and sea. They looked up at the window and waved at Marissa before vanishing once more.

Marissa left the room and ran back down the stairs to the sitting room where the others waited. She told them what had transpired and added, "They wouldn't tell me anymore. They are afraid to because of a curse. It has something to do with the Ring a Ring of Roses... I should go home now."

Marissa ran to the front door followed by Janine who turned to Adam. "I thank you for all you have done but I hope that this is the end of it now, and you won't call Marissa anymore."

Adam nodded. "I hope it is the end of it. But I am sure that if Marissa needs to see me again that you will let her?"

Janine shrugged. "I don't know... All this is very alien to me. I just want her to have a normal life and be happy. Goodbye, Adam, Vanda." She nodded curtly and opened the front door.

Marissa turned and hugged Adam. "Don't worry, Adam. You will work it out. I think you already have," and she sang, "ring a ring of roses a pocket full of posies..." and continued singing until she reached the car and turned and waved. Vanda and Adam watched the car drive away with Marissa's face staring at them from the back window.

Vanda shivered. "Let's get back inside. I suddenly feel cold." Adam closed the door, and they went into the kitchen, where Vanda put the kettle on to boil. "What do you think it all means?"

"I'm not sure," replied Adam, "but I am sure it has something to do with these dreams and visions I have been having."

"To do with the plague?"

"Yes. It all ties in with the nursery rhyme, somehow and we have to work out exactly what it is."

Back at the police station, Vance was interviewing Betty Buswell under caution, for assault, abduction, and attempted murder. She denied all charges pleading that she didn't remember, anything. She had been there for over two hours. Vance pressed her, "What about Shaitan?"

Betty looked harassed as she tried to remember. "The chemistry teacher?"

"The same."

"He was a very charismatic man… handsome." Her brow furrowed. "He had an after school club. I used to help with it… with Mr Draper."

"We'll come on to Mr Draper later. Why did you take that little girl, Sophie Sinclair?"

"I don't know." She was now close to tears.

Vance was uncertain whether she was telling the truth or not. "There are plenty of eyewitnesses who saw what you did and of course we have the statement of the woman that you attacked."

Betty nodded and dropped her head. "I don't know. I have been struggling to remember but I can't believe I would hurt a child. I have grandchildren, I couldn't bear anything happening to them." She flushed guiltily, which did not go unnoticed by Vance who stopped the interview.

"Interview terminated at 12:10." He switched off the machine and turned to Detective Holman. "Please take Miss Buswell back to the cells. We will resume interviewing at two."

The young detective led Betty from the room. Vance sat back and sighed. This whole affair was getting to him. It was all way outside his experience.

Draper was having a tough time of it. He had been interviewed lengthily by the police at the station but because of his help and prior warning, he had been released without charge. Back at the school Draper was being bombarded with questions from the girls about Leonard Shaitan. Their memories had been manipulated, and none could remember why the club had been founded. It was all just a bit of fun. Draper prayed that no lasting damage had been done. To this end, the headmaster had returned early from his holiday to try and get some order into the school and minimise the bad publicity that he felt was sure to follow. So far, the children didn't appear to be harmed physically or emotionally. They just didn't remember. All they knew was that a fire in Moss Woods had spooked them all and that their chemistry teacher had fled.

Draper was in regular touch with Melvyn Thomas, as he tried to bring his life back to God and he was calmer. He had scheduled a meeting for the vicar to come to the school and speak to the girls in order to fully assess the situation. Russell Draper was forming a student Christian Union that he hoped the girls would join. But the biggest problem was the sixth form student Michelle AKA Sabrina.

Michelle had become completely introverted. She wouldn't speak or come out of her room. She was in serious need of psychiatric help. Draper didn't know what to do or how to help. He was hoping Melvyn Thomas would have some ideas.

Adam sat up in bed. He had awoken early again. Vanda stirred beside him. He could hear children's voices singing and laughing. He crept out from under the covers and opened the drapes just a little. It was still dark. He looked out of the window and saw Margaret and Lucy holding hands and dancing around in a circle. They were singing the same nursery rhyme. Adam screwed his face up as he thought, what did it mean? He was sure there was something he should do, and it was all linked to the nursery rhyme and the well. But what?

The sun had begun to rise chasing away the remnants of the shadows of the night in a blaze of fiery glory. The sky was breathtakingly beautiful, and Adam sighed. He was so lucky to live here, thanks to his grandfather. He whispered his thanks to him in his head. A breeze sprang up and ruffled his hair. He felt his mother's hand stroking his cheek. He caught his breath at her delicate butterfly touch. Her voice whispered in his mind, "Revelations 15. Look." Her voice disappeared into the air.

Adam pulled on his jeans, grabbed his robe and quietly left the bedroom. He went downstairs to the study and scoured the bookshelves searching for a copy of the Bible or New Testament. He found one and flipped through the pages to the Book of Revelation of St. John the Divine. He found chapter 15 and began reading and one thing kept being repeated, 'plague'. Adam opened his laptop and started a search for plagues through the years. He shivered as he read of the bubonic plague or Black Death as it was known. Spread by the bite of an infected flea that lived on rodents, exposure to infected tissue or fluid, or inhaling respiratory droplets and even through contact with infected material through a break in the skin. That was why clothes of plague victims, and the dead were burnt. He was horrified to read that although rare, cases of plague still existed today and was a persistent cause of illness in rural areas in the Western United States and certain regions of Africa and Asia. He learned that it could develop into pneumonic plague, which was caused by inhaling droplets from this virus and would develop into a serious lung condition. Adam rubbed his chin and continued searching. He was stunned to discover that there were no vaccines against this pestilence and research into developing one had been discontinued. However, the military in the USA had been vaccinated during the Vietnam war so something must have been available then. He didn't believe the medieval 'cure' of using nutmeg would work.

There were pages of studies on experimental vaccines, and it alarmed him to hear of the plague's use in biological warfare and the fact that a particularly virulent strain had no cure. Most could be treated with antibiotics like streptomycin, gentamycin and fluoroquinolones. If Adam's suspicions were right, how could he get hold of any of these? It looked impossible, but at least if illness struck he could try and get antibiotics from the hospital or his doctor, but it wasn't guaranteed.

Vanda stirred in her dreams as the temperature in the room dropped. She sleepily patted the bed next to her. It was cold but then she felt someone slip in beside her. An arm slid around her waist, and she snuggled into him and murmured, "Mmm, this is nice." He said nothing as he began to caress her and stroke her back. Vanda made little sounds of contentment as she relaxed further and allowed him to massage her back making her groan in pleasure.

Downstairs, Adam continued reading the book of Revelation when his mother's voice broke into his thoughts and spoke with urgency, "Vanda is in danger. Quickly now, hurry." He stopped and raced up the stairs still clutching the Bible. He reached the bedroom and flung open the door. He could see the shape of a man in the bed next to her and shouted to Vanda, "Vanda wake up, NOW!" Hearing Adam's voice Vanda turned sleepily and faced the entity in the bed with her and screamed. Adam rushed across and paraded the Bible in front of him and the entity hissed in anger and dissolved before their eyes. Adam cradled Vanda in his arms. "My god, did you see who that was?"

She nodded, tears blinding her eyes. "It was Shaitan, I'm sure of it." Adam hugged her to him. If the beast had found her they needed to be extremely careful.

"Did you… do… anything?" asked Adam tentatively uncertain how to phrase it.

She shook her head. "No. I thought it was you. He just touched my back, but if you hadn't come in…" she trailed off.

"We are going to have to be doubly careful and set up more protection in the house. I'll speak to Melvyn."

Vanda shivered. "Why didn't the salt stop him?"

Adam crossed to the window and saw that the salt had just scattered. There was nothing on the sill. "The girls. They were playing up here and the window is open." He closed the window firmly and secured the lock. "It won't happen again. I can promise you that."

Vanda rose. "I feel dirty, unclean. I need to scrub myself."

She went into the ensuite and Adam assured her, "I will make sure you are safe." He pulled out the bathroom chair and sat astride it as Vanda turned on the shower. She went inside as Adam kept watch. His nerves were in shreds, knowing what had nearly happened. First thing he would do when Vanda was out and dressed would be to phone Melvyn and then he knew. He had to get to Phillack.

Melvyn arrived at Black Head Ridge House. He had dropped everything instantly and rushed there after Adam's call. Vanda and Adam were waiting anxiously. Adam hadn't left Vanda's side. They had replaced the salt from the blessed salt they had left but Melvyn went around the whole house checking and placing holy items in plain view at all points of entry. Once satisfied he had done as much as was possible, he sat down with them.

"Shaitan will try and come back, but I am positive that with the steps I have taken that he won't be able to get in. However, you will have to be on your guard. Stay together, get up together and go to bed together."

"What about when we are asleep?" asked Vanda.

"Wear your crosses and rosaries and let them be visible. You should be safe."

"Should be?" queried Vanda. "I don't like the sound of that."

"No. But, I feel, somehow, that you are protected. There are elements in this house that are working for you and will warn you."

Adam nodded. "My mother told me."

"And if she hadn't, who knows what would have happened? She will always be looking out for you as your guardian angel. Now tell me about Phillack and the well."

Adam explained what he'd learned and what he'd feared. Melvyn listened carefully.

"It seems that in order to free the children's spirits you will be putting yourselves in danger, so here's what I suggest."

The day seemed drab and heavy with leaden clouds threatening rain. The weather seemed to match their mood, and they were all feeling very subdued as they left Brinkworth. The trio had finally gathered everything they needed for the trip. Adam had advised Vance of where they were headed and was under instructions to let him know when they had discovered its position. He would get there under his own steam with Jacobs as soon as they knew.

They had purchased biohazard suits and masks. The threesome had various other holy items and accoutrements and were now on their way to Phillack. They just had to find the stone well that had been used. It wasn't going to be easy. They needed to do it before the light faded.

The journey to Hayle wasn't too bad at least the roads weren't stogged with holiday traffic. They saw the sign to Phillack and turned off, passing the many caravan sites and seasonal businesses. Melvyn drove while Adam studied the ordinance survey map as the Sat Nav wouldn't be able to pinpoint the hidden location. He had his pendulum in his pocket ready to use once they were in the general area. They arrived at the church of St. Felicitas and Piala and parked.

"From here we travel on foot," said Adam. "We will pass the Phillack well, which was rediscovered in 1993 and renovated. It already has vegetation growing over it. Look out for a granite stone archway with steps. It will be difficult to see. It has been forgotten for so many years. Keep your eyes peeled."

Melvyn and Vanda trod carefully and slowly, looking for any visible signs of ancient stonework. They approached a small copse and as they did so, girlish laughter could be heard. Here the terrain was quite wild and overgrown. It didn't look as if anyone had been here in a long while. They carefully stepped through brambles, nettles and thistles. Vanda swore as she stepped on a large stone covered in a creeper. Adam removed his pendulum, which began dancing around in his hand, and the temperature began to drop. Adam raised his hand to stop them. "It's definitely around here somewhere. Time to get ready."

The threatening rain clouds appeared to dissipate leaving a hole in the clouds where the sun could shine through, but it had no warmth. Although it dappled the ground with golden nuggets of light, it somehow felt tinged with menace.

Melvyn and Adam set down the bags they were carrying and all three donned the biohazard suits that would protect them from any pathogens that might be unearthed. Vanda asked, "What do we say if we meet anyone?"

"We just say we are testing the ground for the source of a pollutant and people should stay away until we know it's safe," replied Adam.

"I hardly think we'll see anyone here," added Melvyn. "It's a bit out of the way and it looks like the ground has not been disturbed in a long while. We should be okay."

They covered their hands with surgical gloves and their feet with protective covers and finally put on the face masks that would filter impurities and infectious agents from the air.

Adam asked the pendulum which way to go, and Melvyn said a prayer for guidance. The pendulum began to swing rhythmically. Adam asked more questions and followed the path directed by the swinging pendulum. They encountered several granite stones that seemed to have fallen from some structure and the pendulum appeared to become excited with dancing energy. Melvyn stepped forward and using a small cleaver-type machete hacked at the undergrowth. He uncovered part of a small stone arch.

Adam nodded and the three tried to clear as much of the vegetation away as possible to reveal the archway. There they found the steps leading down. Vanda took out a torch as they began to descend the stone steps. There was a distinct chill in the air and the air grew musty. Water dripped down the stones covered in moss and algae. At the bottom was a pit with an iron grille, which Adam began to prise up.

Rusty flakes crumbled off the cover and the sound of metal grinding on metal sounded peculiar in the now half-light that pervaded the gloom. "Now what?" asked Melvyn.

"Phone Vance, tell him where we are," ordered Adam. "Use what three words, it's more accurate than anything else. You've got the app."

Vanda nodded. "What are you going to do?"

Adam asserted, "I'm going to lift this thing and send down a rope and bucket. If nothing comes up then I'll go into the well myself."

"I don't like the sound of that."

"Neither do I," said Melvyn. "Phone Vance and wait."

But Adam shook his head. "No. I'll go now. If anyone can end these girls' misery it's me. Vance won't get here in time and the light is beginning to fade. It must be done now."

"You are so damned stubborn, Adam Barrie and impulsive. Remember the trouble that has caused you before?"

But it was as if Adam was blind, deaf and dumb to all of Vanda's pleas. She hurriedly opened the app and got the three words and rang Vance, finishing with, "Please hurry. Adam is going to go in alone."

"You have to stop him," yelled Vance. "I'm on my way."

"He won't listen to me, you know what he's like," said Vanda in despair.

"Keep the line open and tell me what's happening."

Adam attached a stout rope to the bucket tied on his rucksack. He dropped it into the swirling inky blackness of the well and slowly played out the rope until it hit something. He continued to let the rope descend and it appeared to fill and become heavier with some type of substance, and he began to haul it up.

It was as if the bucket didn't want to rise and had snagged on something. Melvyn came to help and the two began to raise the bucket together. As it did so, a weird moaning could be heard, and a wind sprang up from nowhere and rushed around the trio. The words of the nursery rhyme echoed around the well walls. Adam knew whatever was in the bucket would be more than shocking. He steeled himself and instructed Melvyn, "One last big heave-ho. Come on…" They both grunted with exertion and the bucket wobbled to the lip of the well. The rope was now slimy with what seemed like mucus and other matter. Adam yelled, "Watch out, here it comes!"

The bucket crashed against the side of the well but finally emerged. It was full and dripping with blood. Floating amongst the blood and tissue were digits partially severed from a small hand. Vanda turned away and gagged at the sight. Adam yelled, "Don't remove your mask. You must keep it and the protective clothing on."

Melvyn added, "Do as he says. Look at the fingers."

The fingers and hand were covered in suppurating pustules, enflamed and oozing with pus. It was almost as if they were alive. "What do we do with this?" asked Adam. "And how do we recover the bodies?"

"I believe we will have to leave that to the police and medical team. You've done your bit. This is obviously where the girls' bodies were hidden," said Melvyn.

"I am going to have to be certain that the bodies are down there. Then the police can do their work. I'm going down."

"NO! We need to discover why they are plague ridden," said Melvyn.

Adam looked wildly about him. "We need to be scrubbed of any pathogens. These suits will have to be burned. Is Vance on his way?"

Vanda nodded. "I'll check on his progress. Adam, please don't go down there."

"But, I have to see. I need to know."

"But at what expense? Please, Adam. Think," urged Vanda as the open call disconnected and she dialled Vance's number again.

Adam busied himself with securing the rope around him and attaching the other end to a strong oak, one of many trees close to the well. Vanda waited anxiously for Vance to respond, and when he finally did, she said, "I can't stop him. He's going down."

CLUTCHING A TORCH, ADAM GINGERLY climbed over the side of the well. He let out the rope bit by bit and walked down the side, covered in moss and vegetation dripping with water. He paused as Melvyn adjusted the rope outside and helped Adam ease down the slippery sides. Adam's heart was pounding. His foot slipped more than once, and he was relieved that Melvyn was now feeding the rope to him as it jerked tightly preventing him from dropping like a stone into the murk below. He shoved the torch into his pocket.

The descent was agonising, painfully slow and the putrid smell of rancid rotting flesh infiltrating his mask was hard to bear but Adam was determined to see what remains were left even though he believed he would suffer nightmares as a result. A whirling, whirring sound of a devilish wind appeared from nowhere and blew around him as he descended further into the increasing oily blackness. Words from nursery rhymes tumbled around his head together with eerie whispered murmurings. He fumbled for his torch and switched it on. The light played on what seemed to be the floor of the well, which revealed thick red sludge, which Adam assumed to be a mixture of blood and tissue. Sightless eyes in the head of one dead child bobbed up making him shiver and he jumped in fright as a huge black rat that had been feasting on flesh dived off the body and must have swum down to the channel where the water ran. As far as Adam could see there were the remains of two small bodies. He replaced the torch in his pocket and removed his phone. He needed to capture the images of what he could see. He struggled to focus and took several random shots before replacing his phone in his other pocket and grabbing his torch again. He swept the beam around this hideous graveyard of death. The rat returned and began gnawing on the face of one victim. Adam felt his stomach lurch and knew he needed to vomit. He yanked hard on the rope, the signal for him to be hauled back to safety. He replaced the torch and hung on tightly as he made his way back up the slimy walls and reached the lip at the top. As he clambered out he ordered Vanda not to come near him or Melvyn. He shouted for evidence bags and sanitiser, which he knew Vanda had packed. He wiped the torch and his phone and placed them both in a sterile bag before he went to remove his mask.

Melvyn yelled, "No. You are covered in contagion. You need washing down, the suit should be stripped off, bagged and burnt. Vance should be here soon, he's ordered a team to come and deal with what you've found. This site and all its gory secrets must be contained."

"But I need to be sick."

"No. Unless you want to infect all of us."

Melvyn's words appeared to strike home, and Adam whose face was now a greenish white just nodded. He slumped down on the ground against the well wall. He was breathing heavily behind his mask trying to suppress the need to retch.

A white feather fluttered down and landed next to Adam, who knew his mother was around and instantly he began to calm. There was a crashing through the undergrowth and the sound of voices approaching. Vance dressed in a biohazard suit emerged from the copse followed by a team of SOCOs. There was also a man with a backpack containing a sanitising agent attached to a hose.

Vance gestured to the officer and indicated Adam whose suit and his whole figure was blasted with the bacteria killing mixture. The ground where the slough of tissue had run was also blasted. Scene of crime tape was set up and warning signs erected. Adam stood up and crossed to Vance after he'd been thoroughly cleaned. He removed the suit and put it in a sealed hazmat bag ready for incineration. He passed him the evidence bag containing his phone and explained. "I filmed what was in the well, so you will know what you are dealing with."

"That's all very well, but it was a dangerous and stupid thing to do. What if you had torn your suit on the way down or up. The bacteria would be on you, your clothes. It could have got onto your skin underneath your clothes and PPE. This is a serious issue, Adam." Vance didn't mince his words, and Adam had the good grace to look sheepish. "Do you have a change of clothes?" Adam shook his head. "Then, you'd best ask Vanda to go and get some. It may be overkill but better to be safe than sorry." He jerked his head and walked across to her and explained what he needed her to do.

As a special safety measure, both Melvyn and Vanda were blasted with sanitiser and Adam and Melvyn were segregated from the team, while Vanda ripped off her protective clothing and left it with Jacobs in a sealed hazmat bag ready for disposal. She steeled herself and began the journey back to Black Head Ridge. She couldn't explain it, but she felt the situation was filled with urgency and started to drive wildly but she didn't see the black crow with the white tipped tail feather fly out from a tree in the copse.

Cawdor was following her.

Vanda dashed into Adam's house leaving the car running and the door open. She grabbed a bag and selected fresh underwear, a pair of jeans, and sweatshirt, and stuffed them inside. Outside the house, a figure appeared, reached inside the car, switched off the engine, and stepped towards the open door, and recoiled at the salt at the entrance so retreated back towards the shrubbery. Cawdor landed beside him and watched. The atmosphere was thick and heavy. A mist had developed, which slithered in from the sea, sliding on its belly onto the land. It wasn't natural.

Vanda appeared at the door and pulled it to, so it locked. She ran to the car and looked about her nervously. Why had the car engine stopped? The house door clicked open, and Vanda stared in amazement. The serpentine mist began coiling around her ankles and started to rise. Suddenly, Vanda was filled with foreboding and dread. It was then she saw Cawdor hopping towards her, his head on one side. Its beady eyes fixed on her and from the shrubbery stepped Leonard Shaitan. She froze.

"Hello, Vanda. I've been waiting for you."

Vanda was transfixed. It was as if her feet were glued to the floor, and she could not draw her eyes away from his apparently handsome face, but her heart was thumping erratically.

"Shall we go inside? But first... get a brush and sweep away that mess of salt. So untidy and unnecessary, don't you think?" And he smiled revealing his sharply pointed vampiric teeth.

Vanda was unable to move. She struggled internally with her need to escape, and the compulsion being enforced on her to comply. She tried to scream but no sound came out just as Jake, the postman, on his late afternoon delivery round, had reached the path and rounded the corner of the house. He arrived on the scene breaking the spell. Cawdor flew off onto the roof and watched as Shaitan dissolved before her eyes into the encircling mist, which began to retreat back towards the cliff and the sea.

"Hey, Vanda! You're back," he said cheerily and then noticed her face was a ghostly white. "Are you okay? You don't look so good." Vanda swayed and Jake rushed forward to help her and caught her before she fell. He lifted her up onto her feet and stared about him. "What is it? What's wrong?"

Vanda's eyelids fluttered and she whispered, "Did you see him?"

"See who? ... What?" asked Jake looking confused. "There's no one here but us."

"He was just here... And that crow..."

Jake scoured the cliff top for the sign of another person but saw no one. "Let's get you back inside." He looked up as Cawdor flew down and landed on the car. It cawed raucously and began flapping its wings, taking off and flying around Jake's head, which seemed to spur Vanda into action.

"Quickly, shield your face. Come inside." Cawdor attempted to land on Jake who ran with Vanda to the house. They stepped inside and she slammed the door shut, bolted it and leaned against it.

"What's going on? What's happening?" asked a confused Jake.

Vanda murmured, "You wouldn't believe me if I told you."

Jake gazed about him. "What's all this salt on the floor? Shall I clean it up?"

"No!" Her words rang out loud and clear. "Don't touch it."

Jake heard the panic in her voice. "I think you had better tell me what this is all about."

Adam sat in the copse his back against a tree. He was feeling a little calmer but then his breathing became a breathless judder and his heart began to race. His head swam and he felt woozy, and he knew it was some kind of premonition. Immediately, he recognised the feeling, and images of Vanda filled his mind. She was inside his house leaning against his front door. Someone was with her, but he couldn't quite see the person but what he could hear was a crow cawing repeatedly and he shivered.

Adam struggled to his feet, and turned to Melvyn and Vance. "I have to go. Vanda is in trouble."

"What?" exclaimed Vance. "You can't leave, Vanda is getting you fresh clothes."

"You haven't heard me. She's in trouble."

Melvyn responded, "I'll go. Where is she?"

"In my house but there's a crow outside."

"A crow?" questioned Vance. "Like we experienced?"

"The same," said Adam with a nod.

Vance acknowledged Melvyn. "All right. You go but I insist Adam stays here." Adam snorted in frustration. Vance turned to him, "You brought this on yourself. You're just too bloody impulsive and stubborn."

Adam knew Vance was right and hung his head in shame. He went to protest but Melvyn stopped him. "It's best if I go. I'll know what to do."

Reluctantly, Adam agreed. "Okay, but I want it noted that I don't like it."

"Done," said Melvyn.

"And keep me posted," ordered Adam.

"Take my car," said Vance tossing Melvyn the keys. "We can return with the SOCOs."

Melvyn nodded and began to walk back to the place where everyone had parked. His stomach was churning. He had heard about the attack of the crows and witnessed their tenacity in pursuing Adam. He had seen what Shaitan had done with other animals and creatures in the past.

Vanda and Jake had retreated to the sitting room. She had tried to explain things to Jake without telling him everything. She had skirted around the full truth and only talked about the aberrant behaviour of the crows that had attacked Adam and the police. Cawdor was now pecking away at the glass of one of the windows.

"Why haven't they sent out a police marksman to destroy those birds?" Vanda was stumped as to what to say. "You're not telling me everything, are you?"

Vanda shook her head. "I can't. I'm sorry, Jake."

"Can't or won't?" pressed Jake. Vanda didn't answer. "Okay… then what's with the salt? I can see it's by the front door and over there by the fireplace and on the sills of the windows. Why?"

Vanda bit her lip and then blurted out, "Even if I told you, you wouldn't believe me."

"Try me."

"Jake, please understand I really can't tell you. And anyway, it's not something you want to be dragged into. It's too dangerous."

"But I'm already involved."

Vanda sighed. "If you ever breathed a word of it, people would think we are all mad. The police, too. You would think I was mad."

"Look, I don't care. Something is going on and it's now affecting me. If I'm in danger I have a right to know."

Vanda had no more arguments and when Cawdor tapped harder on the glass and was joined by four other crows, she tried to stifle a scream. "All right, all right. I'll try to explain."

Melvyn had driven like the wind and had managed to avoid snarl ups on the roads. He sighed with relief when he saw the sign to Brinkworth. He turned off the main road and followed the sign to Black Head Ridge. As he turned the corner towards the house, he passed the postman's van. It was then that he saw them; a murder of nine crows standing on the grass by the shrubbery in front of the house. They stood like sentinels waiting for something. Melvyn caught his breath. He recognised Adam's car and wondered what to do. He took out his mobile phone and rang the house.

"Vanda? Are you all right?"

"Melvyn! We are for the moment. There are four crows on the windowsill on the side window."

"That makes thirteen."

"What?"

"On the grass outside there are nine others just standing and waiting."

"What does it mean?"

"It means many things but in the Bible at the last supper Judas was the thirteenth guest. That's why it has been considered unlucky."

"What now?"

"Somehow I have to get in to you without being set upon."

"There's something else you should know…"

"What?"

"Shaitan was with them."

Melvyn fell silent. He stared about him. "He doesn't seem to be here now. At least, I can't see him."

"That doesn't mean he's not there."

"No, I know. Now, how do I get in?"

Vance paced in the clearing. He turned to Adam, "So this is all Shaitan's doing?" Adam nodded. "Do you think he'll pop up again down here?"

"I believe so. The South West is littered with wells, holy places, and sites of historical interest that run on ley lines through Cornwall, Devon and up through Somerset and beyond. This is one of them. Spirit activity is more prevalent in these spaces and Shaitan can use it for his own end."

"I thought he'd vanished through that portal, was dragged back you said…"

"It was only a matter of time. Melvyn said it was too easy."

"Once Forensics have cleared this well and identified the remains what can we do?"

"Fill this well up with cement, rubble, anything. We'll need Melvyn to bless the site and exorcise it."

Vance's phone began to ring, he answered, "Vance speaking. Yes? … Vanda…" Adam looked up sharply at her name. "What? … We'll get there as soon as we can." He rang off and looked at Adam. "That was Vanda. She's in trouble. Crows… and she's seen Shaitan."

Adam scrambled up. "We have to get to her."

"Melvyn is there. But he's trapped in my car. The postman is also there."

"It's all my fault…"

"Yes, it is. If you hadn't been so damn impulsive and stubborn, she wouldn't have had to drive home for your clothes and wouldn't be in this mess."

Adam coloured up in shame. "What can we do?"

"I'll phone the station and get someone out there. I'll see if any of the SOCOs came here under their own steam." Vance strode off to talk to members of the Forensic team, while Adam watched, a hangdog look on his face.

Vance came marching back and gestured to Adam, "Come on. We're in luck. One of the team has just rolled up in an official car. We're taking it."

Adam didn't need telling twice, he rushed after Vance and through the copse.

Blackberry juice coloured clouds rolled across the darkening sky. The air was oppressively thick with menace. Adam said little on the journey and was glad that Vance was able to put on the lights and sirens. He heaved a huge sigh of relief when they turned off the Brinkworth road towards Black Head Ridge.

Vance spoke breaking the silence in the car. "You know, I'm not surprised that there is paranormal activity around your house and the ridge." Adam looked at Vance with interest. "You know the history of your place, don't you?" Adam shook his head. "It was a case that shocked Cornwall way back in 1952; over seventy years ago now. I remember my grandfather told me about it when I was growing up and intended to join the police force. He was advising me on the cases I might have to deal with…" Adam listened with interest as Vance went on, "Twenty-six-year-old Miles Giffard had brutally murdered both his parents battering them with an iron pipe. He put their bodies in a wheelbarrow and threw them over the cliff. There was a chase across the country to London where he was caught visiting his girlfriend."

"What happened?"

"The young man was found guilty and hung at Bristol by the well-known executioner Albert Pierrepoint. It was only afterwards Miles' horrific childhood came to light at the hand of an abusive nanny and of his father who was incredibly cruel to him. He spent his troubled school years at different boarding schools, where he was bullied. But he was a talented cricketer and played for the county. There was a move afoot to have him declared insane, but a family friend testified that Miles was a lazy wastrel and knew exactly what he was doing. It went against him and sealed his fate."

"Why are you telling me this?"

"To take your mind off everything. You can look it up. The case has form, locals have said your place is haunted. I wouldn't be surprised if the Giffards are part of the ghosts around the place. Maybe your own house is on a ley line. Maybe, that's why all these things happen to you, what you see and so on."

Adam shook his head. "No. I have seen and felt things all my life not just since moving to Black Head Ridge. But it's a good tale. I grant you that."

"Not just a tale… but truth. You look it up. You'll find it online somewhere with all the gory details." Vance turned the sharp corner leading across the cliff to the house. They parked next to Melvyn, still sitting in Vance's car behind Adam's.

Vance switched off the siren and lights and they saw the crows, all standing stock-still staring at the house until Cawdor flew down from the roof, cawing harshly. And as one body they all flew up into the sky and took off towards the town. Vance looked at Adam. "Do you think it's safe to get out?" Adam was already undoing his seat belt and opening the door. "Adam?"

"They've gone. It's safe."

Melvyn alighted and joined Adam and Vance outside the house, and they went inside where Vanda welcomed Adam into her arms. "I was so worried. Are you sure you're safe to be around."

"I believe so," said Vance, "or I wouldn't have brought him."

They relocated to the kitchen where Jake had just filled the kettle. "Think we could all do with a cuppa," he said.

Adam added, "And with a tot of something to steady the nerves." Vanda retreated to the drinks' cabinet in the sitting room and retrieved a bottle of brandy and they all sat around the kitchen table.

"Now what?" asked Vanda. "What do we do now?"

The group looked around at each other. Melvyn was the first to speak. "I need to do an exorcism at the well. Bless it to prevent evil returning. Adam will, I know, deal with the spirits of the girls."

"What about Shaitan?" asked Vanda.

"It's obvious he's interested in you. Is there anywhere you can go for a while? Cover your tracks so to speak?" asked Melvyn.

"You mean, leave Cliff Head House? And Adam?"

"It's for your own safety."

"But I can't protect her if she's not here," said Adam.

"I don't need protecting. I'm not some little mouse. I can look after myself," said Vanda bristling slightly.

"I don't doubt that," said Melvyn, "in normal situations, but this is somewhat different. Is there anywhere?"

"I suppose I could go home for a while. I haven't seen my parents since Caroline's funeral. Before that it was three years."

"What's the address? Adam can check and see if it's on any ley lines."

"What can I do?" asked Jake who had been silent up until now.

"You can keep quiet," said Vance. "We don't want a panic on our hands. Keep everything that you've seen and heard to yourself."

"How do I know I won't be followed by any crows?" asked Vanda.

"You don't. You will need to be alert and wary. Use the same protections that you used before. Melvyn?"

"Yes, keep all the protection at your house but go and visit your parents. Take your holy items with you. Where do they live?"

"Shropshire... Adam, if I go, can you look after Elsa?"

Adam nodded. "Of course. But will you be safe there? I hate the thought of Shaitan following you there."

"Who knows? But I will be prepared. I guarantee it."

There was a lull in the conversation and Adam burst out, "I don't like it. I think it's wrong. There must be something else we can do?"

Melvyn cleared his throat. "Vanda really needs to get away, believe me... I have some questions, Inspector. How long before Forensics have cleared the site and finished?"

Vance thought for a moment. "The bodies and contents of the well should be cleared by tomorrow and then there will be the final clear up... Why?"

"I don't like the thought that Shaitan is around and looking for retribution and he clearly wants Vanda. However, we will need to know the area is safe. It mustn't be used again for evil purposes. The well must be filled up and exorcised. That will take time. Adam must help those dispossessed spirits to move on and the girls' proper burial will help. It means Vanda will be on her own and she shouldn't be. I can go on to Shropshire to ensure her safety."

"Well, then so could I, but what about the intervening days?"

"Will you two stop talking as if I am not here. I should have a say in this," interrupted Vanda. They all turned to look at her. "Adam, both you and Melvyn are needed here. I have to get home to my parents' house and keep myself safe. I have to do it in such a way that Shaitan doesn't know I've gone."

"What are you suggesting?" asked Vance.

"Try and get someone to take my place so it looks as though I am still here in residence. But she must be careful. You need someone who could pass for me with colouring height and so on and you could keep her safe as we did with Jacobs."

There was silence as they mulled over the idea. Vance eventually spoke again. "It could work. I can set up detectives to watch over your doppelganger."

"I don't like it," said Adam. "Whoever it is would be putting themselves in grave danger and we know from Draper that Shaitan has his own way of finding people. He could find Vanda's parents' house and then they will all be in danger. No. It's not worth it."

"Don't dismiss it just yet," said Vanda. "I don't want to be tied to you constantly. Fond as I am of you, I need my own space."

"This is getting us nowhere," grumbled Vance.

"The other alternative is that I stay here until everything's done and then disappear for a while."

They all exchanged looks. This decision was tricky, and it was obvious that they wouldn't all agree.

It was then that Jake spoke up. "Can I say something?"

"Go on," said Vance as they all turned their eyes on Jake.

"I'm about the same height as Vanda. I am of slim build and could wear a wig to match her hair and dress up as a woman. I could take a few days off work. Use me, safer than using another woman, if this Shaitan is as you say he is."

"He's that and much more," said Melvyn.

"Then what about it?"

They all studied Jake with new eyes. "You know. It could work," said Vance.

"With makeup and a wig, some padding and in Vanda's clothes..." said Melvyn.

"We fooled the crows once before with a disguise. It could work again," murmured Adam.

"We need to get a wig and makeup artist in here and test it out."

They all looked at each other and nodded. The decision was made.

Vanda giggled and laughed, "You make a lovely woman, Jake."

"Thanks a bunch."

"But your walk will give you away. You need to take smaller steps," said Vanda.

"And toss your head. Vanda does that a lot," added Adam.

"I do not!" exclaimed Vanda tossing her head.

"See what I mean?" said Adam.

Vanda blushed and then hooted with laughter as she watched Jake mince around the sitting room tossing his head in the long haired wig.

"Vanda has more of a sway in her hips…" added Vance critically.

"You mean like this," Jake said wiggling his hips.

"No, not like that. It's more subtle," said Adam.

"Oh, Lord," groaned Vanda. "I'm sure I don't walk like that."

"Walk for us," said Vance. "And, Jake, you follow. Go on parade around the room."

Vanda walked around trying not to laugh and Jake followed imitating Vanda's sway.

"That's it!" exclaimed Adam. "Much better. You'll need to try and hide your face… You could wear a hat. Vanda sometimes wears a baker boy cap. And a scarf, pull it up a bit."

Vanda passed Jake a hat and scarf and helped him put them on. "That looks fine. Keep your head down."

"I can't toss my head and look down," complained Jake.

"Then only toss it when you're standing still," ordered Adam. Jake walked around the room some more to the applause of the others. "That's it," said Adam. "I think you'll do. You'll fool the crows."

"But will I fool this Shaitan man?" asked Jake.

"With a bit of luck," replied Adam.

"Then that's it. We're all set," said Jake with a broad grin. "We just have to put it to the test."

18

JAKE DRESSED AS VANDA AND Adam strolled back across the cliff top to Cliff House. Elsa ran to meet them and sniffed Jake curiously. Adam observed, "She's trying to work out what's happened to her mistress."

"At least she knows me. How long do you think you'll need, and do I have to stay here?"

"Until it's done. You did say you'd got some time off?"

"Yes. I must say, I find all this intriguing but terrifying. But anything I can do to help..."

"You already are." A crow cawed loudly making them jump. "So, those critters are still around."

"So it seems. Best keep my head down." They soon reached Vanda's front door and were relieved to get inside quickly followed by Elsa, and Adam closed the door firmly behind them.

Vanda sat in the hallway at Black Head Ridge House. She was dressed like a man with all her hair tucked under a hat. She looked across at Vance and Melvyn and asked, "Are you sure this will work?"

"Who knows?" said Vance. "But it was worth a shot." Vance's mobile rang, "Vance... Ah, Adam, yes... all well? ... Great... how long are you staying? ... I see... In that case, pull all the drapes and blinds, check all the protection... Hold on, Melvyn wants a word," added Vance as Melvyn waved to attract his attention.

"Adam? As soon as you're done, get back here and we can work on those girls. Get them to where they should be. Vance is going back to the site to make sure they have finished there. Vanda will ride with him, and he will drop her off at the station... Yes... she has enough clothes here, so she won't need to go back to Cliff Head. She has things at her parents' house, too. So she'll be okay. Her car will stay there so everyone will think she's at home or here. Yep, okay... I'll call once they've left. Ciao." Melvyn handed the phone back to Vance who looked quizzically. "All sorted. You and Vanda can move off whenever you feel safe."

"What about taking my bag out? Won't it look suspicious?" asked Vanda.

"Depends whether anyone is watching, or those birds are about," said Vance.

"What if they are?"

"I think we can disguise your bag as the postman's bag or something. I'll check the sitting room and kitchen see if any crows are around." Vance strode out of the hallway and into the kitchen while Vanda and Melvyn waited. A few moments later Vance was back shaking his head, and he marched into the sitting room, where he looked at the side of the house as well as the front. It appeared to be clear. He returned, shaking his head again. "No. I can't see any sign of them. It seems to be safe. Tell you what, I'll take your bag out to my car and pack it away and come back. I will be able to see more. We don't want birds flying down from the roof or out of the shrubbery."

"Be careful," said Vanda.

"Don't you worry. I'm not taking any risks."

Vance picked up Vanda's masculine looking bag and exited the house. He stared about him and glanced up at the sky. It was free from crows and the shrubbery was also clear with no sign of Shaitan. He soon returned. "Okay, Vanda, it's now or never. Keep your head down just in case and walk like a man," he ordered.

Vanda was up on her feet and said a hurried goodbye to Melvyn. "Tell Adam, I'll call him when I get there." Melvyn nodded and she slipped out of the door after Vance.

Melvyn was waiting patiently for Adam's return when he heard some piano music. Music was hardly the word as it was nonsensical and discordant. Melvyn went to investigate the hallway and was mesmerised by the sight of the piano keys moving up and down, seemingly on their own.

The front door opened, and Adam entered. He heard the unconnected notes being played and could see the spirits of the two girls giggling and thumping their hands on the piano. He addressed them curtly. "Margaret! Lucy! This is no way to behave." The girls stopped and turned. "We have found your remains in the well and once the pathologist has examined those, you will have a proper burial and service. It is time for you to move on."

Lucy was the first to speak. "What if we don't want to go?"

"Yes," added Margaret. "It's fun here. We can play here and do all sorts."

"You mean, make mischief?"

The girls giggled and nodded. Melvyn touched Adam's arm and as he did, so he saw the shimmering apparitions of the two schoolgirls. "I can see them!" he said incredulously.

"Yes. If you keep hold of me you will see them, too," explained Adam.

"But, if we go our fun will stop and that's not fair."

"Life isn't fair," murmured Lucy.

"No. And neither is what you're doing to Adam when he has tried to help you."

The two girls looked at each other, made a face, and stuck their tongues out at Melvyn.

Adam put his hand up in a stop motion. "Enough... what happened to you was dreadful, abominable. It should never happen to anyone else, ever again. But do you realise that to stay here you'll be giving up so much?"

The girls exchanged a look. "What do you mean?"

"On the other side is so much love such as you've never experienced. You will be reuniting with family and friends who love you. On the other side you will learn, grow and develop. Your energy will go on... Think... It was what you wanted, to be found. I found you, now you must take the next step."

"But I'm afraid," said Lucy.

"Yes. What if we go through the portal and find ourselves in the pit of evil where all our enemies are…"

"You won't. I promise you. Melvyn is here, to bless you and to help me get you to the tunnel of light."

Melvyn began incanting a prayer of deliverance. He started to bless the girls and as he did a vortex of blue pulsating light began to form behind them in the hallway. It spun around in a circle revealing a tunnel of white light. Familiar figures could be seen at the far end and the girls watched.

"There's my Nana!" exclaimed Lucy.

"And my Great Uncle Jack," murmured Margaret in disbelief.

"Are they all family? The ones waiting for us?" asked Lucy.

"All family and friends who have passed across to the other side. They are expecting you; they will help you to heal and cross over. All you have to do is walk to the tunnel's end. It will be wonderful, I promise," assured Adam. "Go on, take the first step. You won't be disappointed. They are calling for you… listen!"

Jubilant voices could be heard, excitedly calling their names, waving and beckoning them to come.

"It's not a trick?" asked Margaret.

"No."

"Mr Shaitan won't be there?" questioned Lucy.

"No. He's not allowed there. Don't you want to be happy and see your loved ones?"

Lucy nodded and said tentatively, "I believe you. But you must be careful. We couldn't warn you definitively… we were threatened with a curse that we and our families still living would be damned to Hell if we spoke." Lucy looked around anxiously as if she expected something terrible to happen.

Melvyn spoke gently, "Go now, go to your families. They will welcome you and you cannot be taken away by evil then. Maybe then you will find a way to speak to Adam and tell him the truth. If not, don't worry. Take the first step. Go towards the light."

Adam nodded in agreement. "Do as Melvyn says. Step into the tunnel and embrace the all-consuming power of love. I'll be all right, so will your families."

The two children clasped hands and nodded. They took their first step into the tunnel and a wind blew up pushing them from behind towards the gathered throng of loved ones. The voices grew louder, and Adam was gratified as they reached the tunnel's end where he saw them being greeted and hugged. Tears filled his eyes. Melvyn, too, was filled with emotion as he watched the girls turn and look back. They waved at Adam and blew him a kiss before disappearing with the crowd. The vortex spun faster and closed up tightly and vanished as if it was never there.

Melvyn looked on in disbelief. "I have never seen anything like it. It was quite beautiful."

Adam nodded. "Yes. The first time is always an experience. It's quite magical."

"What do you think this curse is?"

"I'm not sure. I think it must have something to do with the plague. I've been dreaming about it."

"But we took precautions."

"Yes, thank goodness. But Shaitan was a scientist. If he had somehow manufactured a way to grow this bacteria. Who knows what his plans were?"

Melvyn shuddered. "You do realise we have to try and shut him down for good?"

"Yes, and I am not looking forward to it."

Vanda had arrived at her parents' house luckily enough without any serious incidents, although, she had had a few scares en route. Whenever she saw crows at the roadside, she became alarmed and extra vigilant and wary. However, the birds she saw were nothing to do with Cawdor and his gang.

Her mother, Muriel, came out to meet her. She was an older version of her daughter with her hair swept up in a French pleat. She had long limbs and when she smiled her laughter lines spread part way down her cheeks. She had a certain air about her that many would call poise. Her posture was upright, and she moved gracefully. Her hands were finely tapered and well-manicured. She was clearly delighted to see her. "Vanda, darling. How lovely to see you." She gave her daughter a huge hug. "Come inside, Daddy has put the kettle on. I'm sure you'll welcome a cup of tea after your journey."

Vanda picked up her bag and followed her mother inside after locking her car. She smiled brightly as she gazed around the kitchen. "It's good to be home. Ah, I see you've decorated."

"We had it done while we were away, no mess to work around..." Muriel eyed her daughter with an inscrutable expression. "You know you are always welcome. You can come whenever you want. Bring your young man, too."

"Easier said than done. You are never home. Always jetting off somewhere."

"True. But your father has to keep an eye on his business concerns and that means travel. It is safeguarding it for your future. You know that."

"I know. It's unfortunate that you hardly ever seem to be at home when I am. And when you are, I'm always up to my eyes in work."

"Well, you're here now and that's what matters. Don't forget we keep in touch by phone. It would be far worse without Face Time."

"True."

Muriel hugged her daughter hard. "Here, let me look at you..." She stood back and eyed Vanda critically. "Are you eating enough?"

"Mum..."

"Well, I'm allowed to ask. I'm your mother and you're looking a little thin."

"I'm fine, really, Mum. Just had a lot going on."

"Ah! Stress! That'll knock the pounds off you. Boyfriend not giving you grief?"

"No, Mum. Adam and I... we're fine, honestly."

"Hmm... I know you and there's something you're not telling me." Muriel studied her daughter carefully. "What is it? You know you can tell us anything. We're not judgy."

"No, I know. Nothing to tell, not really. I just needed to get away for a bit.

Now, where's that tea you promised me, and I hope you have some lovely chocolate biscuits for me, too."

Muriel sighed. "All right. I know when I'm beaten. Come and sit down and tell us all your news."

Melvyn and Adam were at the site of the well, where the remains of the girls had been found. A storm was brewing. Black thunderclouds bowled across the sky threatening rain and the atmosphere was leaden and menacing, and Adam was feeling uncomfortable. He stood motionless for a while trying to focus on the here and now and what he and Melvyn were there to do. He wanted to feel his mother's arms around him and her voice calming him but instead there was nothing, and he felt deserted. This was unusual. Adam could only assume that the place was so filled with the remnants of evil deeds that she couldn't come through. Melvyn stood in his vicar robes and regalia. Adam wore the cross that Vanda had given him. Between them was a music stand holding a Bible. There were two bags of holy items in case any were needed. They were standing inside a circle of purified rock salt that lay on top of a chalk circle. On the ground were two receptacles filled with Holy water. Adam swallowed hard as a feeling of nausea overcame him. He shuddered.

Melvyn's voice broke into his thoughts, "Are you all right?"

"As right as I'll ever be. What do we do now?"

"Firstly, we protect ourselves before embarking on the exorcism. Here, take my hand." Melvyn held out one hand to Adam, which he took. In Melvyn's other hand was his big brass cross. "Now, hold onto this with me. No matter how tired your arm gets you must hold on tightly to this and not let go, you understand? We must keep the cross up and level. We have a circle of protection, and we need to pray."

Adam nodded and took hold of the cross, supporting it in his other hand while Melvyn instructed Adam to bow his head, and he intoned a prayer. As Melvyn spoke, a wind blew up and whirled around their feet scattering some of the salt. A pulsing red light began to emanate from the well.

Adam raised his head and interrupted Melvyn who stopped. "The salt, Melvyn. This wind is destroying it."

"Then we must use the Holy water to make a circle. That and the remnants of salt should do it. But we need enough left to finish the exorcism. I'll hold the cross and continue to pray. You have the bottles of Holy water, as well as what's in the receptacles?" Adam nodded. "Good, sprinkle the Holy water."

They dropped hands and Adam took one of the bottles from his pack and covered the circle in drops of Holy water. Where the salt still lay, a strange reaction occurred and it turned into a kind of paste that the wind found difficult to move, and oh, how the wind tried to disperse the water and salt. It whipped around the two men, blowing Melvyn's hair up as if it was electrified. His shock of white hair spread out and he looked more like a mad professor than ever. Adam's hair, too, was parted and blowing back from his face with such force that it was as if it would be ripped out by the roots. The unnatural fierce gale blew with a wild alien strength that almost pushed Adam over as it tried to propel him out of the circle. Melvyn caught hold of Adam's arm and pulled him back towards him urging him above the cacophony of the wind to grab the cross again.

Adam struggled hard against this terrifying supernatural power, but he and Melvyn were holding hands. Melvyn was standing firm, but Adam was not so steady on his feet. He grabbed hold of the cross with Melvyn who continued to incant his prayers of exorcism. The sky above them turned a thunderous bruised black and funnel clouds spiralled down. Rain began to lash over them and soaked their faces as they prayed together.

From the bottom of the well came an eerie wailing that grew in strength until it was a scream that was almost unbearable to hear. As the wind groaned and joined with the agonised shrieks from the pit, the copse of trees surrounding the place bent and swayed into impossible contorted shapes and the leaves were ripped from the branches. Over the copse the sky stagnated; it was immobile and held the oppressive leaden cloud firmly over the area.

Curiously now, the wind was outside the circle and in the copse, but inside the circle it was still, just like the eye of a hurricane. But then…

From the pit came a high-pitched whistling and a terrible thrumming of ratcheting wings. Tarry black beetles with glowing red eyes swarmed from the well, clambering over each other in their multitudes, piling high and forcing themselves against the edge of the circle and as one tumbled from the pile and into the circle it sizzled and burned letting out a whining screech. Following the beetles came a pack of rats, one mischief after another, with black greasy fur, sharp claws and teeth. Their eyes burned like the fiery centre of a furnace. There was a smell of sulphur in the air, and they chattered together, showing their yellow teeth and pointed incisors. They gathered around the edge of the circle surrounding Adam and Melvyn, watching and observing. Fleas could be seen jumping on their bodies and their fur rippled with the parasites. Occasionally, one rat would scratch at its body flinging the flea off into the circle where it instantly combusted.

Melvyn continued to pray but Adam had started to tremble and shake. His aversion to rats had manifested into a panic attack and he found himself gasping for air as his heart thundered in his chest. Melvyn opened his eyes and studied Adam looking gravely concerned. "Adam, are you all right?"

Adam swallowed hard and shook his head. "No, I can't stay here. I have to get back to the car. I'm sorry, Melvyn."

"No!" Melvyn's voice was firm. "If you leave the circle these creatures will jump on you. I'm convinced this is the threat the girls spoke of. Those rats have fleas and carry Bubonic plague. Hold on tightly to me and the cross. Close your eyes, focus and breathe. Shut them out. You must stay inside the circle." Melvyn's voice sounded desperate as he tried to urge Adam to stay still.

Melvyn gripped Adam's hand so tightly his fingernails dug into his skin. Adam winced. Adam closed his eyes tightly. The thought of what surrounded him filled him with terror. He gasped, "I don't know if I can... I feel as if I must do something, anything. The sounds these creatures make are piercing my brain." Almost as if the rats heard him, the click of their claws became louder as they scratched around the circle.

Melvyn pleaded, "That's the idea. Shaitan wants you to make a move. You're safe if you stay here. Come on, Adam you can do this."

"Yes, but for how long? We can't stay here all day and night."

"No, I don't think we'll have to."

"Why say that? You don't know."

Melvyn's tone was measured. "No, but I feel it. I truly believe the Lord will only let you bear so much. Adam, please."

Adam held his breath and to his surprise a warmth spread through his body as he felt his mother's touch and heard her voice, "Listen to him, Adam. He speaks the truth."

"We must do something," Adam's voice was calmer. "Can't we use the Holy water?"

Melvyn nodded. "I'm going to let go of your hand. You hold onto the cross. Keep your eyes closed. I will spray all the critters at the edge of the circle. Are you ready?"

Adam spoke breathlessly after a moment's hesitation. "Yes. Do it."

Adam clung to the cross. He swayed unsteadily, with his eyes remaining tightly closed as Melvyn released him and delved in his bag. He removed a half litre bottle of Holy water with a spout and flipped open the cap. Using it like a water pistol he moved inside the circle spraying the creatures, which screeched in agony and retreated from the circle's edge. Melvyn continually showered the critters and then scattered some sanctified salt over the ones he could still reach until the ones that remained alive fled back into the well. The remaining oily mass of rodent bodies rippled in pain as they clumped together, finally disappearing from sight, vanishing as if they had never been there.

"It's all right, Adam. They've gone. You can open your eyes."

"But for how long? Will they back?"

"I don't know. But they've gone for now. The wind has dropped. We are safe for the moment."

"What's next?"

"The pit must be filled. We will have to get onto Vance. If they pour concrete made with Holy water into the well that will suffice for the moment. We will have some work to do to bless enough water for the mix."

"What about us? When can we safely leave?"

"I'm not sure. Give it a few minutes and see if anything else happens... Look!" Melvyn pointed to the heavens. "The clouds are clearing, and that wind has finally dropped. We may be able to move."

"Not quickly enough for me," muttered Adam whose heart was still thumping in his chest and resounding like rapid gunfire in his head.

Melvyn scouted the trees around them, the area of the well and the sky above. "It all seems to be clear. No crows, no rats. Let's pack up our things and head for the car."

"You don't need to tell me twice," said Adam scooping up his bag of items. "What about the pots of Holy water?"

"Leave them. They can't do any harm. We can complete the exorcism once we have all the equipment in place to seal the well," assured Melvyn. "Let's get back to the car and alert Vance. They cautiously stepped out of the circle and began to walk out of the clearing to the trees. What they didn't notice were a few fleas lying in wait that jumped on Adam's trouser leg.

They crashed through the undergrowth and hurried their way through to the road where the car was parked. As soon as they reached the road they stopped and stared in horror. Lounging against the driver's door was Leonard Shaitan.

19

THE SKY HAD TURNED A blackcurrant juice purple and the rolling cloud cover seemed imprisoned and confined above Melvyn and Adam's heads. Shaitan smiled superciliously. It was a dangerous, cold smile that didn't manifest as human. He eyed the two men and spoke officiously. "You believe that with all your God trappings you can beat me?" There was no response. "Well, you're wrong."

He began to move towards them. His eyes flickered with the burning light of unholy fire. Adam and Melvyn stepped back towards the coppice and Shaitan grinned. His teeth appeared sharp and pointed as if they had been filed to inflict acute pain and damage with one bite. Melvyn ordered, "Back to the circle now." The men hurried back towards the safety of their circle of protection.

As they retreated, a car raced into view and pulled up behind Adam's vehicle. Vance alighted with Jacobs, who stopped and stared. He alerted Vance and pointed at them. Vance just caught sight of Adam and Melvyn returning to the trees and the back of Shaitan. He urged Jacobs to follow. "That's him. That's Shaitan. We have to arrest him," and Vance plunged after the demonic figure.

Jacobs muttered, "How is that even possible?" He paused for a moment before following Vance into the coppice.

Back inside the sanctity and safety of the circle, Adam and Melvyn stopped and laid down their bags. There was a sizzling sound and a puff of smoke as the fleas fell out of Adam's trouser leg and burned up. Melvyn nodded meaningfully at the vessels they had left, and each man picked up a pot of the Holy water.

Shaitan snorted derisively, "As if that will stop me."

"On my count throw it over him," ordered Melvyn. "One, two, throw!"

They each moved to the inside edge of the circle and chucked the contents of the pots at Shaitan, who raised his arms to shield his face and screamed. Vance and his detectives rushed forward to apprehend Shaitan and take him into custody. But Shaitan ran to the well, now a swirling red vortex and disappeared inside.

Vance and his detectives stopped in amazement. "What the hell just happened there?" exclaimed Vance.

Melvyn tried to explain, relating what had happened.

Adam called out, "Watch out for fleas. Step inside the circle just in case."

Jacobs didn't hesitate and Vance joined him. There were two more sizzling puffs as the pests incinerated.

Adam insisted, "This could be a problem. We were surrounded by rats; some of those parasites could still be left on the ground."

"What can we do?" asked Jacobs.

"I suggest soaking the bottoms of our trousers and shoes with Holy water," urged Adam.

"And check no one has been bitten. When fleas bite they inject an anaesthetic so you won't know until the bite comes up and starts to itch. If you have been bitten, you will need a course of antibiotics. We don't want to be plague carriers," said Melvyn.

"What about Shaitan?" asked Vance.

"He's a demon. You won't be able to arrest him. He will need to be exorcised or killed," replied Melvyn.

"And just how do we do that?" asked Vance sceptically.

"It won't be easy, but we have the tools," and he related his idea of making the concrete with Holy water to fill the well.

"But it won't stop him from popping up elsewhere," said Vance.

"Probably not," agreed Melvyn. "But it may deter him from our area. I last encountered him in Derbyshire."

"That would, at least, be something," conceded Vance.

"And you never know, it may defeat him for good," said Adam optimistically. "Let's pour the rest of the Holy water in the well."

"There's not much left," advised Melvyn.

"And, as they say, every little helps."

"So we step out of the circle, now?" asked Vance.

"Now or never," affirmed Melvyn. The three men engaged eyes, nodded as one and stepped out of the circle half expecting something to happen… It didn't.

Adam moved to the well and gazed into its inky depths and shuddered as he heard the scratching of tiny claws. He took the remaining bottle of water and poured it into the well. There were a number of loud squeals and squeaks and silence. Adam glanced at Melvyn and Vance, "Quick. Let's go while we can."

No one needed telling twice and they all hurried back through the clearing and copse and into the road to the cars. Vance clicked his key fob and Jacobs wrenched open the doors and dived inside.

Adam and Melvyn tried to open their car doors, but they wouldn't budge. It was as if they had been superglued. "Leave it," said Melvyn. "We'll go with Vance. We can collect the car when the well is filled. I expect the doors will open easily then." Adam waved at Vance and pointed at their car. Vance seeing their difficulty gestured them across and they climbed in. They sat there a moment to compose themselves as their breathing was harsh and ragged. Feeling calmer, Vance started the vehicle, and they moved off.

On the way back, all in the car were extra alert watching out of the windows in silence. Vance spoke and everyone jumped as his voice cut through their thoughts. "More alarming is the Forensic report from Shaitan's lab." He stopped and took a deep breath. "Shaitan has been modifying the bacteria that contaminates us with Bubonic plague." There was a pause. He continued, "Don't ask me anything technical I can only explain in simple terms. Bubonic plague, as such, is not transmitted from person to person, except by infected tissue but he has tampered with it to the extent that the bite of the flea from infected rodents becomes pneumonic plague and that is transmitted easily by droplets from people's breath. Pneumonic plague is deadly. What he has done is create a biological weapon that could rage out of control."

The silence in the car was dramatic. Adam finally spoke. "This has to be the threat the girls spoke of."

Vance nodded. "I'm sure it is. Another thing. You warned me about a reporter, said he would be persistent?"

"Yes?"

"Well, he hasn't been pestering *me*. I asked Jacobs to take the press conference, hoping it would stop the premonition, but now Jacobs is being hassled by some reporter from Truro."

"Yes, he's a pain in the butt. Brian Thompson. He caught wind of something. What, I don't know but he realises that there is more to these cases than people are aware of, and he believes, you, Adam are a big part of it. I should watch out."

Jake was sitting in Vanda's living room playing his guitar. He was still dressed in Vanda's clothes and kept his face away from the big window. There was a loud caw outside and Jake stiffened. He put down his guitar and keeping his head down he stood up and closed the blinds. He checked the thresholds of doorways, and windowsills, all over the house and closed the drapes and other window coverings so that no one could see inside. It made him feel better. He had to admit he was feeling spooked especially whenever he caught sight of himself in the hall mirror. He just hoped the disguise was enough to fool the birds. He had done some research and discovered that crows could recognise faces so was being particularly careful about keeping a low profile.

He realised it wasn't going to be easy, pretending to be Vanda for such a long time but he was determined to help. He so regretted not being able to help Caroline Mitchell in her hour of need. He knew he had a week of this and groaned. He sat down with a bump and Elsa jumped up onto his lap and began to purr. She kneaded her claws through Vanda's skirt, and he winced. "Ouch!

Elsa, hold on." He reached across for a cushion and tried to ease it under the cat who was not amused and jumped down. He put the cushion on his lap and patted it, "Come on, Elsa." Elsa turned her back on him and walked to the hallway. "Elsa, please!" The cat must have heard the pleading in his voice and stopped. She turned around and padded back and jumped up again. Jake made a huge fuss of her, and she dug her claws into the cushion and purred contentedly before tucking her front paws under her and settling down. "That's better," murmured Jake.

Jake leant back in his seat and continued to fuss Elsa who relaxed under his attention and nudged his hand with her head each time he paused in the petting, making him laugh. There was another raucous cawing outside and a fierce pecking at the window. Jake shuddered. He was feeling like a prisoner. There was only so much TV he could watch. He yearned to be outside. That's why he had finally become a postman. He loved his round and walking in the countryside as well as the town. He enjoyed a chat with his mail recipients. Stuck in the house he realised how much he missed the interaction with people, as well as the fresh air.

Adam was missing Vanda. He was feeling none too well, believing all the activities over the past few days had depleted his energy. He was feeling washed out and decidedly fluey and now his leg was itching. Adam rolled up his trouser leg and there just above his ankle was a bright red lump, a swelling that was begging to be scratched. He resisted the urge as it suddenly dawned on him that this could easily be a flea bite.

Adam was feeling achy, and his head was beginning to swim. He was running a fever and had begun to tremble. He picked up the phone and called Melvyn, who answered swiftly.

"Not a good time, Adam. Can I call you back?"

Adam dismissed Melvyn's words and continued, "Melvyn, I've been bitten. I need antibiotics. Are you all right?"

He heard Melvyn sigh deeply. "I have to go. I *will* call you back. And no, I don't think I have been bitten." He ended the call.

At the site, rubble had been tipped into the well and the cement had been made with Holy water. Melvyn was just about to begin a ritual that would seal the well and entomb the portal forever. He turned to Vance who had brought him and was inside the protective circle with him. "Adam needs antibiotics, he says he's been bitten."

Vance looked alarmed. "Oh no. What now?"

"We believe this was the danger the girls spoke of. He needs antibiotics urgently or it could develop into something very serious like pneumonic plague and then we will all be in trouble."

"I'll get onto the police doctor. Get him to see Adam. It will be easier keeping this under wraps than if he goes to see his regular GP. But now… Let's finish this."

Melvyn closed his eyes and raised his cross in one hand and his other hand was lifted in blessing. He intoned another prayer of exorcism and blessed the site.

A green mass shimmered by the well taking the hazy form of a man, as the well appeared to explode. A sulphurous smell tainted the air making them gag. A black tarry substance began to bubble from the site and pour over the side of the well opening and across the ground, stopping as it hit the salt circle. In the bubbling liquid were the bodies of rats and cockroaches. Faces leered up and dived down, horror struck faces of terror distorted with suppurating pustules that festered and oozed pus. A mournful wailing began that reverberated around the clearing chilling both men to the bone. Vance began to shiver, and he whispered, "We have to get out of here, now."

Melvyn stopped him. "No! That's what he wants. Trust me, please. Close your eyes and hold onto the cross with me. Keep saying the Lord's prayer."

"But…"

"Just do it!" The authority in Melvyn's voice was hard to ignore and Vance shut his eyes tightly and he began reciting the Lord's prayer under his breath. "Louder!" ordered Melvyn. "Say it with confidence and meaning."

Vance chanted the familiar holy words. His voice grew in power becoming stronger and filled with intention as Melvyn uttered his final words of exorcism. The black substance stopped bubbling and Melvyn's mouth dropped open as Lilith stepped out of the slime and fixed her eyes on Melvyn who shuddered as he tried to avert her brazen look. He swallowed hard as she began to approach the edge of the circle accompanying her seductive walk with lewd gestures as her forked tongue flicked in and out of her mouth exploring her index finger, which she inserted in through her lips and sucked hard.

Melvyn screamed out at the top of his lungs, "May the Lord Jesus Christ banish you, Lilith, to the bowels of the earth. Let God suppress and hold you in Hell for all eternity so that you and your minions cannot terrorise and abuse innocent men. Feel the weight of the Lord's hand on you, drowning you in the sludge from whence you came." He stared in amazement as Lilith appeared to shrink back from his words at which point Shaitan manifested fully as a man. His eyes turned from red to a venomous black and Melvyn fervently intoned another prayer of exorcism until like a sputtering screen on an old movie Shaitan visibly retreated. From the well escaped a plume of smoke that twisted and writhed in serpentine coils around Shaitan's feet that rose up and devoured him. He seemed to disappear inside it and the smoke, heavier and thicker now, pulled the demon back to the well and down into the ground. Melvyn was shaking. He nudged Vance. "You can open your eyes now. They've gone."

Vance looked about him in wide eyed astonishment. The sludge had vanished, the space inside the copse was clear and the air was free of the sulphurous smell that had enveloped them. Songbirds landed in the trees, which had been forever silenced while the pit was active. They trilled and sang staking out their territory and claiming it for good.

"Is it safe to move now?" asked Vance, his eyes scanning the area.

"It's safe," affirmed Melvyn. "I can't see this portal being used again. But we will check it, just in case." Melvyn stepped out of the circle and waited. Nothing happened. No crows appeared nor any creatures from the depths. Melvyn strode towards the well brandishing his cross. He peered through the grid down into the depths. He could see the cemented rubble was intact. There were no breeches in the material. The air smelled pure and fresh. He lifted the grid and placed his stout cross on top of the sealing layer of cement and replaced the lid. Satisfied he grunted. "There, it's done."

Vance stepped out of the circle and looked around cautiously. "Come on. Let's get out of this place." The two men picked up their accoutrements and hurried back to the car.

Once safely inside and the engine running Vance took out his phone and called the police physician. He briefly explained what was needed and told him to deliver the right amount of antibiotics to Black Head Ridge House telling him that they would be there as soon as they were able.

Adam sat hunched in the kitchen feeling miserable. He had a raging fever, pounding headache and aching joints. He alternated between feeling uncomfortably hot and being extremely cold with attacks of shivering. He had a burning throat and had developed a cough. He knew exactly what had caused his symptoms and he had done enough research to know what it was and what he was in for.

His doorbell rang and as Adam shuffled to his feet he was hit by a bout of coughing that produced a watery mucus. Each step was hard, and he was out of breath and wheezing. He opened the door to admit, three people in dressed in biohazard suits, goggles and face masks with breathing apparatus and gloves. Adam blinked, was he hallucinating? He turned and walked back to the sitting room where he pulled a blanket around him, as he was beginning to feel shivery again.

Vance spoke. "Adam, this is Dr Sharpe he has come prepared with antibiotics that could prevent this from developing further."

Dr Sharpe explained as he rattled a bottle of Levofloxacin, "Take 750 mg every twenty-four hours. Start now. Take it with a large glass of water at the same time each day. It's imperative that you drink plenty of water to keep hydrated to stop crystals forming in your urine. You can take these tablets on an empty stomach or with food but do not drink alcohol or eat bananas. There is enough here for a seven to fourteen day course but be aware, some people may recover in a little over three days. If that's you, take the full seven day course anyway and then, stop, as even when the symptoms subside you can still be infectious for a few days afterwards. All of you involved and in contact must also take a course. Better to be safe than sorry. Your friend Melvyn has volunteered to stay with you, so you won't be alone. If these pills are ineffective we will resort to intramuscular injections. Also, no antacids or dairy products – no cheese. And no grapefruit. In fact, there should be a difference in two hours, if so you could be over this inside three days. Let's hope that's you. Oh, and one more thing, stay out of the sun."

Adam shook his head, he was feeling woozy. "How am I supposed to remember all that?"

"I'll remember for you, Adam," said Melvyn gently. "Now, take your first tablet. I shall be taking them with you, so we won't forget."

Vanda paced her mother's kitchen. "Something's wrong. I know it is. It's not like him. He should have called by now." As she spoke her phone rang. She answered immediately. "Adam? Is everything all right?"

Adam relayed all that had happened, and Vanda sat down in the kitchen chair with a bump. Her face registered shock and her mother looked on in concern. Vanda listened some more. "Perhaps I should come back?"

"No, you are safe there. No one knows where you have gone. Look, I'll call you later. Meanwhile, try and relax and enjoy being home. Vance will be posting some antibiotics to your parents' address. Take them as a precaution, please."

Brian Thompson sat in the main office at the Newspaper building in Truro. He jiggled his knee in agitation and chewed his pencil. He was a tall man, some would say lanky. He had striking blue eyes and straw coloured hair that just clipped his shoulders. He was working on a piece about the death of Melanie Parker and crossing out the names of various people on his list. Question marks remained at the side of Leonard Shaitan's name and others including Russell Draper, Margaret Lake and Lucy Ward.

He had made copious notes on Inspector Vance, Jacobs and Harding as well as Adam Barrie with arrows linking him to other people and the story of Ted Johnson and his abhorrent crimes. Brian scratched his head and threw down his pencil in frustration. He needed to speak to Adam Barrie, but he couldn't get any joy through official channels. He sighed heavily and grunted as he rose from his desk and grabbed his jacket, murmuring aloud, in his Brummy tones, "If I can't get to him, maybe I can find out more from Ted Johnson's last victim." He referred to his notes. "Angie Hartman, now Mrs Luke Armitage." She would be his first port of call, and her parents, he'd visit them, too. One of them might let something slip.

He picked up his car keys and flipped them in the air before putting on his jacket and snatching his notebook and pencil. Whistling cheerfully, he sauntered out of the office and ran lightly down the stairs to the underground car park and made for his car striding purposefully as he worked out exactly what he was going to say.

~ 2 0 ~

MR AND MRS HARTMAN WERE enjoying an afternoon pot of tea and a crumpet, toasted twice, the way Angie's mother always did them. They were crisper on the outside and not soggy in the middle and the lashings of butter spread more easily. Their bell rang and Rita, Angie's mother looked up. "Now, whoever can that be?"

"You won't know unless you look," said her husband, Peter, with a twinkle in his eye and his mouth full of crumpet with the butter dribbling down his chin. He grabbed a napkin to wipe it off and hurriedly popped the rest in his mouth spoiling his enjoyment, As his wife went to the door.

She returned followed by Brian Thompson who studied the room carefully, noting the furnishings and the space. "Nice house," he said appreciatively.

"Thank you," Rita replied looking pleased.

Peter interjected, "And you are?"

"Sorry," he apologised. "Brian, Brian Thompson with the West Briton."

"Oh, I know. Comes out every Thursday. We sometimes pick one up in town." There was a pause. "What do you want with us?"

"It's er… a bit of a delicate matter," said Brian hesitantly.

Rita gestured to a seat. "Do sit down, Mr Thompson. Would you like a cup of tea?"

"That would be very kind. Thank you," he replied as he settled onto the settee.

Peter eyed the young reporter. "Been in this neck of the woods long?"

"Two years. I moved here from Birmingham."

"I thought you were a Midlander."

"Yes, the voice gives it away, doesn't it? An accent, something you never lose, not completely."

"No, I suppose not," said Peter as Rita returned with another cup and plate and some assorted biscuits.

Rita asked, "So, how do you like it?"

"As it comes, milk no sugar."

Rita poured him a cup and handed him a plate indicating he should help himself.

"Thanks very much," he said with a nod and took a chocolate digestive.

"So, what's this delicate matter that makes you seek us out?" asked Peter his eyes narrowing.

Brian cleared his throat. "I am doing an article on some of the strange events that have happened around here, and I was fascinated by the story of your daughter's abduction... I know that Adam Barrie was instrumental in helping find her, wasn't he?"

At the mention of Adam's name Peter closed up tighter than a sealed paint pot that had been closed with wet paint on the rim and had dried. Rita watched the two men and said nothing. She drank her tea silently. Brian finished his chocolate biscuit as he studied both of them.

Peter finally answered, "He was."

"Perhaps you can tell me, How did he know where to find her?"

Peter cleared his throat and feeling pressured stuck to the official story. "From what we understand, he was out walking and heard screams coming from a shepherd's cottage. He broke in, found her and called the police. That's it."

Brian screwed his face up and blew through his teeth before responding. "That's the official story. But why would anyone go walking in the dead of night in an horrendous storm?" Peter was stuck and didn't know how to respond, he began to colour up. Brian pressed on, "It doesn't make sense."

Rita attempted to rescue her husband who she knew would flounder under persistent questioning. "It does to a woman."

Brian turned to her and fixed his eyes on her. "What do you mean?"

"Adam had had a disagreement with his girlfriend."

"A disagreement?"

"A row. They had a huge argument. He flounced out to clear his head."

"In a storm?"

"There wasn't a storm when he started his walk."

"Then why didn't he turn back when it started?"

"Because he'd gone too far and was looking for somewhere to shelter," Rita said as if the answer was obvious.

"I thought they were walking together?" he said staring hard at her.

"She chased after him, wanting to make up." Rita was now feeling very uncomfortable and worried that she might say the wrong thing. "Look, if you want any information on this then it's best if you speak to the man himself. We only know what we've been told."

"Oh, I intend to and to speak to your daughter."

"I don't think you ought to speak to Angie. She's been through enough. It would be cruel to dredge it all up again and make her relive it. She's trying to forget it. Questioning her won't help her, at all." With that Rita rose and took her cup out to the kitchen to escape Brian's searching gaze and probing questions. Her hands were trembling. She didn't like being interrogated and she didn't know what else to say.

Peter spoke again. "If you're not satisfied with what you've heard then I think you should leave. You're upsetting my wife, and I won't have you upsetting my daughter, needlessly."

Brian Thompson drained his cup and rose, brushing the biscuit crumbs from his front. He moved to the door and turned. "I think I have what I need. Thanks for the tea." He sailed out whistling.

Peter muttered under his breath, "Damned reporters," and he closed the door firmly.

Rita came out into the hall. "Has he gone?"

"Yes. And I hope he's not going to come back."

"I think we should ring Adam and warn him, don't you?"

Peter nodded. "I'll give him a call now."

Adam sat in the living room flicking through the channels on the TV. He sighed and put down the remote after switching it off. "This is no good," he grumbled. "I can't settle. I need to be doing something."

"What you need is to switch off and recover. It's going to be a rough few days for you," said Melvyn through his face mask and covered in PPE.

"Not so good for you either in all that lot."

"I'll manage."

Adam was hit with a wave of electricity, he seemed to step outside himself as the vision took hold and he watched as he answered the phone, which was jangling so much that it almost jumped out of its cradle. He saw himself stopping the infernal ring, which was distorted and loud. The instrument appeared to have a life of its own and he heard himself, "Hello? …Yes… I see… Okay, thank you." He replaced the receiver. "That was Peter Hartman. Something about a reporter coming to question me. He can't come now and see me like this." Adam explained what the Hartmans had said. Adam wavered in his speech and swayed as he tried to stand.

He could hear Melvyn muttering, "That's not good. If any of this gets out, we'll have a panic on our hands. What are you going to do?"

"Best not to answer the door. Let him know I'm unwell and can't see anyone."

"I can't answer in this lot. He'll know something is up."

"True. Best sit tight then."

As quickly as the vision had started it was over, and it was back to reality. Melvyn stood looking questioningly at him. "What is it? What did you see?"

Adam seemed to come around from his stupor, he was wearing a face mask sitting in the kitchen with Melvyn who was in full PPE with breathing apparatus. He was about to explain when the phone rang startling him. Adam picked up, "Hello? … yes … I see…" He listened carefully to the person on the other end of the phone. His tone was measured. "Thank you for letting me know." He replaced the receiver.

Melvyn studied Adam's face that was screwed up in uncertainty and enquired, "Problems?"

"Could be. Some reporter chap has been around to the Hartmans' asking questions. They gave him the official story, but he was very persistent asking all kinds of questions. He intends to come here to see me."

"What are you going to do?"

"He can't come here. I'm not well enough. And you can't answer the door in that lot. It would only bring more questions. I won't answer the door… I'll sit tight, pretend I'm not in."

"It might work once but then he'll be back. You can't keep hiding away."

"I will until I'm better. I don't want to infect anyone. What else can I do?"

Melvyn shook his head. "We'd better stay out of the sitting room. The front bay windows face the cliff path and drive. Anyone parking out there will see us."

"In that case, I'll retreat to my bedroom. Watch telly in there. There's a couple of chairs in there. You can watch with me. We can't go in the kitchen. If he's a reporter, he's a snooper. He'll wander around the outside of the house and peer in where he can."

"Maybe," said Melvyn. "If I were you I'd get upstairs now. Is this chap coming today?"

Adam shrugged. "I don't know." He began to cough. "Damn this cough. It hurts my throat. I'm feeling shivery again."

"Time for your next antibiotic. How are you in comparison to what you were?"

"Better. I'm no longer hallucinating."

"I didn't know you were," said Melvyn abruptly.

"No, I kept it to myself. Didn't want to worry you."

"Listen, you must be honest with me. I can help."

"You should be getting back to Helen."

"She understands. Don't worry. It will only be a few more days, I'm sure. After all, the doctor said you could be better in three days. It's only been two. I need to finish my course, too. I can't go home before that."

"Hmm," said Adam getting up from his seat. He shuffled towards the door and went into the hall. "I'm going up."

The bell rang and they both froze. "Quickly!" hissed Melvyn. "Be as quiet as you can. I'll follow."

Adam began to climb the stairs wincing at every creak. Melvyn followed and they crossed the landing to Adam's bedroom. The bell rang again persistently. A male voice shouted out, "Mr Barrie!"

Melvyn tiptoed to the window and peeped out keeping well to the side. He just caught sight of a tall man, with fair, straw coloured hair wearing jeans, a check shirt and a light coloured jacket. The man appeared to peer in the bay window and then proceeded to walk around the back of the house. Melvyn and Adam sat tight and waited. Melvyn peeped again. The reporter had parked his car further along the cliff top towards the path that crossed to Vanda's house. He reappeared from behind the mansion and began to walk along the cliff path towards Cliff House. Melvyn observed, "He's off to see Vanda."

"Damn, Jake is there. He mustn't answer the door."

"No, that chap will think Vanda is some sort of transvestite or something." Adam began to laugh and ended up with a coughing fit.

"I'll call the house and warn him," said Melvyn.

Adam managed to splutter out, "You'd better hurry."

Jake answered the phone at Cliff House and listened as Melvyn explained. He thrust down the receiver and ran about the place closing curtains that weren't already shut and fled upstairs followed by a curious Elsa. He disappeared into the bedroom and waited, feeling uneasy.

Some minutes later there was a ring on the doorbell followed by a pounding on the front door. Jake sat tight.

Outside, Brian stared at the salt all over the doorstep and frowned. There was salt at the front of Barrie's mansion, too. What did it mean? Brian peered up at the upstairs windows and squinted, and he thought he detected a movement at one or was it his eyes playing tricks? No... there was nothing. Just a crow with a white tipped tail feather that had landed on the roof and had just fluttered down onto a windowsill. Brian turned to walk away when something else caught his attention. He stopped and stared along the cliff path. A police car had driven up to the front of Black Head Ridge House but the men that got out, there were three, were all dressed in white hazmat suits or something similar. Brian squinted to see but couldn't distinguish any faces just that one was carrying a bag. They all walked to the door and were admitted by another person similarly dressed. What was going on? Brian decided he needed to find out. He moved to the cliff path but didn't notice a number of other crows landing on the roof of Cliff House. As he walked a sound assailed his ears. He could hear the distinctive sounds of Haitian Tanbou drums. He'd heard them before on a trip to New Orleans where there was some kind of voodoo festival that he had gone to cover for an online magazine when he was just starting out in journalism. Brian hesitated, just what was going on?

Brian quickened his step. He would jolly well wait by the police car until they came out and then they would be forced to tell him something. The drumming suddenly became louder and more oppressive, and thirteen crows fluttered down in front of him. They stopped like a barricade as if to intimidate him from continuing. Brian waved his arms about to scare them off, but they remained stock-still. "Shoo!" he shouted. "Stupid birds."

One crow hopped forward, the one with the white tipped feather and eyed him beadily. Immediately the drumming stopped, and Cawdor flew at Brian and landed on his head. Brian thrashed around trying to dislodge the creature when the others all flew at him, landing on his body and head in a full blown attack. He began to run, stumbling blindly. He screamed at the top of his voice as the weight of the birds dragged him down to the ground and he began to crawl. Birds pecked at his face, his eyes, and his neck. One bird hit his carotid artery and jugular vein, which sprayed the others in blood, and they began to squabble as each wanted to drink from the fountaining vein. A wailing wind blew around and muttered whisperings were heard on the breeze. There was another burst of drumming, which stopped abruptly, and the birds stopped.

Brian's screams had been heard inside Black Head Ridge House and across at Cliff Head House. Jake peered outside and saw the attack and shuddered. He got on the phone to Adam but didn't dare venture out himself.

Inside Black Head Ridge House, they all heard Brian's screams. The call from Jake confirmed what had happened. Vance went to the front door and looked out. He saw the mass of crows around Brian's body, which unexpectedly cawed loudly and flew up as one. The murder of crows departed into the sky and across to the woods at the back of Cliff Head House.

As soon as Vance saw the crows leave, he called to Doctor Sharpe for help. Jacobs joined them and the three ran to the journalist and tried to stop the bleeding. Doctor Sharpe exerted pressure on the wound and tried to halt any more loss of blood. He yelled, "Ambulance, quickly. This man needs a hospital, now. I'll do what I can while we wait." Jacobs put out the call.

"We have to get him back to the house. Those birds might return and attack us. Besides an ambulance can't reach us here," said Vance.

The doctor nodded. "Help me with him." The three men pulled a semi-conscious Brian to his feet. Jacobs and Vance half carried, and half dragged him along the path as the doctor kept the wound in Brian's neck under pressure. The doctor waited outside with him for the ambulance to arrive.

Vance and Jacobs returned inside to Adam and Melvyn to explain what was happening. "This is Shaitan's doing," said Melvyn. "Who else would order the attacks? Can't you get a police marksman out to shoot those devil crows?"

"But why would they attack that journalist?" asked Jacobs.

"To stop him discovering the truth," replied Melvyn. "It would throw all of his plans and schemes into disarray. He doesn't want the truth coming out any more than we do."

Vance snorted in frustration. "Bastard man!"

"But he's not a man. He's a demon," insisted Melvyn.

"I know, I know. But imagine what that would do to our credibility?"

They all paused for a moment whilst they thought about the consequences of the truth getting out to the public. Melvyn broke the silence. "What did the doctor say about Adam?"

"After examination he believes the antibiotics are proving effective. He feels he's one of the lucky ones and should be clear of the infection very soon but needs to stay out of circulation for a week."

The sound of an ambulance siren interrupted them, and Vance went out to meet them. "Think I'll have some explaining to do dressed like this."

"You'll be okay, just tell them Mr Barrie has an infection, and the suits are a precaution. Thinking about it, it's a good job we were here."

Outside, the paramedics had taken over from Doctor Sharpe and were loading Brian into the ambulance. Whatever the doctor had said seemed to satisfy them and there were no searching questions. Dr Sharpe stood there and watched as the ambulance drove away before returning inside.

Shaitan addressed his crows in the woods behind Vanda's house. "You have done well my beauties. Now away. Return to Moss Woods and if I need you I will summon you." The crows flew off and soared over the treetops and took the direct line to Gilbert Bray School and Moss Woods.

Shaitan watched them go before he moved back towards Cliff Head House. He descended the steps and walked along the beach until he reached the cave entrance, which he disappeared inside. He needed to make another portal and what better place to create one than under Black Head Ridge House? There was strong spirit activity around it, and he could keep a watchful eye on Mr Barrie and the beautiful Vanda and when the time was right and they had dropped their guard, he would strike.

He raised his arms and closed his eyes muttering some kind of mantra in another tongue. "Lilith! Come forth!" he ordered.

A shimmering green mass began to develop and soon the alluring body of Lilith manifested before him. "Why do you call me?"

"A man has just been removed from the top of the cliff and taken to the local hospital. I want you to seek him out. He mustn't live. He is too inquisitive and meddling. He must not know about me or you, or any of our other plans."

"What about the protection?"

"There will be none there. You can enter safely. Do what you do best and drain his life and you will have done well. Then you can move onto other prey and repopulate your line. Do you understand?"

Lilith grinned and licked her lips. "I do. I have a hunger for men, to enslave them and captivate them. Then and only then will I be satisfied and have revenge on God's curse and those that made me flee the garden of Eden."

Shaitan nodded. "And we can continue our plans to bring our dominion here on earth." As Lilith dissolved, his mouth stretched into a wide but chilling smile, and he disappeared from view.

THE HOSPITAL WAS BUSTLING WITH energy as nurses, doctors and orderlies scurried here and there. There was a backlog of ambulances waiting to discharge patients to hospital wards. Brian Thompson lay in Ambulance number six. He was wired up to some machines and had an IV line transfusing blood. His neck was packed to prevent more blood loss, and his facial injuries were being attended to. His eyes, however, were more severely damaged. One of the paramedics, Luke Foster, shifted in his seat opposite the patient. He was bemoaning the fact to his partner, Jeff Fleetwood, that hospital beds were scarce and emergencies like this were being forced to wait until something suitable became available.

"It's ridiculous. We go out on an emergency and race to get here and then they can't be admitted. This guy is in a bad way. He needs help, now," grumbled Luke.

Jeff got up. "He's as stable as we can get him for the moment but that's not enough. I don't expect it to last." There was a lull in the conversation until Jeff spoke again. "I'll take a look inside A & E and see if anything can be done. Why don't you get us each a coffee. We could be here for hours and he's not going anywhere."

"But what if something happens? We can't leave him alone. We have a duty of care. I'll stay until you get back."

Jeff nodded. "You're right. It's just my stomach is rumbling, and I could do with a good hot drink."

"You go, see if it can be speeded up, you can grab us a couple of drinks and bring them back," said Luke.

Jeff slipped out through the doors and hurried into A & E to find someone, anyone who could give him some idea of the length of time before handover. He spotted a junior doctor who was talking to a nurse and dashed up to him.

"Excuse me. Sorry to interrupt, we have a patient in a critical state. We have done all we can, but he needs proper medical attention urgently. Isn't there anything you can do?"

The junior doctor looked frazzled and exhausted. "See for yourself, we're struggling enough as it is."

The paramedic persisted, "He really is in a bad way. Lost so much blood and his eyes have been damaged as well as his face. He's been sedated to ease the pain. There must be something you can do. We've already gone way past our shift and we're both hungry. Please."

The doctor sighed in a long suffering way. "All right. I'll take a look. We may be able to get him a spot in the corridor but there'll still be a wait."

"Fine. He'll be in your care officially now and we can knock off," said Jeff. "The man suffered a complete nightmare. It's a horror story," and he explained to the doctor as he led him to the waiting ambulance. The doctor took one look at Brian Thomson and nodded. "You're right. He doesn't look good. Let's get him on a trolley and he can wait in the corridor outside the Medical Assessment Unit. We can try and make space in Intensive Care. I'll get one of the nurses onto it now."

Luke and Jeff manoeuvred their patient out of the ambulance, into the hospital to where the doctor had directed them and with relief they left Brian in their care, and went up to the canteen. "After our snack I'll go back down and check on him. It's an absolute horror story as I explained to the doc."

"Yeah. Who'd have thought it? Attacked by crows..." and he shuddered.

Brian remained sedated on the trolley as he was triaged. It was clear he needed urgent care, and he was transported to I. C. U. straight away as a bed had become available. There was no hanging around in corridors. He was ushered into a recently vacated private room where an auxiliary was washing down the mattress with sanitiser and cleaning the room. She made up the bed and Brian was transferred to it from the trolley. A chart was made up for him and his vitals checked. His pulse was weak but his heartbeat seemed strong. The doctor was satisfied he would be okay until they decided what to do about his facial injuries and eyes. He left the room.

Once the door was shut, a greenish mass began to manifest and hovered over Brian's chest. His breathing became constricted, and he gasped for air ripping the oxygen mask from his face. He pawed at the mass sitting on his chest, finding her breasts, and Lilith sighed. She stretched her talons and caressed him before gently drawing her nails down his arms and traced circles down his sides and across his stomach, avoiding the painful pecks and scratches he'd received from the attacking birds. She played with his body, nibbled his ears and licked the blood that began to ooze from his wound below the dressing before turning her attention to his nipples as she straddled him.

Even in his sedated state Brian Thompson was aroused and Lilith utilised his manhood and rode him until he was spent. She gave a small joyous cry as he ejaculated inside her and he began to come to consciousness. It was then she dug her talons into him and bit his chest and he groaned in both pleasure and pain. Lilith threw back her head and laughed as she watched his spasmodic reflexive movements subside and lay her hands on his chest. Once Lilith was sure his heart had stopped, she moved off him, drew back the covers to hide her deed and vanished. The machine monitoring his vitals gave out a shrill alarm and a nurse came running to the door and opened it.

The nurse called urgently for the crash cart and other medics came running. She couldn't find a pulse and pulled open the bedding to begin CPR as she waited for the emergency team to arrive. She stared in disbelief at the journalist's body, marked with scratches and bite marks. She couldn't help but see, his hospital gown was rucked up but couldn't explain it. The team worked on him for almost fifteen minutes. It was no good. Brian Thompson was dead.

Word soon went back to Vance at the station that the man who had been transported from Black Head Ridge to hospital had died. The doctors were puzzled. He was being well looked after and although seeming critical, he was stable. He had somehow sustained further injuries in his hospital room, but CCTV had proved that nothing and no one had entered his room and the marks on his body were a mystery.

Vance had an idea what had happened but was unable to enlighten the medical staff without arousing more questions, questions he was not prepared to answer. He thanked the clinical lead in the ICU and got on the phone to Adam.

Adam was feeling much better. His shivering fits had stopped, and the achy flu-type feeling was slowly evaporating but he was not cleared to go out, yet. He still had a few days of antibiotics to take and once he had the all-clear, the house would need a thorough deep clean just to be on the safe side. There should be no trace of any bacteria no matter how small. The phone rang, making them both jump. Melvyn answered. He was feeling fine and had been put on a course of antibiotics as a preventative measure and they appeared to be working. He had no hint of illness or even side-affects from the medication at all. "Yes?"

Vance relayed all that had happened at the hospital and about the death of Brian Thompson. Melvyn's face was grim. "This is far worse than I anticipated. I know the man was a pain, but he didn't deserve to die. This is Lilith's doing. She needs to be chained in Hell along with Shaitan, if that is at all possible." Whatever Vance said next was short and to the point. Melvyn muttered a goodbye and hung up.

"What?" asked Adam.

Melvyn explained and continued, "Vance is concerned about Jake. Believes it's time for him to pack up and get back to work."

"But if he does that, Shaitan will know Vanda's gone."

"Don't shoot the messenger. It's just what he said."

"I understand but Shaitan has resources and many ways to find people. Look how he found Marissa. I feel he could easily try again."

"But she's safe for the moment," said Melvyn.

"Possibly but you never know…"

Marissa sat absorbed in her My Little Pony colouring book. Her face was creased in concentration as she tried to keep within the lines, and her small pink tongue protruded from her mouth as she selected her next colour. Abruptly she stopped and put down her pencils. "Mummy?"

"What?" asked her mother as she washed the dishes.

"I need to see Adam. It's important."

Her mother hurriedly dried her hands on a tea towel and crossed to her daughter. "Sweetheart we have been through this before. Yes, Adam helped you and things have got back to normal, but I don't think it's a good idea for you to see him again. The things he is involved in are… well, just not suitable for a child. It's not good for you."

"But, Mummy…"

"No. And that's an end to it. No more Adam. Please."

"Even if we're in danger if we don't see him?"

"What?"

"That bad man. He is going to come after me again. Adam and his friends are the only ones who can help."

"How do you know this?"

"I just do."

Janine was flummoxed. She had hoped all the previous problems were at an end. She sighed and made a decision. "We will telephone him, and you can speak to him. Tell him what you know."

"Then will you let me see him?"

"We'll see."

"That means no."

"Not necessarily." Finally, Janine relented. "You can speak to Adam and then we can decide if it's important for you to see him."

Marissa jumped up and hugged her mother. "Thank you, Mummy. You'll see that it's best. Can we call him now?"

Vanda had enjoyed time with her family but now, she was bored. She had already begun writing a novel based on her experiences at Black Head Ridge and had done some more research on defeating demons. Once she had separated all the fantasy and information on video game play from the very real threat she discovered much more on a Roman Catholic site and knew to get rid of Shaitan completely would require prayer, fasting and reading the scriptures. It was something very new to her. She had always dealt in reality and truth but this… this was something that she had never experienced before and now, she knew first-hand the power of evil.

Vanda wanted to return, and she decided to call Black Head Ridge House. Melvyn answered. "Hello?"

"Melvyn. It's good to hear your voice. How is Adam?"

"He's getting there. The medication is working. Nearly safe now. We will soon be able to burn the PPE and get the house fumigated. Do you want to talk to him?"

"Yes, please. But first, are you able to stay and help us rid the world of Shaitan?"

"We have tried twice but nothing seems to have lasted."

"We can't do it without you. Everything I've learned in my research requires God's help and you are his instrument."

"Vanda don't worry. I shall see this through."

"That's what I thought. I'll speak to Adam now."

Melvyn passed the phone across to Adam who had been listening on loudspeaker. He took the receiver eagerly and switched off the loudspeaker as he and Vanda chatted privately. He was more animated than Melvyn had ever seen him in a long time. It was a good sign he was sure.

Shaitan had gathered his demon crows, Lilith and three fallen angels, Berith, Astaroth, and Belial. Angels that had turned to darkness and rejected God to follow Heylel previously known as 'Spreading Brightness' or 'The Shining One' who changed his name to Lucifer. The cave walls were illuminated in a blue phosphorescent light, which glowed eerily in the developing darkness. A pentacle had been drawn in the sand. The birds watched as Shaitan murmured an incantation and the incandescent light grew. At the back of the cave the spirit of Ted Johnson manifested together with that of Miles Giffard and two other unknown entities. A whirling wind grew up that groaned and whistled in the cave. Other spirits joined the clamour with agonising sounds of pain and a shapeless mist twisted and turned as if hollowing out the rocky cavern. There was a sudden explosion, and a blue portal revolved in the back of the cave into which the birds flew one by one.

Shaitan's eyes turned from red to black and he heralded the portal in glee and called to his fellow conspirators who followed him inside the portal, which swirled and then vanished with a snap.

Inside Black Head Ridge House there was a loud bang-like explosive sound that shook the house. Melvyn and Adam looked at each other. "What the hell was that?"

Adam replied, "I don't know. I've never heard anything like it before. It's almost like an eruption, a bomb going off…"

"Or the opening of a fissure in the earth!" exclaimed Melvyn.

The two men looked at each other and said as one, "Shaitan." There was an uncomfortable silence between them as they digested this information, when the telephone rang again, startling them. This time Adam picked up.

"…Hello?"

Janine Porter's voice came through loud and clear. "Adam?"

"Yes?"

"We need to talk."

The bright day had turned to one of gloom and cloud as the skies were wrapped in rolling leaden clouds blocking the light of the sun. A moderate breeze was whipping up the seas and white horses frothed in the expanse of the water. Seagulls called as they soared on the thermals patrolling the coast and the beach.

Adam gazed out of the window and noticed several crows on the sand watching the waves. Unusually the tide seemed to be taking longer to come into the shore. It was as if the barrier of birds were holding it back, but Adam knew that was impossible. He gasped suddenly as he saw the spirit of Ted Johnson emerge from the cliffside and hover on the sand as he stared up at the lighthouse before turning and peering at Black Head Ridge House. He could almost feel Ted's eyes on him looking right through him to his heart and he shivered.

"What is it?" asked Melvyn sensing a change in the atmosphere and drop in temperature.

Adam tried to turn away but found it impossible when Ted's eyes locked onto his. Adam couldn't speak and he couldn't move. Melvyn moved closer and took his arm. It was then he witnessed what Adam could see, and he shivered. He managed to spin Adam's view away from the window and back into the room, where he found that he could speak and move again. He had to explain about the man on the beach, what had happened to him and the part Adam had played in the lighthouse keeper's death.

Melvyn listened carefully and nodded. He took Adam's hand and urged him to pray and as Adam recited the Lord's prayer he felt a freedom growing inside him. When Melvyn looked out of the window, Ted had vanished, and the crows had taken to the skies mingling with the gulls who shied away from the creatures and flew inland.

Melvyn sat Adam down. "This can only mean one thing."

"What?"

"Shaitan has opened up a portal under the cliff and the ghosts of the past have re-emerged for whatever reason. This isn't good. The man has opened up a well of evil right on your doorstep."

"What do we do?"

"We have to shut it down. You and me in a final showdown. Vanda must *not* return until it's safe. Jake must return to work. This is something so terrifying that we dare not involve any others."

"But how?"

"I don't know. We must fast and ask for guidance. Call Vance and get him to take Jake away."

Adam picked up the phone and dialled.

CLIFF HEAD HOUSE WAS A hive of activity. Jake had divested himself of Vanda's clothes. He was now dressed in his own gear and Vance was checking all possible entrances and ways into the house ensuring the protection was there and had not blown away. The curtains were pulled in the rooms Jake had occupied, the others left open. Jake was eager to get away, he felt as if he had been there forever. Elsa had been picked up and popped in her cat basket, and all her kitty equipment, food and toys had been bagged up. Jacobs was in situ expecting to transport Jake back to Brinkworth in his car. Vance had the cat and all the accoutrements ready to take to Black Head Ridge House. He slipped into his Hazmat suit as he waited to see Jake and Jacobs off site. Once they had departed safely without seeing any crows or any other entities, Vance drove around to the old mansion taking the long route. He didn't fancy walking the cliff path with the cat and just in case the malign crows made an appearance. He didn't relish that thought at all.

He could see a large van had arrived that housed a clean-up crew to disinfect the mansion. Cleaners in protective suits were marching out with mops and buckets and loading the van up with various other cleaning equipment. Vance was relieved, it meant he wouldn't have to wear a hazmat suit again. He picked up his pace and just caught the van before it drove away.

"Is it all clear?"

"It's safe," said a lean man with a swarthy complexion. "It's had a thorough deep clean and been tested."

Vance nodded in acknowledgement and watched the van drive away before he went and knocked on the door. Melvyn answered with his hazmat suit pulled down over his shoulders. "I'll be glad to take this thing off," he murmured as he admitted Vance and the cat.

Marissa was agitating with her mother, "So, tell me... what did Adam say?"

"He said it wasn't safe for you to go to the house. He's not well enough, yet."

"But he will be. His seven days are up, and he can get out and about again."

"Marissa, the house has to be sanitised. You don't want to go there and pick up something nasty, do you?"

"No, but..."

"No buts. You cannot see him. Not now."

Marissa's face crumpled and she acted totally out of character and stamped her feet, insisting, "I have to see him. It's important. He needs to know he's in danger. At least let me talk to him." She eyed her mother and in a wheedling tone added, "Pleeease!"

Janine sighed in frustration. "Let me finish what I'm doing, and I'll call."

"That will take ages. Let me call him on my own. I know how to use the phone..."

"Oh, for heaven's sake." Janine stopped what she was doing and sat with her daughter. "I promise I will ring him but just not yet." And with that Marissa had to be satisfied although she folded her arms in a huff and made a face.

Vance stood in the kitchen and eyed Adam. "I must say, you're looking a hell of a lot better."

Adam nodded. "Thanks for getting the doc to me and antibiotics as quickly as you did. Otherwise, it would have been a totally different story. I see you have Elsa." He jerked his head at the cat basket.

"Yes, well Jake has returned home and to his job. So, Elsa is now in your care." Vance opened the basket, and Elsa flew out and ran to Adam rubbing herself around his legs and purring. He picked her up and she nuzzled into his neck and face clearly delighted to see him.

"Have you anything to report?"

Adam shook his head. "Not really, except…"

"Except…?" pressed Vance.

"It's just a feeling…"

"Which we know not to ignore," interrupted Melvyn.

"Agreed," said Vance.

They were interrupted by the phone's strident ring. Adam crossed to answer. "Yes?" It was Janine Porter and Marissa. Marissa was incredibly excited and desperate to make Adam understand. Adam put the phone on loudspeaker so they could all hear.

"I'm sorry, Adam," said Janine. "Marissa is insistent, she's been pestering me for days to come and see you. I told her that was impossible, but she claims she has to talk to you."

"That's okay. Put her on."

There was some fumbling before the phone was passed to the little girl. She spoke clearly, "Adam you are in danger. Great danger."

Adam exchanged a glance with the others. "I was… but I am fine now. Honestly."

"No! You have to listen. You heard a big bang earlier. It shook the house."

"How do you know that?"

"I just do… Adam, it's him, the very bad man. The one who wants me. He's somewhere underneath you. Under the house."

Adam paused. "But Marissa there is no cellar here."

"No, not in the house. In the cliff. He's doing something to… oh I don't know how to explain it." The little girl had begun to cry.

Melvyn spoke gently, "Marissa, it's Melvyn the vicar. You remember?"

"Yes. Adam needs you to get rid of him. He can't do it without you."

"How do we do that?"

"I don't know but he's making something…"

"What? Like a bomb?"

"No, nothing like that… a way… a path… a… like in Moss Woods."

"You mean a portal? A way between two worlds?"

"Yes… yes, a… what you said. And he's doing it in your house."

The three men were dumbstruck. Adam finally spoke. "Is this portal open?"

"No, not properly. He can come and go, and a few others but it soon will be open properly and then he will come looking for me again so he can keep it open forever." Marissa began to sob, and Janine took the phone away from her.

"I'm sorry, Adam. That's enough for now. She is getting far too distressed."

"Of course," said Adam looking alarmed as he took in the expressions of Melvyn and Vance. "Janine look after Marissa and thank her for us. I will ring when I have some good news." Janine muttered something and hung up the call.

Adam sat with a bump in a kitchen chair. The three men looked around anxiously and the worry on their faces grew as there was a loud caw from outside and Cawdor flew onto the windowsill and began pecking at the glass.

"I've had enough of this," said Vance and he crossed to the window and hammered on it. "Go away! Shoo!" But the bird remained and continued to peer in the window at them.

"We need to move to another room. One where he can't hear us," said Melvyn. The trio moved into the hallway and the sitting room. There on the sill were another two crows.

"Follow me," said Adam and he led the way to the study and switched on the light. There were no windows in there. "They can't hear us in here," said Adam but he spoke in low whispered tones as if to make certain.

"What now?" asked Vance.

"If you can get a police marksman out here. Do it. These crows need to go," said Melvyn assertively.

"What will I tell them?"

"Tell them… the truth. That these birds have been attacking people and are a menace. People are afraid to go out."

Vance nodded his head slowly. "Very well. I'll see what I can do." He took out his mobile and dialled. It was soon answered and Vance explained what he wanted. He put his hand over the mouthpiece as he turned to the others. "Someone has been dispatched they should be here shortly." He spoke into the phone again. "Tell them to wear protective gear. These birds are dangerous." A few more words were exchanged, and Vance ended the call. "That's done. What next?"

"We'll wait until the birds are dealt with and then we'll move on to the next part of our plan," said Melvyn.

"What plan? We haven't got one," said Adam.

"Then we'd best formulate one now," asserted Melvyn. The three men looked at each other. Melvyn rubbed his hands together and announced, "Right, let's get on with it."

It was a little while later when a vehicle was heard at the front of the house. Vance went into the sitting room and peered out of the window. Two police marksmen in full riot gear emerged from the car with Glock 17 pistols and Sig MCX carbines and gazed about them. A crow flew down from the roof and landed on one man's shoulder and began pecking at him. He managed to shake the bird off and the other officer raised his pistol and shot the creature, which flapped around before finally stopping and lying still.

The gunshot had reverberated around the cliff and there was a flurry of wings as more crows fluttered down to the path and fixed their gaze on the two marksmen, Max and Raymond. Max shouted across to Raymond, "Back in the van, now. We'll fire through the window. They scrambled inside and lowered the window a fraction, enough to get the muzzle out of the window and began to fire. Several birds fell and twisted together in a clumping feathered mess. The remaining birds soared up and dived down the cliff out of sight.

The two marksmen sighed in relief.

Max nudged Raymond and pointed at the oily black mass of birds. "Look!" he said and before their eyes the birds began to dissolve and finally disappeared. "What the?" Max alighted and walked to where the birds had been shot. There was no sign that anything had fallen there, not even a speck of blood.

Vance had been watching through the window and swore softly. "Bugger! Now how do we explain that?"

"What?" asked Adam.

"The shot birds… they've vanished."

Melvyn interjected, "We don't explain it. We act as flummoxed as them. We can't explain it either. It's the only way."

The doorbell rang and Vance went to open it, and Max and Raymond tumbled inside. "DCI Vance!" exclaimed Raymond. "Just what the hell was that?"

Vance shook his head. "Never seen anything like it in my life. Did we have a mass hallucination or something?" He looked around at the others.

Adam answered, "It was more than weird. It was…" he searched for a word, "inexplicably bizarre. I don't understand it. Don't understand it at all."

"Well, I for one am not saying anything to anyone," said Max. "No one would believe it anyway. They'd think we were all loopy."

"That's putting it mildly," said Melvyn adding his weight to the conversation.

"Are you all right now?" asked Raymond.

"As right as we'll ever be after that," stated Vance. "You get back now and if we need you again, I'll ring."

Max nodded. "What do we say if anyone asks?"

"Tell them you solved the problem. That a number of the birds were dealt with but some escaped. That way, if we do need you again we can call."

"Yes, sir. Thank you, sir." The two marksmen took their leave and left.

"So, what now?" asked Vance.

"I have to get down there. He must be in the cave under the house…" said Adam.

"What are you going to do?" asked Vance.

Melvyn interrupted, "We'll go together, and we must prepare. We have fasted and prayed. We will pray some more and take our holy items with us."

"How do you perform these rituals without the bishop's permission?" asked Vance.

Melvyn turned to Vance and said seriously, "I am the official undercover priest for exorcisms. The Church doesn't like to talk about it or attract attention to any situation involved in the paranormal. Ever since the trouble in Derbyshire, I am the one chosen for this type of work. But please respect the Church's secrecy."

"Of course," said Vance looking shocked. "Is there anything I can do?"

"Stay out of the way, make sure this house is well protected. We don't want any nosy reporters or anyone else getting wind of this."

Vance nodded. "I'll stay out of the way. I don't want to invite trouble to my own door."

Melvyn nodded. "That's wise and no matter what you hear or see, stay put. Do not come running. Do you understand?" Vance nodded and Melvyn continued, "Then come, Adam we must prepare."

The inside of the cave dripped with moisture and roots of vegetation that covered the top of the cliff dangled down like shredded ribbons. A small spring gushed through a fissure in the rocky wall and spattered the sand. Melvyn stood there in his full vestments with a purple cassock, for healing, and white surplice for purity. He wore a stole embroidered with Christian symbols that hung around his neck to his knees.

Adam was dressed in an alb, a white gown with long sleeves that covered his whole body down to his ankles with a girdle tied around his waist. He wore Vanda's cross around his neck and clutched a Bible in one hand, and a bottle of Holy water in the other. He shifted his feet uneasily. Around them was a circle of salt and inside the ring a number of iron implements.

Melvyn asked him, "Are you all right?"

"As right as I'll ever be," murmured Adam. "What can we expect?" As if in answer to his question there was a grating sound like bone on rock and a rash of guttural heavy whispers floated around the cave. An orange flare flew up from the cave floor like a Roman candle and in the shower of sparks the image of twenty-six-year-old murderer, Miles Giffard appeared in cricket gear with a rope around his neck. His youthful fresh-faced appearance was deceiving. He looked as if he was appealing for help but when Melvyn raised his hand with the cross to bless him, the young man's eyes flamed red, and he pulled back his lips in a vampiric smile revealing pointed sharp teeth. He opened his mouth and roared. Green smoke shrieked out of the cavernous mouth and swirled about them, but it couldn't penetrate the air around Melvyn and Adam.

Melvyn's voice rose and he uttered a prayer finishing with, "In the name of Jesus Christ I banish you from this place. Go back from whence you came, and may God have mercy on your soul," to which the apparition threw back his head and laughed hollowly before dissolving to nothing and vanishing through the cave floor. Melvyn asked, "Who was that?"

"I believe that was Miles Giffard hung in 1953 for murdering his parents. Vance told me the story." Adam was about to explain when a fissure cracked open in the cave floor and spread from the rocky walls across the cave floor and glowed red, orange and amber. A red ball of fire flew like a cannon ball all around the cave hitting the cavern's walls and ricocheting like an out of control missile. Adam flinched as it whistled around the circle before it stopped, and a figure began to form pointing an accusing finger at Adam. A voice, sounding like its vocal cords had been cut, rasped, "You took my life. Now it's my turn."

Melvyn moved and stepped in front of Adam and again he prayed in Christ's name to release the man's tormented soul and confine him forever in the realm where he belonged. The spirit of Ted Johnson clawed and pawed the air in front of him until he was propelled back into the rock wall and seemed melded to it. His eyes remained wide and staring as he was sealed inside the granite wall. His mouth lay open as a multitude of insects like scarab- type black beetles swarmed from his mouth and crawled across the sandy floor only to be met by the Holy salt. Adam also sprayed Holy water over the creatures, which screeched and curled up in their death throes before shrivelling and falling into the fissure where lava bubbled.

By this time, Adam was shaking and Melvyn asked, "Do you want to tell me about him?"

Adam shook his head. "Not until we're done here." He shivered, what was he to see next? His face was covered in a thick sheen of sweat and contorted in fear of what he had seen, and he had begun to shake.

The wind abruptly stopped and there was an eerie but uneasy silence in the cave. All that could be heard was the bubbling of molten lava emanating from the crack in the cave floor. The smell of sulphur was radiating from the wound in the floor. But then... the cave walls began to run with what looked like blood. It dripped from the roots of trailing plants and oozed from the rock walls, sliding and dripping onto the sand and pooling in gelatinous puddles all around the protective salt circle.

The sound of Haitian Tanbou drums filtered through the air, at first faint, they grew louder and louder, and the suffocating odour of sulphur grew thicker like thick fog, which surrounded the circle. Lilith in all her voluptuous glory slithered forward like a green serpent and stood like a sentinel before them. She wiggled her body seductively and sighed as if in rapture and sucked at her index finger as if teasing it to attention. She ran her tongue around her lips and pouted provocatively before stretching her lithe limbs and staring beguilingly into Adam's eyes. Her eyes were like bottomless pools and her face promised forbidden delights. No words were said but Adam could hear her in his mind and her voice like whispering grass urged him to step outside the circle and to enjoy the fruits of her body. Adam was mesmerised and took a step forward.

"That's it, Adam. Come to me. I want you so. I need you so. Step outside and I will share with you delights you have never known. Come, throw away that cross, leave that water bottle and lock yourself in an embrace with me and I promise you all that you could ever desire. Her words were like honey running over his ears and he took another step forward as Lilith continued to hypnotise, plead and cajole.

Melvyn glanced across at Adam and warned, "No, Adam, turn away. Close your eyes. She will devour your soul. Look away... Now. Think of Vanda." At the mention of Vanda's name Adam stopped. He was right on the edge of the circle. But his eyes were still fixed on the succubus. "Adam! Don't! Step back, now." But Adam raised his foot to step over the salt, when Melvyn picked up an iron poker and threw it at Lilith who screamed as the metal seared her skin. It was enough to break the spell and Adam blinked and drew back. He opened his water bottle and squirted the Holy water over her. Her skin bubbled and blistered and she screamed in agonising pain. A torrent of abuse rushed from her lips and Melvyn threw another piece of iron at the creature who fell back into the fissure screaming in anger. Adam collapsed onto the cave floor and Melvyn rushed to his side and helped him to his feet. "You must never engage with these monsters, they will sap your will and strength and force you to be compliant, stealing your soul."

Adam nodded. He was still trembling when the sound of the drums heightened, and a fierce snarling was heard. Demon dogs with gargoyle type faces and muscular bodies walked alongside the familiar figure of Shaitan whose face rippled with feasting maggots. His eyes were a pool of venomous black. He raised his arms and speaking in a strange tongue he incanted orders to the newly dead and faceless shapes of horror gathered around him. A cacophony of vicious sounds accompanied the rising wind that swirled around their feet trying to blow away the salt and leave a gap to allow entry into the circle. Melvyn retaliated by lifting his Bible and calling on the Lord Jesus Christ to deliver them from this vile evil. Adam, finding strength from somewhere, raised his water bottle and sprayed the devil dogs, which whimpered and turned to stone.

There was a flash of lightning and a rumble of thunder. Rocks began to tumble from the cave ceiling. Melvyn shouted above the shrieking wind, "Adam... Pray!" Adam fell back to his knees and began to repeat the Lord's prayer over and over again. A swirling blue portal appeared behind Shaitan, which imploded sucking the demon inside. A jet of fire played around the portal entrance and began to erase the entrance to the pit of evil and more rocks dropped down from the ceiling. Melvyn grabbed hold of Adam's hand, pulled him to his feet and dragged him from the circle and out of the cave entrance. Melvyn called aloud, "Lord please deliver us, your servants, from this pit of evil. Save our souls."

A mighty explosion ripped through the cave, spewing out flames and rock. Boulders fell down from the shaking cliff and the cavern entrance filled with rock, molten lava and rubble sealing it forever.

Melvyn and Adam stood and watched in awe as the molten rock solidified into basalt pillars. It would take huge plant equipment to pierce or reopen the entrance. Adam and Melvyn fell to their knees and holding their Bibles prayed their thanks together. The clouds that had been bowling across the cerulean sky seemed to cling together and form a heart and Adam heard in his head his mother's voice, "Adam, you are blessed by the hand of God. Use your talents wisely and well."

The sky cleared and the sound of birdsong could be heard elsewhere. Adam stood up and gazed about him in wonder. He turned to Melvyn. "Melvyn… your hair."

"What about it?"

"It's white… all white."

"At least it won't look as if I have dyed it," he mused.

The two men wearily trekked their way up the beach to the cliff path and returned to Black Head Ridge House. They settled in the kitchen while Adam filled the kettle. He turned to Melvyn. "So, do you think it's over?"

Melvyn nodded. "Adam, I believe it finally is."

And the two men appraised each other and smiled.

Author Thanks

Many thanks for reading the next book in the *Adam Barrie paranormal investigations*. If you have a little time, I would appreciate a review. I really value my readers' thoughts about a book. It often helps me craft future stories. They are vital for indie authors like me.

You are welcome to contact me at elizabethrevill@protonmail.com or visit the website: www.elizabethrevill.com

****

I have free stories for you as well, all I'd like in exchange is your email address and you can unsubscribe at any time.

The first is called *Dead or Alive* just follow the link.

I'd like to keep in touch. Either via the newsletter, I'll send out once a month, or you can join my Facebook page: Elizabeth Revill. If you join either, there will be notifications of new stories, releases of covers and the occasional giveaway and special deals just for you. There will also be an opportunity to join my *Advanced Reader Team*.

Acknowledgements

I would also like to thank my commissioning editor and mentor Sarah Luddington and her team at Mirador. Sarah is a tower of strength to me; my terrific proof reader Jeff Jones who works very hard to get everything right. My son, Ben Fielder who helps me with all my newsletters and my husband Andrew Spear who encourages me to write and supports me.

Other titles by Elizabeth Revill

DCI Allison Thrillers:

Killing me Softly

Prayer for the Dying

God Only Knows

Would I Lie To You?

Windows For The Dead

Dead Eyes Opened

Mother's Not Dead

Llewellyn Family Saga:

Whispers on the Wind

Shadows on the Moon

Rainbows in the Clouds

Thunder in the Sun

The Adam Barrie Paranormal Investigations:

The House at Black Head Ridge

Portal To Evil

Against the Tide

Turn of the Tide

The Electra Conspiracy Part 1

The Electra Conspiracy Part 2

Stand Alone Novels:

Sanjukta and the Box of Souls

The Forsaken And The Damned

Web of Fear

The Dreamtime of the Artful Dodger with Norman Eshley

Children's book

And an illustrated children's book *The Secret of Gidon*

www.ingramcontent.com/pod-product-compliance
Lightning Source LLC
Chambersburg PA
CBHW031222260626
47169CB00007B/2154